ME, Suzy P.

Karen Saunders
xxx

templar

A TEMPLAR BOOK

First published in the UK in 2013 by Templar Publishing,
an imprint of The Templar Company Limited, Deepdene Lodge,
Deepdene Avenue, Dorking, Surrey, RH5 4AT, UK

www.templarco.co.uk

Copyright © 2013 by Karen Saunders
Cover illustration by AT Rock

First UK edition

MIX
Paper from
responsible sources
FSC® C020471

ISBN 978-1-84877-296-0
Printed and bound by CPI Group (UK) Ltd, Croydon, CR0 4YY

For my wonderful Mum.
With love, always.

CHAPTER ONE

Oh no, oh no, oh *no*... I can't *believe* I'm so late.

How can I be out of breath this flipping quickly? I am seriously, seriously unfit. And these new shoes aren't helping. They may look great, but they sure aren't easy to move in at speed.

In my jacket pocket, my mobile vibrates for the bazillionth time. I don't need to check it, because I know exactly who it is. It'll be my best friend, Millie, asking yet again:

Where r u??!!!

Like I have time to reply.

Besides, doesn't she know I'm moving as fast as I can?

I feel majorly guilty because I promised Danny that nothing short of a meteor decimating the school would make me miss his football match. As a loyal girlfriend, of course I'd be there to support him. He said he'd do a lap of the pitch in the buff if I actually made it in time for kick-off.

Tsch. Anyone would think I had a reputation for being late or something. Which, actually, now I think about it... I suppose I kind of do.

But this time, it totally wasn't my fault. Miss Evans, our über-anal maths teacher, went all CSI on us after a school protractor went missing. Like anybody would *seriously* steal one. It was only after a full-scale investigation verging on fingerprinting and waterboarding that it was discovered she'd counted wrongly, but by then it was twenty minutes after the bell. I had to go to my locker and dump my stuff, then I needed the toilet, then I went back to my locker because I'd forgotten my English reading, then I bumped into my science partner, Rachel, who waffled on for ages about our photosynthesis homework and made me realise I needed to go back to my locker *again* for my science textbook, and, well... yes. I'm late.

Which is why I'm legging it through the school, risking life and limb to get to the football field as quickly as humanly possible.

This match is pretty big deal to Danny. The fact he's only been picked because of a clash with the French exchange – meaning most of the regular squad are currently larging it up in Paris – means nothing. As Danny's told me proudly, and practically hourly over the last few days, he's never played for any sports team before. Ever. And this isn't just any old match. It's the quarter-final of the regional cup.

Secretly I think Mr Barnes, one of the PE teachers, might have been desperate to make up the numbers. I'm not being mean. I'm really not. But since Danny's major growth spurt, any vague coordination he might once have had has totally disappeared. It's like he doesn't know how his arms and legs work any more. And football's never been a strong point. I don't think he's ever kicked a ball straight in his life, so let's just say the England squad won't be quaking in their boots anytime soon.

But I should still be there to show my support. That's what girlfriends are supposed to do. Like those WAGS. They show up in their designer clothes and inches of make-up, look stunning and cheer on their menfolk.

And I'm sure I look stunning right now – not at all red-faced and flustered with my brown curly hair zinging all over the place like I've had an electric shock.

I stop for a rest, but when I check my watch I let out a tiny yelp of horror.

Nearly half four?! Gnargh, I am *so* late.

No time for stopping, then. I've got to keep going

and hope my lungs eventually forgive me. I'm now so short of breath I'm practically *wheezing*.

Trying to ignore the painful stitch in my side, I speed past the science blocks and veer onto the wet grass, squelching my way across the field. The pitch, not far away now, is at the bottom of a small, steep slope, and there's a crowd of spectators on the sidelines. Millie's down there somewhere because Jamie, her boyfriend, is playing today too. He's actually good at football, though, and one of the team regulars.

I hear a familiar scream, then a whooped cry of "Goooooo, Colinsbrooke, go, go, go!"

Oh-kaaay, so *that's* where Millie is. You can't exactly miss her, given she's leaping around like a hyperactive kangaroo, bellowing at the top of her voice. Her blonde hair, with its newly acquired purple streak, has been tied into wildly bouncing bunches, and she's found some pompoms from who-knows-where, apparently appointing herself cheerleader for our team. It never fails to amaze me how much energy Mills has. It's exhausting keeping up with her sometimes.

"Millie?"

"Give us a C... C! Give us an O... O! Give us an L..."

"Millie," I yell again, starting to jog down the slope.

"L! Oh, hi, Suzy. Where've you been? The game started forever ago," Millie calls, shaking her pompoms vigorously. For such a tiny person (152 centimetres if she's stretching), she sure is loud. As she bounces forwards towards the sidelines, I suddenly notice the person standing behind her.

Danny.

His face is downcast, his light brown hair is a mess, and his shoulders are slumped inside his muddy football shirt.

Huh? Danny's meant to be playing, not watching. What's happened?

Although... I don't think I can worry about that right now. Because I've been so distracted looking at Danny, I've not realised just how slippery this grass is. I'm going a *teensy* bit faster than I feel comfortable with, and I don't seem to be able to stop. My lovely new shoes don't have any grip.

Okay. I'm all right. All I need to do is act calm, even though my legs are out of control and I'm careering along at a crazy speed. I'm cool and collected. Everything's fine. Nothing to see here, people.

Oh help, this is not going to end well...

Everything spirals into slow motion when I reach the bottom of the hill, stumble onto a patch of mud, and skid spectacularly towards the pitch. My arms windmill as I struggle to keep my balance, and just when I think things can't get any worse, I trip over someone's outstretched foot.

I can feel myself falling... falling...

In a final, desperate effort to prevent myself landing face first in the mud, I flail around frantically for something to grab hold of. Which, somewhat unfortunately, happens to be Ryan Henderson, our star player. He's got his back to me, and is about to take a corner. And as I hurtle downwards, my hands grab, well, erm, slightly *lower* than is ideal... onto the legs of Ryan's shorts.

As I crash to the ground, the shorts come with me.

A growing roar of laughter fills my ears. When I dare open my eyes, Ryan's standing over me in the geekiest pair of Bart Simpson tightie-whities I've *ever* seen.

O. M. G. Someonekillmedeadrightnow.

"Nice pants," shout several of Ryan's teammates, over a chorus of wolf-whistles, cheers and people singing *The Simpsons* theme tune. Someone else yells, "Now we know why you got changed in the bogs!"

"These were the only clean ones I had. Mum's away and Dad can't work the washing machine, all right?" Ryan mumbles, quickly hoisting his shorts and glowering at me with such hatred I practically shrivel on the spot.

"Suzy Puttock, get off the pitch this instant!" snaps

Mr Barnes. A pair of scruffy white trainers appear in my eye-line. "What the hell are you doing, young lady?"

I stare up at him pathetically. Given that I'm lying at his feet covered in mud, I'm not exactly in a strong position to make a case for my defence.

"You, madam, are the most disaster-prone individual I've ever had the misfortune to know," Mr Barnes says. "Get out of my sight. Immediately."

I'd love nothing more than to get out of here, but when I try and stand, I slide around all over the place. Yeeeeew! My hands are covered in gross, slimy mud.

Mr Barnes sighs deeply and reaches out his arm.

What? Oh, come on, you have *got* to be kidding me. I thought I'd hit the pinnacle of my humiliation, but it seems not. Now, on top of everything else, I've got to hold a teacher's hand. And not just any teacher. This is skanky Mr Barnes, who honks of BO and has back hair that pokes out of the neck of his T-shirts. Gag.

I gingerly grab onto his fingers and try not to grimace too obviously as Mr Barnes hauls me to my feet. Once I'm safely vertical, I scuttle off through the crowd, refusing to make eye contact with anyone.

When I reach Millie and Danny, they're leaning against each other, laughing like lunatics.

"Oh, stop, stop, my belly hurts," Millie moans.

"*Simpsons* pants!" says Danny, and they're off again. Millie's actually got tears streaming down her cheeks.

It's forever before they start to calm down.

"That's cheered me right up," Danny says, trying to compose himself.

"Why aren't you playing, Danny?" I ask, refusing to acknowledge anything out of the ordinary ever happened.

"Suze, you're hilarious, you know that?" He straightens his face hurriedly when he sees me scowling. "Not quite ready to see the funny side, huh?"

"Nuh-uh," I say. "So are you going to tell me what happened?"

"Oh. Um. Well, I kind of... got sent off," he says sheepishly.

"You what? How? What did you do?"

"There was a bit of a miskick..."

"A bit of a miskick?" Millie interrupts. "Danny, you scored two own goals and the rest of the lads decided they'd rather be a player down than keep you on the pitch."

"Don't listen to her," Danny says, frowning. "Anyway, you should have been here to see for yourself. Now you've missed my one moment of sporting glory. There may never be another."

"Evans kept us all back after class," I explain. "I came as quickly as I could."

"We noticed," Millie says, making a strange snorty noise

as she struggles to hold back more giggles. Even Danny starts to smile again.

Hurrmph. Time to change the subject. Sharpish.

"What's the score?" I ask, wincing as Ryan makes a particularly violent tackle and St Edward's is awarded a penalty.

"Thirteen-nil to St Edward's," Danny replies. "No, wait... now it's fourteen-nil. Our goalie's glasses broke in the first ten minutes so he can't see a thing. And Ryan appears to have gone into meltdown since the pants thing, which is thanks to you..." Danny grabs me in a headlock and rubs his knuckles across my scalp.

"Gerroff," I say, trying to pull away, but admittedly not too hard. I've got to take affection where I can. Danny doesn't really get how to demonstrate his feelings in public. Rubber-band fights, whacking my head with a ruler, pulling my hair – it's all very juvenile and the way Danny shows he cares. Who said romance was dead, eh? Although I guess I should be used to it by now. I've known him long enough.

We've been mates with each other, and Millie and Jamie, since we were four. We were all at the same primary school, our parents became friends, and as a result we've been shoved together at family barbecues, birthdays and Christmas parties for as long as we can remember.

When we hit thirteen, Millie and Jamie used each other for kissing practice, then kind of hooked up, so Danny and I figured we'd get together too. It just made sense.

Danny's always been there for me. He came along to meet my newborn sister Harry in hospital and caught her as she tipped out of my arms (she still doesn't believe it was an accident). He hauled me out of the canal when I was practising cartwheels, aged eight, and got too close to the edge. Then there was the legendary Big Bicycle Crash the day after I got my new bike and wasn't too hot at the whole steering thing. We've both still got the scars – me on my left temple, Danny above his right eyebrow.

He is also the first person I ever kissed.

Actually, he is the *only* person I've ever kissed...

A huge cheer from the St Edward's supporters and the whistle blowing jolts my attention back to the game. St Edward's has scored yet another goal. Danny groans in agony as Millie bounces around encouragingly, but her enthusiasm's fading rapidly.

"Talk about a disaster," I say, hopping from foot to foot, trying to keep warm. "We're getting battered out there."

"Tell me about it," Millie says. "Jamie's going to be in a right mood after." She sighs heavily, but then her face brightens. "I know what I wanted to ask you. You guys around this weekend to come shopping? I need some new boots, and *ta-daaaa*, oh yes, it's a miracle: Mum's actually given me some money."

"Count me out," Danny says quickly.

"That sounds great," I reply. And then I remember. "Oh no. Wait. I can't."

Millie frowns. "How come?"

"Amber and Mum are taking me to choose my bridesmaid's dress," I say gloomily.

"Ooh, new clothes," Millie says, rustling her pompoms in my face. "Sounds good to me. Do you know what you're getting? Something slinky and chic?"

"I wish." I grimace and push her away. A couple of the fronds have gone up my nose and now I want to sneeze.

"C'mon, it can't be that bad. It's still a new dress, right?"

"Er, you have met my sister before, yes?"

"Oh, right." Millie bites her lip. "How bad are we talking here?"

"The words 'lime' and 'green' have been mentioned."

Millie winces. "You're *kidding*."

"Wish I was. What normal human can wear lime green, for God's sake? It's all Conni G's fault. Her bridesmaids wore that colour, and you know how obsessed Amber is with all things Conni."

Conni G is one of those celebrities with gravity-defying breasts who is regularly photographed leaving nightclubs wearing teeny-tiny outfits, usually while sucking the face off a premier-league footballer. Amber worships her. But Amber has weird ideas about a lot of things. Half the time it's doubtful whether she even inhabits the same planet as the rest of us, but instead wafts around in Amber-land, a sparkly place filled with fluffy clouds, harp-playing kittens and candyfloss.

A while back, there was a brief second when I was excited at the thought of being her bridesmaid. But that was before I heard what Amber wanted me to wear. For a start, I don't do dresses. And the colours? Hot pink with lemon polka dots was the first suggestion, and that was horrifying enough, but even that would be better than lime blooming green. Conni G has a *lot* to answer for.

From the field comes several long whistle blasts, followed by a cheer from the opposition's crowd. The match is over and as the players troop off, all of our team, Mr Barnes included, glower in my direction.

"What a massacre," Jamie says as he joins us, pushing his dark fringe out of his eyes. Millie leans over gives him a kiss.

A proper one.

With tongues and everything.

I watch them wistfully, wishing, not for the first time,

that Danny didn't have such a complex about affection in public.

"Ahem." Danny coughs loudly and punches Jamie in the shoulder, proving my point.

Millie and Jamie pull apart and laugh.

"You okay?" Millie slides her arm around Jamie's waist.

"Not really. We were slaughtered out there. And you didn't help," Jamie says, before prodding my ribs with a grin. "Though at least you gave us a laugh. But, mate, seriously, what were you thinking?" His attention turns to Danny.

"Don't start," Danny says. "And it wasn't *all* my fault. The ref was totally biased towards the other team."

"You're not wrong. Did you see that goal he gave when the ball hadn't even crossed the line?" Jamie asks. As we trudge towards the school, the boys wander ahead, dissecting the match, kick by disastrous kick.

Millie opens a packet of jelly babies and gleefully chomps off an orange head.

"Want one?" she asks, mid-chew.

"Nah, thanks."

"Ooh, there's that new guy," Millie says, pointing at a figure with the ball tucked under his arm, dawdling behind the other players. "Have you seen him yet? Well worth a squiz."

"Where?" I stand on tiptoes at the exact moment the guy fumbles with the ball. It drops to the floor and bounces in our direction.

As he chases after it, I swallow. Hard.

How did I miss him on the field? He is seriously, *seriously* hot. He's got tousled blondy-brown hair and amazingly chiselled features, like someone from a magazine. He's tall, too, much taller than a lot of guys in our year. Plus I've never seen anyone look so sexy in our school PE kit.

The ball stops a short distance from us. The boy scoops it up, glances in our direction, and for a brief moment, our eyes meet. A crackle of electricity surges through me, leaving me all kinds of tingly.

Blimey. Where did *that* come from?

"Isn't he gorgeous?" Millie says dreamily, as all too quickly, the boy runs off again.

"Shhh, Mil, Jamie's right there," I remind her guiltily. After all, *my* boyfriend's right there too.

"Oh, big whoop. I'm only looking and they aren't bothered. We could talk about anything and they wouldn't pay any attention. Watch." Millie raises her voice. "There's a pink donkey somersaulting over the fence!"

The boys carry on chatting, completely oblivious.

"See? Told you. Nothing," Millie says. "His name's Zach.

He moved here from Cornwall and has the sexiest arms I've *ever* seen. I think he's so buff from all the surfing. He's in my maths set and even makes algebra appealing. I could literally watch him all day and not get bored."

"You're unbelievable," I say, giggling.

"Hey." Jamie turns abruptly. His forehead crinkles in bewilderment as we stare at him guiltily. "Mills, did you just say something about a somersaulting donkey? What are you going on about now?"

Danny catches my eye, and we both start grinning.

So what if I've never felt anything for him like I just felt for Zach? It doesn't matter, because it's not as if it means anything.

I don't *think* so, anyway. Does it?

CHAPTER TWO

ONE OF life's most irritating mysteries is the reason why, every weekday, without fail, I'm knackered when I have to get up for school, but at the same time on a weekend, with all the hours in the world for zeds, I wake up at silly o'clock.

It's Saturday. I should be asleep.

I *want* to be asleep.

Snuggling deeper into my cosy nest of pillows and duvet, I try and distract myself with nice, comforting thoughts to send me back to Dreamsville. Thoughts like, my hair has turned sleek and straight overnight. I've got backstage passes to meet my all-time favourite band, The Drifting. Amber's decided I don't have to be a bridesmaid... All I'm going to do right now is sleep, sleep, sle—

"*Hehehehe!*"

Eh? What's that noise?

It'll go away.

I'm probably hearing things.

22

Ah, blissful, lovely sleep, come to me. . .

I'm finally dropping off when I hear it again.

"*Hehehehe!*"

Slowly my brain begins to creak into action as I start to figure out what's going on.

"*Hehehehe!*"

And then I sit bolt upright, because I've worked it out.

Harry. My seven-year-old sister, and more irritating than itching powder in your pants. Harry specialises in appalling practical jokes and to say she's annoying would be the understatement of the century. I've often wondered if I might be adopted, because I have no idea how my sisters and I come from the same gene pool.

Although I can't actually see anything suspicious, the curtains are still closed and it's pretty dark in here. I flick on the bedside lamp, remembering some of the hideous things Harry's done in the past, like the time she put slime from the pond in a tray by the side of my bed, so when I got up, my feet hit slippery goo and I completely freaked out.

Or the Monday she set my alarm clock two hours fast. I was halfway to school before I figured out what was going on.

Or the morning she hid a frog in my bed...

So the question is, what's Harry done now?

"*Hehehehe!*"

I gingerly lift the duvet and peep underneath. No amphibians in sight, but she's definitely up to *something*.

"Harry? I know that's you. I'm not falling for any of your dumb tricks, so get lost," I shout.

The giggle gets louder.

"Ugh, you need putting down," I say, clambering out of bed and flinging open the door. Before I know it, a cascade of cold water and ice cubes lands on my head as a Tupperware tub bounces onto the floor.

"YEEEEEEEEWWWW!" I scream.

Harry appears on the landing and collapses in hysterics onto the carpet. "I got you, I got you. That was the funniest thing ever!"

My mind speedily rewinds a couple of seconds. The door was ajar. And I always, without fail, sleep with my bedroom door firmly closed, to keep the poison dwarf out. I can't believe I've fallen for the 'water on top of the door' scam. It's the oldest trick in the book, and I'm *soaking*. Not to mention freezing cold.

I scrape my hair back from where it's clinging to my face in soggy rat tails, before peeling my now obscenely see-through pyjama top away from my body.

"I. Am. Going. To. Kill. You," I tell her, my teeth chattering.

I must look pretty terrifying, because Harry scrambles to her feet and backs away. "It was just a joke."

"Do I look like I'm laughing?"

"Dad," Harry yells, dodging my outstretched hand. "Suzy's picking on me."

"Suzy, stop teasing your sister," I hear Dad shout.

What the... ? How unfair is this?

"I'm so getting you back," I say darkly, as Dad bounds up the stairs.

I clamp one hand across my chest to cover myself before Harry and I start speaking at once.

"Dad, look what she did..."

"It was just a joke, Dad..." Harry's the very picture of innocence.

Dad's mouth twitches at the corners. Harry is Dad's favourite, and he's not ashamed who knows it. He always felt outnumbered living with Mum, Amber and me, so when Mum got pregnant for the third time, he was convinced he'd finally be blessed with a boy. Apparently when the midwife announced, "It's a beautiful girl," he cried louder than Harry did. Unable to tolerate another female in the house, Dad decided to treat the new baby like an honorary son (hence why she's Harry, rather than Harriet).

Of course, Dad isn't the only man in the house since Mark moved in while he and Amber save up for a place, but as Mark doesn't like football, monster trucks or beer (he prefers bird watching, musicals and gin and tonic),

Dad feels Mark might as well be another woman.

Harry grins winningly at Dad and he bursts out laughing.

"It's only a bit of water, Suze," Dad says. "Go and get yourself dried off. As for you, monkey child, come and get a towel to clean up that carpet." Dad slings his arm around Harry's shoulders. I hear him chuckling as they clatter downstairs. "Now, what are we going to do today while the womenfolk are out shopping?"

The favouritism in this house is totally unfair. Harry *always* gets special treatment. She's even managed to weasel out of being a bridesmaid. When Mum and Amber told her she'd have to wear a dress, she lay on the kitchen floor and screamed with fury.

And then screamed again.

And then she screamed a bit more, just for good measure.

Harry was blue when they eventually gave in. I tried the same tactic, but Mum told me to stop being childish as I was being a bridesmaid (the only bridesmaid, at that) whether I liked it or not.

If you ask me, it's blatant discrimination. I should probably sue.

"No, no, *no*," Mum says loudly, emerging from Harry's room, a handful of dirty clothes in one hand, the phone clamped to her ear with the other.

"What's all the shouting for?" Amber peers out from

behind her bedroom door, yawning widely. Her long brown hair's tousled and her big blue eyes seem confused.

"I don't want to cancel the appointment," Mum explains, sounding exasperated and pretending to bash her head against the wall. "I want to make it an hour later, that's all. Something's come up. It's booked in the name of Puttock, we're coming to try on some bridesmaid's dresses. Yes, Puttock, with a P... a *P!*"

"You look weird," Amber says to me, blinking as her forehead creases. Her brain's probably unused to so much activity this early in the morning and is feeling the strain.

Mum pulls a frustrated face as the woman in the bridal department still seems to be having difficulties, then covers the mouthpiece. "Suzy, what have you been up to? Your pyjamas are transparent. And what on earth is going on with your hair? You look like the wild woman of Borneo."

Well, that's just charming. I open my mouth for a sarky retort, but Mum gets in first.

"Go and get changed, we're going soon. And stop dripping everywhere, you'll ruin the carpet."

"Oh right," Amber says, snapping her fingers. "You're all wet. Did you shower with your clothes on? Why would you do that? Were you in a rush or something?"

"Aaaaargh," I yell, stamping back into my room and slamming my door so loudly that the Drifting poster over my bed falls down. What did I do to get lumbered with a family this nuts? It must have been something really, really bad. I raise my gaze heavenwards and offer silent apologies to anyone up there who I might possibly have offended. But clearly my plea for forgiveness isn't heard, because a few moments later there's a knock on my door.

"What?" I'm balancing on my pillows, trying to stick the poster back up and make sure it's straight. Once it's in place, I give it a fond stroke. I love, love, love this band. Their music is the best.

Mum sticks her head inside. "Are you nearly ready?"

"Funnily enough, no. In the two seconds since you last saw me, I've not dried off. I'm drenched, thanks to that mutant halfwit you insist is my sister. You should have sold her at birth," I reply, jumping off the bed to grab a towel before dabbing at my head. The merest whiff of moisture and my curls take a turn for the mental, so today is set to be a seriously bad hair day.

"Why are we leaving so soon, anyway?" I ask grumpily. "Didn't I hear you move our appointment back?"

"Er, we'll be taking a little detour," Mum says, sheepishly.

"A detour? Where?" I squeeze a new serum into my hand. Maybe this will be the one to tame the untameable. I stare hopefully into the mirror, but as I start smoothing it in, it's quickly apparent it's not to be. How disappointing.

I add it to the pile of failed bottles in the corner of my room and wrestle my hair into a ponytail with a sigh.

"I was speaking to Aunty Lou yesterday, and she mentioned she'd really like to come with us," Mum explains. "We're going via the home to collect her."

Oh no. Not Great Aunt Loon.

Great Aunt Loon is proper bonkers, with the kind of selective deafness that can drive a person insane. She's tiny and gives the appearance of a fragile old lady, but that shouldn't fool you. More spiteful than a snake with a toothache, her hobbies probably include sacrificing kittens and eating newborns. Unfortunately, as Aunt Lou's practically the only relative left in Mum's family (I suspect the Loon sold her soul to the devil in return for immortality), we're stuck with the old bat.

"Come on, Suzy," Mum says, when she sees my dismayed face. "She's not that bad, although I appreciate she can be a little... er..."

"Evil? Vindictive? Poisonous?"

"*Difficult*," Mum continues, pretending not to hear, "but this is a special occasion for Amber so I'm sure she'll behave. Everyone loves a wedding. Now, get yourself changed, so we can go and find you a dress."

"Yeah, Mum, about that. Does it have to be lime green? Seriously?"

"I know it's not the most flattering colour in the world..." Mum begins.

"It's disgusting," I say flatly. "Who has lime green as the theme for their wedding anyway?"

"Well, you know she wants what Conni G had," Mum says, "and if it's what she's set her heart on, Suzy, couldn't you just wear the dress? It's only for one day."

"One day where I'll be photographed a billion times. The pictures will haunt me for the rest of my life. Please can't you talk to her? Try and make her see sense? Just think about it. What if she wants your Mother of the Bride outfit to match as well?"

Mum goes pale. Hah! I guess she hadn't thought about that possibility.

"Maybe you're right. I'll see what I can do," Mum says. She walks over and wraps me in a squashy embrace. "Ugh, you're still all clammy. Finish getting ready and then we can go. It's going to be a lovely day, us girls together. You'll see."

What an absolute porker! And from my own mother, too. I squeeze her back, then quickly leap away, just in case she gets struck down by lightning for her fibbing. I don't want to be anywhere near if that happens. My hair's insane enough already without a zillion volts of electricity helping it along.

CHAPTER THREE

"**Young lady**, would you slow down?" Aunty Lou bellows in my ear, gripping my arm with the strength of a vice. "I'm eighty-six. Have some consideration."

I somehow manage to refrain from pointing out that if I slow down any more we'll be walking backwards. It's taken ten minutes just to get across the car park and we're still nowhere near the inside of the department store, where Mum and Amber will be waiting impatiently in front of the escalators.

I can't believe I had to turn down shopping with Millie for *this*.

Mum fake smiles as we approach, and starts to speak v-e-r-y s-l-o-w-l-y and LOUDLY, enunciating every word. "All right there, Aunty Lou? We're going up to the bridal floor now."

"I'm never going to manage those stairs," Aunty Lou

says, waving her walking stick and nearly decapitating a nearby toddler. His mother glowers in our direction as we all pretend not to have noticed.

"It's fine, there's a lift," Mum says.

"My hips? Yes, they're awful. They're thinking about surgery, you know, but they operated on Glynis Jones two weeks ago and she never woke up."

"No, there's a LIFT!" Mum shouts.

"Well, why didn't you say so? Come on, hurry up. I need to be back at three for my bingo."

Mum looks like she wants to grab Aunt Lou's walking stick and poke it in a very rude place. I can hear her teeth grinding.

When we eventually make it to the lift, disaster occurs on a catatonic scale. The flipping thing is out of use. It seems that the store is reorganising their stock in a major way, and they need the lift to move clothes around. And of course the bridal section is right at the top of the five-storey shop. As we slowly make our way up the escalators, I decide even climbing Everest can't be this challenging. But I suppose Edmund Hillary had the sense not to take any geriatric relatives with him.

Good Lordy, I'm knackered. Who knew that manoeuvring wrinklies was such hard work?

When we finally make it to the top floor, we appear to

have arrived in a parallel universe — a universe where a small child has run amok with glitter, lace and frills. In front of me there's a sea of white froth, silvery tiaras and bridesmaids' dresses in every pastel colour imaginable.

It's like a Barbie factory spewed up in here.

I want to go home.

Now.

But that's not going to happen any time soon, given the way Amber's staring around in delight, making guinea-pig squeaks of excitement and clapping her hands. But then a place like this is heaven to Amber, who's a twenty-two-year-old die-hard romantic.

She got engaged to Mark on their fortnight anniversary. Yes, that's right, after fourteen whole days. There are *cyclones* that move slower than these two. The best bit is that she only found out his last name after they'd got engaged. It's Mycock. I laughed for a week once I heard, because only Amber could have found the one person in the world with a surname worse than Puttock. But she doesn't care, because she's so vomitously in love with her hubby-to-be.

"Oooh, they've got new ring cushions in," Amber says, picking up the most revolting satin and gold monstrosity with the words *Love and Cherish Forever* embroidered on it. "Aren't they beautiful?"

Aunty Lou scowls, grabs the cushion and shoves it under her bum as she collapses into a chair, muttering something disturbing about piles.

"Hello there. Can I help you?" A lady with radioactive orange foundation and bright pink lipstick is bearing down on us.

"Yes," says Mum. "We have an appointment at eleven. We're here to find a bridesmaid's dress for my daughter."

"Lovely, lovely." The woman beams. "Could you confirm the surname for me please?"

"Puttock," Mum replies.

The woman gives a snort, which she hastily turns into a cough when she sees three stony faces glaring at her, and consults her book. "Ahem. Right, here you are. If you'd like to follow me…" She spins around on unfeasibly high heels and sets off at a *click-clack* trot across the floor.

"Don't forget your aunt," Mum hisses at me over her shoulder.

Why is she my responsibility all of a sudden? It's not even as if she's particularly portable, like a lip balm or something.

"Come on, Aunty Lou." I offer my arm.

Aunty Lou glares. "What?"

"We're going to see the dresses," I explain.

"The what?"

"The dresses!"

"But I've only just sat down," Aunty Lou moans.

I pretend not to have heard and heft her onto her feet. We shuffle towards Mum and Amber – Aunty Lou grumbling every slow, painful step of the way.

As we get nearer, I hear what the startled shop assistant is saying. "I'm sorry, I'm not sure I understand. You *do* know what colour lime green is?"

"Yes," Amber says, beaming.

"And you want a *bridesmaid's* dress in that colour?"

"Yes," confirms Amber.

"In *satin*? You realise how shiny that is?"

"Yes." Amber nods.

The shop assistant gulps and shoots me a sympathetic glance. "Um, I see. How very… unusual. I'll just go and have a chat to my colleague about what we could do for you."

"Mum," I say, meaningfully.

"Hang on just a minute," Mum says to the shop assistant. "Amber, are you sure lime green is the colour you want? It's very… um… *lurid*. And perhaps not the easiest for Suzy to wear."

"Mum, it's the theme," Amber says, pouting. "Lime green. You know that. Suzy's dress has got to match."

"But have you seen this?" Mum says, and in a rare

stroke of brilliance produces a celebrity magazine from her bag. She flips through the pages and stops at Conni G's *What's Hot/What's Not* list. How Conni got a column in a magazine when it's doubtful she's even literate is baffling.

"Look at the *What's Not* list," Mum says.

Amber reads the page painfully slowly, mouthing the words and twizzling a strand of hair around her finger. Then she gasps in horror.

"Conni says bright colours are totally over," Amber wails. "Oh no. This ruins *everything*. What are we going to do?"

"But she also says pastels are in," Mum says quickly, smiling at me. "Especially pink. And you love pink, Amber."

"Do you think that pink would work? Really? Oooh, I can't breathe. And I think I'm going to throw up," Amber says, clutching a hand to her chest. "I'm feeling really pukey all of a sudden. Oooh, this is a disaster."

"Now, calm down," Mum says, rubbing Amber's back as she inhales and exhales slowly, urging Amber to copy her. "I think pink would look stunning."

"You're sure?" Amber gasps, between breaths.

Mum nods.

"I guess pink would be pretty," Amber says. She inhales deeply one last time and nods shakily. "Okay. If that's what Conni says, she must be right. I'll change the theme to pink."

Yes! Saved. My mother is an evil genius. I flash her

a grateful grin. I mean, it's still pink, which isn't my favourite colour in the world, but it's preferable to the hideousness that would have been a lime green dress.

"So we're decided on the pink?" the sales assistant asks warily.

"We're decided," Mum says.

"Lovely," the sales assistant says. "Wait here a moment and I'll go and pick out some gowns."

"This is soooo exciting!" Amber says, clapping her hands. Her mood has completely transformed. "Are you excited too, Suzy?"

"Er…"

"Suzy," Mum warns.

"So excited I could burst," I squeal, ignoring Mum's death glare.

Amber beams happily. She has no comprehension of sarcasm.

"These are a few of our most popular styles," the shop assistant says, returning with a stack of clothes.

Hmm. They don't look too great from where I'm standing. And they definitely won't go with my Converse.

Mum sees my expression. "Suzy, these dresses are lovely." She comes closer and hisses in my ear, "Be thankful they're not green." Deftly, she whips Aunty Lou off my arm and pushes me in the direction of the changing rooms. "Off you go and try these on."

Before I know what's happening, I'm standing in a cubicle wriggling out of my jeans and retro Wonder Woman tee, only to be faced with a giant reflection of myself in the mirror.

My hazel eyes, carefully rimmed with brown eyeliner, blink in surprise.

Blimey. Talk about a close-up. You can see *all* the pores on my nose. And I really should have worn some better undies. My pants have gone grey in the wash, and there's a hole in my bra.

"How are you getting on in there, Suzy?" Mum says loudly. "Do you need a hand?"

Does the woman think I'm still a child? Honestly. I'm perfectly capable of dressing myself.

"Just a sec," I call back.

Right. There's clearly no escape, so I'm going to have to do this. Which is the least hideous?

Taking a deep breath, I pick one out and tug it on. It's not good. There's a huge bow that rests at the bottom of my back while the material sags unattractively, cleverly avoiding any of the curves of my body. I might as well be wearing a pink sack.

I rummage through my backpack and find my mobile, tapping out a quick text to Danny.

**Am in shopping hell, trapped in the world's
worst dress. Kill me now. Or better still,
come 2 my rescue.**

Danny replies within seconds.

Hah! No way. You're on your own.

Pfff. Some knight in shining armour he is. I stamp outside the changing room.

"Hideous," Aunt Lou says with a disdainful sniff.

"She's right. It's terrible. It doesn't fit her properly, and the dress has to be perfect – perfect, Mum!" Amber's voice has gone high and panicky again.

"Amber, calm down, for heaven's sake. There are lots more left for Suzy to try. Go and put on the next one, Suze," Mum says. "And cheer up, this is supposed to be fun."

I huff off to try dress number two.

It's equally nasty, much too long, and the strangest shade of pink I've ever seen. Kind of like gammon, I guess. I very much doubt gammon is the theme my sister has in mind for her wedding, and sure enough it gets the thumbs down from the judging panel outside. As do dresses three to thirteen.

By the time I pull on dress fourteen, I'm losing the will to live. Even Aunt Lou had the sense to fall asleep at dress seven; her rumbling snores have been drifting over the curtain for the last half hour.

This one's not too awful, I guess, although there are way too many fabric flowers and ruffles for my liking. It's a pale baby pink, and A-line, fitted under the bust. It's the best so far, apart from one ginormous hitch: the top appears to have been designed with a glamour model in mind. You could fit at least another four pairs of bazoomas in here, so there's no way it'll stay up with just my chest to cling on to. And it's about twice the length of my body. I step into the huge heels I was given for trying-on purposes, and teeter gingerly outside, holding onto the neckline for dear life.

"Ooh, that one's pretty," says Amber, a huge smile on her face. "Yes, I think we might finally have found it."

"It's lovely," Mum says, bustling up and fiddling with the skirt. She slaps at my hands. "Let go, Suzy, we want to see."

"You'll see more than you bargained for if you're not careful," I say, fighting her off with my elbows. "If I let go, I'll be wearing it round my ankles."

"That doesn't look much like a wedding dress to me," Aunty Lou says, waking up with a start. "Is this what they're wearing nowadays?"

"Aunt Lou, it's Amber who's getting married, remember?" Mum says. "Suzy's the bridesmaid and we're shopping for her today."

"The what?" Aunt Lou says, cupping her hand around her ear.

"Suzy is a bridesmaid, not the bride," Mum says more loudly.

"You said we were shopping for the bridal gown," Aunty Lou says, sounding appalled.

"No, I said we were shopping for Suzy. You told me you wanted to see what she was going to be wearing. Doesn't she look lovely?"

"If I'd known it was only the bridesmaid's outfit, I'd never have come," Aunt Lou snaps. "I missed bridge for this. You lied to get me here."

"I didn't lie, Aunt Lou," Mum says, taking a deep breath. Her hands are starting to clench. "I told you exactly what we were doing today. Now, what do you think of this dress?"

"It's a bit big, isn't it?" Aunty Lou says, extracting her glasses from their case and fumbling them onto her nose. She hauls herself onto her feet and hobbles closer before jabbing at my right boob with a bony finger. "She hasn't got much in the way of a bosom, has she?"

"Get off," I say, twisting away. "I'm perfectly happy with my breasts, thank you very much."

"You what? Speak up. You youngsters are always mumbling. No proper elocution."

"I said, I'm perfectly happy with my breasts," I shout.

A whole floor of shoppers falls silent before their

gazes universally swivel in the direction of my chest.

"If you say so," Aunty Lou replies dismissively.

She is truly more evil than Satan himself.

"I'm going to see if I can find you a padded bra," Mum says. "We need to see the fit properly to make a decision. Wait here. And ignore her," Mum adds out of the corner of her mouth.

"I heard that," Aunty Lou says. "Don't think because I'm old that you can get away with being rude about me. Your mother would be ashamed."

"My mother loathed you, you mad old bag," Mum mutters as she goes off in search of the lingerie department, Aunty Lou following behind. Luckily for Mum, it's not long before a nearby chair provides a distraction and Aunt Lou gives up, deciding a snooze is the preferable option.

"Wow, look at these," Amber says, holding up some pink, shimmery fairy wings. "I could have some fairy flower girls – that'd be lovely, wouldn't it, Suzypoos? But we don't have anyone young enough in the family who'd do it. I know Harry won't. Maybe you'd..."

"Don't even think about it," I tell her firmly.

"Oh well. Perhaps you'll change your mind. I'll be back in a bit, I'm going to try on some tiaras."

Well, thanks *very* much everyone. Just abandon me here, why don't you? It's not like I can move, because there's a distinct possibility I'll fall over, let go of the dress and end up semi-starkers — and *nobody* needs to see that. Good job it's not too busy in here, so there're not many people around to witness this.

Although... that girl walking towards me looks a lot like Jade Taylor from school.

Exactly like her in fact.

Wait a minute... it *is* Jade Taylor.

Universe, why do you hate me so?

Of all the people I don't want to see right now, Jade Taylor tops the list. She's super gorgeous, with her pouty lips, huge eyes and perfect, ruler-straight, honey hair. The boys all fancy her, which isn't surprising, given the way she sashays through the corridors in her too-tight shirts and short flippy skirts. The boys, she's nice to. The girls... not so much. You don't want to get on the wrong side of Jade. She'll make your life hell.

Maybe it's not really her, and it's just a lookalike.

Nope. It's definitely her.

My life is over.

Please, go the other way, go the other way... I wish harder than I've wished for anything before in my life, but she's not going the other way. In fact, she's heading straight for me.

I cannot, under any circumstances, let Jade see me like this.

Gazing around in desperation, I duck down behind the nearest clothes rail. But somehow I get tangled in my hem and trip over, ending up on my bum and clinging to the dress's bodice for dear life.

I lower my head and stare at the ground, trying to pull the hanging clothes around me. Please, please, let me be invisible...

"Suzy?" Jade pokes at me with the toe of her Ugg boot before pulling apart the clothes hangers. "Is that you? Why are you scrabbling round on the floor?"

I scramble to my feet, which isn't the easiest when you're wearing massive heels and don't have use of your hands. "Oh, um, hi, Jade. I was, er, checking they swept the floor properly. I'm here with my great aunt who gets asthma and dust is, um, really bad for people with allergies."

What am I *saying*? Brain to mouth, brain to mouth, change the subject. Now.

"So, um, what are you doing here?"

"Trying to find the toilets," Jade says, rearranging her armful of shopping bags. "You're not seriously buying that dress, are you? It's vile."

"My big sister's getting married," I mumble. "I'm the bridesmaid."

"And that's what she's making you wear?" Jade says meanly. "She doesn't like you much, does she?"

44

I'm saved from having to reply because Jade's stopped paying attention. "Over here," she calls. "God, where have you been?"

I swear my heart stops beating as Zach, of all people, walks up. What's he doing here? And why's he with Jade?

"Just around," Zach says, sounding bored. "Who's this?" he asks. "Oh... you. I know you from somewhere."

Yes, you do, I want to scream with delight, thrilled that he remembers me. *I'm the girl you dropped the football in front of. We shared a look! There was a connection!*

"You look really familiar. You go to Collinsbrooke, right? Are you in one of my classes?"

"Er, no."

C'mon, keep thinking, the football field, you saw me on the football field...

"Hang on, now I remember," the boy says, clicking his fingers and starting to laugh. "You're the girl who pulled down Ryan's shorts, aren't you? That was one of the funniest things I've ever seen. I only wish I'd filmed it."

Oh. So that's why he remembers me.

I'm standing in front of the fittest guy I've ever met and, miracle of miracles, he's aware of my existence — but it's only because he witnessed my most cringesome moment *ever*.

Thank goodness he didn't film it. The last thing I need is to be plastered all over YouTube, my humiliation broadcast on a global scale.

"This is Suzy Puttock." There's an evil glint in Jade's big brown eyes as she places extra emphasis on my surname.

Zach snorts. "Puttock? Seriously? As in, rhymes—"

"And this is Zach," Jade coos, interrupting him.

As if I need telling.

I can't seem to drag my eyes away from Zach's light brown hair, flecked through with blond highlights from the sun. Or his dark green eyes, which have the longest lashes I've ever seen on a boy. Or his achingly-cool outfit, a red printed tee over designer jeans.

Trust Jade to already have her perfectly French-manicured claws in him.

"That's certainly an interesting dress," Zach says, his gaze flicking up and down my body.

Crikey. The way his eyes are scanning me *everywhere* is making me feel all kinds of peculiar.

I should probably say something to show what a witty and amusing individual I am, and how I totally see the funny side in this whole situation.

"Um, thanks," I say, swallowing awkwardly. "It's not my choice. I don't like ruffles, or dresses even. I usually look perfectly normal, honest, in jeans or leggings or something, but you know what weddings are like, they send people crazy and you can't stop my mother and sister when they get going. They picked this out but the top's way too big so I'm stuck here because I can't walk in these heels and I didn't want to flash my boobs..."

The moment the word 'boobs' exits my mouth, I stop talking and my cheeks burn hotly. What is *with* me? Did I *seriously* just say 'boobs' in front of him? That little speech was about as far away from witty and amusing as you can get. I am *such* a loser.

"Suzy, where are you?" Mum calls from the middle of the shop.

"Over here," I reply, without thinking.

"I've got you a bumper-boost bra to try," she hollers, shaking it in the air. "It took ages to get your size as you're so small but I've finally found one with plenty of extra padding."

For the second time in twenty minutes the shop falls silent and everyone stares at my chest.

I can hear blood pumping in my ears. "I... er..."

"We have to go," says Jade, whipping an iPhone out of her bag. She holds it up and snaps a quick photo.

"Hey," I protest as Jade starts to text at top speed.

Great. Just great. That'll be my photo posted all over the internet, then.

"Bye, Suzy," Jade says, pulling Zach away before I can make a grab for the phone.

"Yeah, bye," I mutter.

Thanks for nothing, Mum.

CHAPTER FOUR

"IT WAS such a nightmare," I wail down the phone. "Stop laughing."

"Okay, okay, it's just..." Millie's off again, giggling madly.

In your own time, Mills. Don't mind me.

"Oh, Suze, I'm sorry," Millie says, trying to stifle her laughter.

"Liar."

"No, I am, honest. It must have been beyond awful. But you have to admit, it is pretty funny..."

"It's not," I protest. "There's not enough brain bleach in the world to erase the image of Mum waving around that bra. How can I go back to school now? Jade will have told *everyone*, *and* she's probably plastered that photo everywhere online. I don't even want to know what Zach thought. As if remembering me because of what happened on the football field wasn't hideous enough."

"Well, to be fair, it's not exactly forgettable," Millie says, unhelpfully. "So do you think Zach is Jade's boyfriend?"

"I guess. But aren't we getting off topic? We're focusing on the fact that this time, I am actually going to die of embarrassment. Over the last few days, my humiliation quota has been reached, and death is the only way out. You'd better come to my funeral, or I'm going to haunt you for all eternity and focus my paranormal powers on throwing stuff at your head."

"It's really annoying Jade's nabbed him already," Millie says.

"Er, haven't you forgotten something? A small matter of Jamie? Your boyfriend?"

"Oh shush," Millie says. "I'm only saying. So, did you get a dress in the end?"

"Yeah," I say with a sigh. "Luckily Mum talked Amber out of the lime green, so we've gone with the pink one requiring the bumper-boost bra of shame, but only on the condition some serious alterations take place. I have no desire to end up semi-naked in a church."

"That would be pretty horrific," Millie says. "Anyway, what are you up to tonight? You and Danny want to come out with Jamie and me?"

"Can't. Mum and Dad have taken Aunty Loon home and are going out for dinner on the way back. Amber's gone with Mark to choose stuff for their gift list, and I'm the sucker lumbered with babysitting Harry."

"Just you and Harry? In the house on your own?" Millie sounds alarmed. "You'll kill each other."

"Nah, it's all right, Danny's coming over. He's bringing a DVD. I'm planning on locking Harry in a cupboard so we can have a romantic evening together."

"Sounds great," Millie says. "After blackmailing Jamie into coming shopping, I had to promise I'd see a dumb martial arts film with him. No romance for us, just a whole lot of karate chopping."

Buzzzzzzzzzzz!

The sound of the doorbell echoes through the house and moments later Harry races past. "Danny's here! Danny's here!"

"Blimey, someone's keen," Millie says.

"Tell me about it. He's the big brother she never had. I'd better rescue him."

"Flipola, I've gotta go too," Millie says. "I'm supposed to be at Jamie's in five, and that's not going to happen. See ya."

In the mere milliseconds it takes to press the button that ends our call, Harry's attached herself to Danny's arm and is telling him everything she's done over the past week. Danny even seems interested, the freak.

He's always saying he's jealous of my sisters and loud, crazy family. It's just him and his dad since his parents divorced, so his house is always really quiet. I think it's heaven. Danny says it's boring.

"Hi, Suze." Danny leans over Harry's head to give me a kiss. I suppose at least I get some affection in the privacy of my own home. As long as my parents aren't around, that is.

"Yuck!" Harry says, sticking her fingers down her throat before running off.

"I brought supplies," Danny says, holding up a carrier bag from the corner shop. "Crisps, popcorn and triple-choc ice cream."

"Yum, you star."

"Thought you might need them after that shopping trip." As Danny takes off his coat, I see he's wearing battered jeans along with his ancient *Star Wars* T-shirt, the one with the hole under the armpit and a picture of Darth Vader pointing a finger at you above the caption *I AM YOUR FATHER*. Sometimes it seems like he wears nothing else. I wonder if he'd be up for wearing clothes more like the ones Zach was wearing, but when I've tried mentioning it before, he's just not been interested.

"So on a scale of one to ten, just how bad was today?" Danny asks.

"Easily hitting a hundred. Hey, Harry, go steady!"

Harry has hurtled back towards us, unable to stay away long, and grabbed Danny round the knees in a rugby tackle, barrelling head first into his crotch. Danny's eyes water and his face takes on a purple tinge.

"Danny, Danny, come with me," Harry orders. "I've got a new joke to show you."

"Give me a sec," Danny says, wincing, his voice a few notches higher than normal. "I don't know what you think is so funny," he reprimands, when he sees me sniggering. Finally he straightens up and breathes deeply. "Okay. I'm ready." Danny thrusts the carrier bag at me as Harry drags him away. In the kitchen I empty the snacks into bowls and grab a couple of spoons for the ice cream. I check to see what film he's brought.

I should have guessed. *Star Wars: A New Hope.* Sure, I thought the film was good the first time I saw it, and the second time it was still pretty entertaining. By the fifth viewing it was losing its appeal a smidge. I've lost count how often we've watched it now. And if the boredom wasn't bad enough, Danny insists on reciting all of the lines along with the actors. Which is really, *really* annoying. Plus, it's hardly conducive to a romantic atmosphere, is it?

Honestly, boys have no idea. And this particular boy is about as romantic as a warthog.

Although... if I set everything up in the lounge, I can

stick another DVD in the machine and pretend I never saw the one he bought.

Genius!

I gather up the food and head towards the front room. All the lights are off, and I'm nudging the door open with my shoulder when I hear something weird. It sounds like a scratching noise but then becomes a kind of moan. My heart starts pounding.

Then I realise what's going on.

"I know that's you, Harry," I say wearily. "You're not getting me twice in one day."

"No, Suzy, it's me," says Danny.

I take a deep breath, putting the bowls down on the floor as I move to flick on a lamp. Danny's got his hands clasped over his eye, his face scrunched in agony.

"What's wrong?" I ask, alarmed.

"My eye... it really hurts. Would you mind checking it out?" He groans again as I rush over. When Danny pulls his hand away, I scream in horror as his eyeball falls out and bounces against his cheek.

Danny bursts out laughing and Harry pops out from behind the curtain, squealing with delight. They reward each other with a triumphant fist-bump.

"You *idiot*." I thump Danny on the arm as hard as I can. Jeez, my heart's *racing*.

54

"Sorry," Danny says, still amused. "Harry asked me to road-test her new fake eyeballs. You have to admit, we got you pretty good."

"I'm only forgiving you because you bought ice cream," I say grumpily, "but don't you dare pull something like that again. And by the way, I refuse to watch *Star Wars*, no matter how much you pout."

"Oh c'mon, Suze, it's a cult classic," Danny says.

"Well, for once, I'd like to see something else. Amber's got some good movies in her room we can check out."

"I'm watching too, I'm watching too," Harry says, jumping up and down on one of the chairs.

"No, you're not," I tell her firmly, as Danny says, "Sure."

"Danny, we're supposed to be spending the evening together," I protest.

"We are," says Danny, infuriatingly logically. "You're here, I'm here, we're together."

"Spending the evening together *on our own*," I say meaningfully. "The film I pick might be a fifteen. I can't let Harry watch that, can I?"

"But you're babysitting her, remember?" Danny says. "And anyway, Harry texted earlier to tell me to bring *Star Wars* over."

"You stole my phone again?" I scowl fiercely at

Harry, who smiles back smugly.

"C'mon, Suzy, we love *Star Wars*," Danny says.

"Yeah, Suzy, we love *Star Wars*," Harry echoes.

What choice do I have? Defeated, I curl into the corner of the sofa while Danny retrieves the DVD and sticks it in.

"Yay!" says Harry, sticking her tongue out and grabbing my spoon.

"That's mine," I object, trying to snatch it back.

Harry stuffs the spoon in her mouth. "Mine now."

There are many occasions when I could cheerfully dismember my little sister, limb by limb. This is definitely one of them.

Danny kicks off his shoes and leaps onto the seat next to me, stretching his legs out over my lap.

"Move your stinky feet," Harry orders. She wiggles her way in between the two of us and takes control of the ice cream tub. Soon my sister and Danny are 'Daa daa, da da da daa daahing' along to the familiar theme tune happily.

I sigh loudly and shove a handful of crisps into my mouth.

So much for the plan of a romantic evening for two.

CHAPTER FIVE

"Right, everyone, the field is too muddy for team sports today, so we're doing a cross-country run," Miss Lewis says, striding into the changing rooms on Monday morning. 9C is loitering in various states of undress, and she's met with a chorus of groans and whimpers.

"I don't want to hear it," Miss Lewis says, shaking her clipboard. "I want positive attitudes, people. Running is a wonderful way to get our bodies feeling alive, and it's good for the soul."

Hmm, I beg to differ. Nothing that makes me want to die can be good for my soul.

If there was ever any doubt that the Head, Mr Parker, was a sadist, scheduling PE for first thing on a Monday morning proves it for sure. Like that's going to get a person bouncing out of bed with excitement, screaming, "Get me to school, pronto!" I'm scarcely able to prise my eyes open at this time of the morning, never mind wield a hockey stick, leap around a netball court or, worse still, brave the cross-country course. I hate running with every fibre of my being. I was not born to run. To sit or lie, yes. I am marvellous at those things. Can't get enough and could do them for hours. But running? Nuh-uh.

"We'll be doing a warm-up lap of the school field, then out onto the usual route," Miss Lewis continues. "And don't even think about taking shortcuts – there are TAs stationed around the course that will be checking you off as you pass. Anyone found cheating will be given detention. Now quickly finish getting ready, we need to get moving. I'll be back in two minutes to get you; I'm just going to see how Mr Barnes and the boys are getting on."

I pull up my joggers and slump onto the bench to tie my trainers. Next to me, I see Millie's tucking jelly babies into her sports bra.

"Emergency rations," she explains. "Sugar to keep me going. It's cold out there this morning."

"Freak," Jade says from the opposite bench. She bends down to pick up her clothes and her Aertex shirt gapes open so I get a full-on, in-your-face flash of cleavage. Most of the boys on the planet would maim their own mothers for the view I've just had. Jade would have fitted in the bridesmaid's dress without the bumper-boost bra, no problem.

I should probably stop staring at her chest, though.

58

People will get the wrong idea.

"You ready to get thrashed, Ka?" Jade asks her best friend, Kara.

Kara stretches out her hamstrings and snorts. "You wish. You know I'm a better runner than you."

"In your dreams," Jade snaps back.

I'm not entirely sure how Jade and Kara's friendship works. They're supposedly best mates, but don't actually seem to like each other that much. They're two of the most competitive people I've ever met. If they're not competing over boys or who can wear the coolest clothes, they're competing over sports. Everything comes down to who's the best, which if you ask me, must be exhausting.

"Right, girls, off we go," Miss Lewis calls, reappearing at the door.

Ugh. I so don't want to do this.

As Suzy and I follow behind Jade and Kara, we can hear every word of their conversation. They cackle about their mutual friend Bryony, who's off today. She cut her hair at the weekend and isn't in because her fringe looks like it was attacked by a goat. Then they start discussing Tasha, who got off with the spotty bloke from the chippy and is mortified in case anyone finds out. Which they will, because Jade and Kara plan on putting it on

Facebook, Twitter and every other social networking site they can think of, and find this notion highly hilarious.

As we arrive at the field and begin to warm up, Jade starts going on about some boy she fancies called Max, who apparently has the tightest butt she's ever laid eyes on.

"Aren't you going out with Zach?" The question pops out before I can stop myself, and immediately I regret it. Never, ever, draw Jade's attention to yourself, especially when you've been eavesdropping. Rookie mistake, Puttock!

Fortunately Jade looks too horrified to be narky. "Zach? God no! What made you think that?"

"Oh, um, because you were together on Saturday and I s'pose I, er, assumed y'know…" My voice trails off.

Jade stretches out her arms above her head. "Zach's my cousin. He moved here last month and my lame-o Mum is making me show him round. Total dullsville, but you know what parents are like."

I nod vigorously. Do I ever.

"Ugh, the idea of me and Zach… that's too pukey for words," Jade winces. "There was this one time when we were younger – he ran around my bedroom naked and peed in my wardrobe. I would never, not in a million years, not if he was the last person left on the planet, fancy him."

A vision of Zach running around with no clothes on burns my mind and my face gets hot. Luckily, we're bending down to touch our toes (or knees, in my case) and nobody notices.

"What do you care about Zach for, anyway?" Jade huffs her fringe out of her eyes and glances over at me. "You're with Danny Williams, aren't you?"

"Uh-huh."

"Fancy Zach though, do you?"

"No, I..."

But Jade isn't listening, because Miss Lewis has blown her whistle and she's sprinted off, Kara hot on her heels.

"What am I going to do?" I hiss at Millie. "Jade thinks I like Zach."

"Then you need to tell her that you don't," Millie says. "You know what a gossip she is. It'll be all over the school by lunch."

"But she's miles away," I wail.

Jade and Kara are already running out of the school gates, while we're barely halfway round the field.

"I guess you're just going to have to catch them up," Millie says. "You can do it, you were fast enough running onto the football field. Only don't do the falling over part this time."

Curse Jade and her motormouth. But I can't have a rumour spreading that I fancy Zach. It would be mortifying – and what would Danny say?

Okay. If I can run super-speedily to get to a football match, I can run super-speedily now. At least I'm in trainers today, so the risk of landing on my face should be minimal.

"See you later, then." I take a big breath, and start to force my feet forwards.

One, two, one, two, faster, faster, keep going, don't think about how much it hurts, don't think about how much it huuuuuuuurts...

As I race past Miss Lewis at the gates, she gives me an enthusiastic thumbs up and calls, "Fantastic, Suzy, great you're making an effort at last. Don't forget to pace yourself!"

In the distance, Jade and Kara are nearly on the golf course. As if running in public wasn't bad enough, part of our cross-country route is the footpath that runs through Collinsbrooke Golf Club. So while you're busy trying not to pass out from oxygen deprivation, you also have to keep your wits about you ducking the golf balls whistling past your ears.

"Jade!" I call, as I get closer. She doesn't hear me. Probably because what came out of my mouth was "Jaaa..." accompanied by a wheezing pant.

My lungs are burning and I think I'm in real danger of passing out, but I have to keep going.

"Jade!" I try again. This time she turns slightly and looks surprised to see me so nearby.

"Suzy? What do you want?"

"I, um, y'know, just wondered if I could keep pace with you guys for a bit," I lie.

Jade and Kara laugh. "Only if you can keep up, Puttock," Jade says, and they start to run even faster.

How are they doing that? They're not even out of breath. They're just pad, pad, padding along, ponytails swishing, like it's no big deal at all to be moving at such speed, while I'm on the verge of a heart attack.

"So, um, about earlier, I just wanted to say I don't like Zach," I say as casually as I can manage, when I finally catch them up again.

"What?" Jade frowns.

"Zach. You thought I liked him?"

"*That's* why you're running with us? Whatever."

"I didn't want you getting the wrong idea. Because I'm with Danny."

"Like I care."

"Well. Just in case. I'm with Danny, and not interested in Zach. Just so you know," I reiterate, leaving no room for doubt.

"It's not like you can tell you and Danny are together, though, can you?" Kara butts in. "We figured you two were just mates."

Ouch. Harsh. But there's no way I'm telling Jade and

Kara about Danny's weird showing-affection-in-public issues. And what does she mean they figured we were just mates? Have they been talking about us?

"Well, he's definitely my boyfriend," I say, forcing myself to smile extra-brightly as we run past a large group of golfers. They stop what they're doing to gawp.

"Hmm." Jade sounds disbelieving.

I blink as black spots appear in front of my eyes. I have no idea how much longer I can keep running like this; I can feel blood pumping in my ears. Am I going to pass out? Right here, in the middle of the golf course?

"Suzy?"

"Hmm?" Jade's been talking and I completely missed what she said.

"How long have you and Danny been going out? It must be forever."

"Oh. Yeah." It's taking a while to get my words out. "I guess since we were about thirteen."

"*Thirteen?*" sneers Kara. "You're *kidding.*"

"Er, no?"

"That's, like, so completely wrong," Jade says. "You're seriously saying you've never gone out with anyone else?"

I shake my head, my tummy beginning to flutter uncomfortably in a way that has nothing to do with the running. Jade's acting like I'm a complete freak. I mean,

I know it's kind of an unusual situation, but I've never felt weird about it before.

"Don't you think that's kind of tragic? Like, don't you wonder what you're missing out on?" Jade asks.

I'm confused. "What do you mean?"

"I've had eight boyfriends, and that's just this year," Jade says.

"And I've had nine," Kara interrupts.

"Shut up, Kara. What I was *trying* to say, before Kara butted in, is that getting different boys to like you is all part of the fun," Jade says. "I'm so good at it now, I'm pretty sure I could get anyone I wanted."

Wow. Clearly Jade wasn't at the back of the queue when egos were being handed out.

"Anyway, you're boring me now," Jade says. "C'mon, Kara, let's go." And with that, Jade and Kara sprint off across the field.

Ohmygod. That's it. I'm going to have to stop. I bend double, hands on my hips, desperately trying to get some air. There's a pain in my side every time I inhale. Ow, ow, ow, ow, ow. *How* is this good for you?

I can hear people running past me, a couple of them pausing to ask if I'm okay, but I wave them on. Then someone rubs me on the back.

"Hiya, Mills," I say, straightening up and wincing.

"How did it go?" she asks, jogging on the spot.

"Well, I cleared up the whole Zach thing, so, y'know, that's a good thing. But on the downside, I'm going to require a lung transplant and may never recover."

Millie fumbles around in her top and there's a wolf-whistle from somewhere. Some pervy golfing granddad, I imagine. "Jelly baby?" she offers.

"Um, gross, much? Funnily enough, I don't want to eat anything covered in your boob sweat," I say, and Millie laughs.

"Oh, you're such a cranky-pants. You ready to go now? I want to be back in time for break."

I start to run again, but stop after about three paces. It hurts too much. "You go ahead," I tell her. "I could be a while."

I wander on slowly, still clutching my side. Soon I think everyone's passed me, and I'm the last one left out here.

Ooh, look at that horse, peering over the fence. He looks friendly. I'll just stop for a moment to rest next to him, and then I'll make a proper effort to at least jog back to school, no matter how much pain I'm in.

I lean against the fence and pat the horse's nose. Then I jump out of my skin as I hear Miss Lewis, bellowing my name.

"Suzy Puttock, what do you think you're doing? I've got

66

three teachers out searching for you, thinking you must have suffered some kind of horrible injury and I find you lolling about, fondling a horse? It's not good enough. Detention, tomorrow after school."

CHAPTER SIX

"**Are you** still coming over later?" Millie asks after school the next day. She shoves books into her already full-to-bursting locker before forcing the door shut.

"Yep," I reply. "Soon as this dumb detention's over. Lewis is such a witch. Mum went mental when I gave her the detention slip."

"And you're sure you don't mind helping me walk Murphy? He—"

Down the corridor I see Ryan heading in my direction. Immediately I start searching for a place to hide. There has to be somewhere around here. Maybe I could fit into one of these lockers...

"Suzy, are you listening?" Millie asks.

"Ryan's coming," I hiss. "I can't let him see me."

"What? Don't be mental," Millie says, laughing. "Ryan can't still have it in for you. That thing on the football field was days ago."

"Yeah, well, he seems to have the memory of an elephant. Mills, you have to help me."

Millie shrugs then swoops forwards, holding her coat out wide like bat's wings.

"Oh, good one, subtle," I say.

"What?" Millie says. "You said help, so I hid you. Only obeying instructions."

"Has he gone?"

Millie checks up and down the corridor. "Yeah, you're safe. So you'll help me walk Murphy, then?"

Oh. I'd forgotten about that. Rats.

"Um, well, actually there's something I'm supposed to be doing," I say.

"Suze, you're such a liar." Millie sounds dismayed. "The boys have already vanished off somewhere. You promised you'd help. You know what Murphy's like."

Yes. I know exactly what Murphy's like. Which is precisely the reason I want to get out of going. After Millie's dad had too much to drink in the pub one night, he bought Murphy as a puppy from some random man. The guy promised it was a small dog, but Murphy's never really stopped growing. He's the size of a Shetland pony and probably weighs more than I do. Last time Millie took Murphy out, she almost got hauled into the duck pond on the common, but she completely adores him.

"Suze, you have to come," Millie begs. "Please, please, please, please. Say yes or I'm going to hold onto your leg and drag you over to Ryan."

She would, too.

"All right, all right," I surrender. "I'll be round in about an hour. But I've got to go, I'm late for Lewis."

Further down the corridor I bump into Jade, who's grabbing GHDs, a hair dryer, three different brushes and an armful of products from her locker.

So *that's* how she always looks so perfect. She carries an entire blimmin' salon around with her.

"Hi, Suzy," Jade says coolly. Her mobile starts to ring. "Here, hold these for me would you?"

Jade dumps everything into my arms then answers her phone. She starts giggling madly, while I stand laden down under the weight of all her things.

"Sorry about that," Jade apologises insincerely, when she finally ends the call. "Drew won't stop calling me."

"Drew?"

"He's at St Edward's," Jade explains. "He's goooorgeous. Nothing serious of course, but we're having a good laugh flirting, y'know? Oh no, silly me. Of course you don't."

Ouch. Score one for the bitch.

"That's because I never needed to," I retaliate.

Hah. Score one back for me.

Jade's face darkens.

Eep. Maybe I should have kept my mouth shut. Do I never learn?

"Um, see you later, I've got detention with Lewis," I say, hurriedly.

"Yeah, me too," Jade says.

"You? Why?"

Jade's one of Lewis's superstars, so what did she do wrong?

"I missed one of her stupid checkpoints yesterday and didn't get marked down, so now she's got it in her head I cheated to beat Kara," Jade says dismissively as I trail after her into the gym, still laden down like some kind of packhorse.

That'll mean she cheated then.

"You're late," Miss Lewis tells us sternly. "And what's all that, Suzy? This is a gymnasium, not a beauty salon."

"It's not mine, I—"

"I'm really not interested," Lewis says, striding over to the equipment cupboard and flinging the doors open, gesturing inside. "Right, I need all this stuff sorting. Year Seven were in here earlier and have left it in one hell of a state."

Is she for real? This place is a dump, plus it stinks of feet. There are quoits and hoops and unihoc sticks and a whole load of other stuff I don't even recognise in a massive tangle on top of the crash mats. And are those lacrosse sticks at the back of the cupboard? When has anyone at this school ever been posh enough to play lacrosse?

Jade and I are sorting through the beanbags and hockey pucks when Mr Patterson, my English teacher and the only decent-looking member of staff in this place, walks in.

"Miss Lewis, can I have a word?"

"Of course you can." Miss Lewis smiles girlishly, and Jade and I exchange a shocked glance. Lewis is actually batting her eyelashes. Blimey, I never knew she had it in her.

"I'm sorry to ask," Mr Patterson says, "but I've got a pupil in detention and I've been called to a departmental meeting. Nobody else is about. Can I leave him with you? He's got homework to finish."

"Not a problem," Miss Lewis says, smiling and fluttering so madly her glasses slide down her nose.

"In you come," says Mr Patterson, gesturing to someone in the corridor.

Oh flipping heck. Of *all* the people in this place, why did it have to be Zach?

Zach seems majorly grouchy until he spots Jade and me, then his face brightens a little. "Hi," he says.

I smile back and duck my head quickly, but not before I notice he's even cuter than I remember. His hair's flopping over his forehead and his green eyes are blazing. Mmm. Yummy.

No. I did not just think that. Behave, Suzy.

"This isn't a social club, young man," Miss Lewis says sharply. She hauls out one of the exam tables and a chair from the other cupboard, and gestures to it. "Get on with your work. I don't want to hear a peep out of you until you've finished."

Miss Lewis sits down and starts reading the paper.

I've been trying to untangle one of the badminton nets for what feels like five hours when Zach coughs loudly. The next thing I know, he's chucking a piece of tightly folded paper over in my direction. It skids along the floor and lands by my feet.

A note? For me?

The piece of paper has a couple of sentences written on it in Zach's loopy, practically illegible handwriting.

I'm very bored. Entertain me.

I tell myself Zach's only given it to me as Jade's buried deeper in the cupboard, and I'm easier to reach. He said himself he's looking for a way to pass the time. But even so I get a small flutter of butterflies.

I shrug and mouth back, *"What do you want me to do?"*

Then it's his turn to shrug, before he grabs his phone and starts texting.

Oh. Is that it, then?

Why didn't I do something more interesting? Now Zach probably thinks I was being totally dismissive. He wanted me to entertain him — I could have done, I don't know, a tap dance, perhaps. Well, maybe not that. But I should have done *something*.

Zach's still texting away, but finally he puts his phone down and starts scribbling something. Please let it be another note for me...

When I look around to see if Jade's noticed what we're doing, I realise she's given up with the tidying and is leaning up against the crash mats, texting at top speed, glancing up every now and then to keep an eye out for Lewis.

Zach's piece of paper comes skidding across the floor and I grab it, trying not to look too eager.

Wanna go and get a burger after school?

I stare at the note in shock. Huh? Is Zach asking me out? No. That can't be right.

Can it?

I read the note again.

I think he is.

But everyone knows that I'm with Danny. Although... Zach's new. So maybe he doesn't. What should I do? I bite my lip and risk a look at Zach, but he's texting again.

Miss Lewis clears her throat. "How's that assignment

coming along, Zach?"

"Nearly finished," Zach replies, hiding his phone as quick as a flash. When Miss Lewis has returned to her paper, he mouths, *"Well?"*

I gesture for him to chuck over his pen, trying to buy more time while I think of how to answer. Obviously I can't say yes. I mean, I wouldn't. I don't want to, because of Danny. But I don't want Zach getting the impression I'm a total dullard.

And then it hits me.

Is this *flirting*?

Wow. Maybe this is what Jade was talking about. She's right, this is kind of fun.

Wait. No. I shouldn't be thinking that. I shouldn't be flirting with someone else.

But then, Danny wouldn't *really* mind, would he? It's only a bit of fun, like Jade said. Danny probably flirts with girls all the time. I just don't know about it.

And it's not as though I *fancy* Zach or anything. I need to give him an answer.

Although I know I should tell Zach I've got a boyfriend, I find myself writing, *Can't tonight. Off to the park to help a friend walk her dog. Sorry.*

When Zach reads it, he shrugs yet again, and goes back to his essay.

And I'm left feeling strangely disappointed.

What feels like ten years later, we're finally out of detention. I hover by the door for a moment, waiting to see if Zach says anything to me, but Jade grabs hold of him the second Lewis lets us leave. Part of me thought I heard my name mentioned, but I'm probably being paranoid. Or Jade's über-nosy and wants to know what was in those notes. When I realise Zach's not leaving Jade's claws anytime soon, I give up and leave.

It's a good job I can walk the route to Millie's backwards and blindfolded, because right now I'm so befuddled I can scarcely remember how to put one foot in front of the other. I can't get my head round the fact someone so utterly amazing was flirting with me.

Yes, *me*!

But it's not like it *means* anything. Because I have Danny. My very lovely boyfriend.

Although… I don't remember when Danny last made me feel so fluttery and kind of, well, *alive*.

What if Jade was right and I am missing out?

No. She's wrong. She has to be.

I'm sure Zach was probably just trying to make the time go faster and make new friends or something.

Anyway, I can't ponder this any more. I'm at Millie's

front door. A furious barking erupts when I press the bell, and as usual, inside I can hear people shouting.

"Shut that dog up, the neighbours will complain again!" (Millie's mum.)

"I'm trying to. Stop it, Murphy, it's Suzy! Friend, Murphy, friend." (Millie.)

"What's for dinner, Mum?" (Millie's big sister, Sophie.)

"Suzy, if Murphy has anything to do with it." (Millie's mum.)

"Move, Murphy, darling, so I can get to the front door, would you? Move. Move!" (Millie.)

Eventually Millie manages to wrestle the door open. She looks exhausted, and we haven't even left the house yet. This isn't a good start.

"Hi, Suze. Sorry about that. I'm not quite ready yet, so can you help me get Murphy ready?"

'Getting Murphy ready' is a lengthy process, which the crazy mutt considers to be an excellent game, and even more exciting than the walk itself. It consists of us chasing him all over the house, behind the sofa, through the kitchen, up the stairs, across the beds and into the bathroom where we eventually trap him in the bath and bribe him with dog biscuits to get the leads (yes, two leads – one for each of us) attached to his collar.

When we're done we're knackered and sweating like pigs.

"Are you sure this double lead thing is going to work?" I ask dubiously on the way to the park. Murphy still feels way too strong for my liking.

"You can walk him with one, but it's slightly more risky. I thought with both of us holding him we might have more chance of keeping control... Oh flipping heck, distract him quick, there's Pansy."

On the opposite side of the road, a tiny Yorkshire terrier is prancing along in front of a little old lady.

"Murphy, Murphy, a jelly baby for you!" Millie calls.

As Murphy chews happily on the sweet, I realise it's no wonder he weighs so much and is constantly hyper. The mutt's permanently wired on sugar.

"Okay, it should be all right now." Millie sags with relief. "That dog lives with Miss Pepper – you know, the lady at number twenty – and Murphy's besotted with her. Murph got a little, um, carried away a few months ago and Miss Pepper's been dead moody ever since."

"What did he do?"

"Got loose and broke into her garden. He chased Pansy round for about an hour and trampled every plant in sight. He also ate most of the vegetable patch, so he wasn't popular. Were you, Murph?"

Murphy wags his tail happily and woofs loudly as he

canters through the park gates. As we're tugged along behind him, I'm not entirely sure who's walking who.

"Can't you get him to slow down a bit?" I plead.

"If you'd like to have a go, knock yourself out," Millie says.

Pulling on Murphy's lead has no effect whatsoever, so eventually I give up. I'll have to accept Millie and I are careering around a public park at speed, with no way of hitting the brakes. It's only when Murphy finds a tasty stick and lies down for a chew that we get a much-needed breather.

Millie's phone buzzes, and she reaches into her pocket for her mobile. She smiles when she reads the text.

"Who is it?" I ask.

"Jamie," she says, holding out the phone for me to see.

Soz i bailed on u. Will help u wiv Murph tomoz. Luv ya! Xx

"Weasel," Millie says, shaking her head. "I so knew he was avoiding me."

I stare at the phone, chewing at my lip. Millie doesn't even realise how lucky she is, getting texts like that. Jamie's so sweet. Danny never mentions the L word. Or uses kisses. But Jamie chucks love in at the end of his message, like it's not even that big a deal.

And then Zach burns into my head again. Which makes

me think about what Jade was saying in PE.

Is it lame I've only ever been interested in one boy? I wonder if I should ask Millie if she's ever had wobbles about having been with Jamie so long.

But what if she says no and it's only me that feels like this?

Yes, I'll feel ten times worse, but I have to know.

"Mill?"

Still puffing, Millie glances at me expectantly.

"Nothing," I say hastily, changing my mind.

"Okay," Millie pants. "Murphy, you're such a nightmare."

"Actually... there is something," I say before I can change my mind again. "You know Danny and Jamie?"

Millie pulls a face of exaggerated puzzlement. "Danny and Jamie, Danny and Jamie... I'm sure I know those names from somewhere..."

I punch her arm. "I was wondering about something. Don't you... did you... do you think it's weird we've been going out with them for so long?"

Millie frowns. "Huh? Where did that come from?"

"I don't know," I mumble.

"It must have come from somewhere."

"I guess... maybe Jade and Kara. They made me feel like a bit of a freak for only ever having had one boyfriend."

"And you actually listened to them?" Millie says. "Suze, you nutter. They don't even have proper boyfriends.

They only ever get off with people."

"Well, yeah," I say, pulling at a hangnail and wincing. "Exactly like everyone else does. There are girls in our year who keep tallies of the people they've snogged in one evening and I can count the guys I've got off with on one hand. One finger, even. As can you."

"So?"

"So, don't you think we might be missing out?"

"Um... actually, no, not really. I'm happy with Jamie. Suze, what's up?" Millie says, concerned. "Have you and Danny had a fight?"

"No," I say quickly. "Nothing like that. I was just wondering what you thought, that's all."

"Well, I love Jamie to bits," Millie says.

"But you're always eyeing up other boys."

"So?" Millie laughs. "That doesn't mean anything. I'm only looking. Like with Zach. He's yummy, but I wouldn't do anything about it. I'm just happy the view in maths got better since he arrived."

I smile weakly.

"Hey, speaking of Zach, isn't that him?" Millie grabs my arm.

I blink a couple of times to make sure, but it is. It's definitely Zach, bouncing a football as he saunters down the path towards us.

Hang on a minute. He knew I was coming to the park. Surely he hasn't come here because of me? No. That would be stupid. Jeez, I really need to get over myself.

"Hi, Suzy," he says, brushing the hair out of his eyes. "How's it going?"

Murphy clambers to his feet and goes to investigate Zach, sniffing suspiciously at his trainers. I ignore the stunned expression Millie's shooting in my direction.

"Hiya," I say, doing my best to sound casual.

Zach points at Murphy. "That is officially the biggest dog I've ever seen in my life. What kind is he?"

Millie's blushing furiously and seems to have lost the ability to speak.

Blimey. That's never happened before. Millie's mouth is silently flapping open and shut, so eventually I decide to answer for her.

"Er, this dog?" I ask, like a total spanner. As if there's some other massive canine around that Zach's referring to. Pull it together, Suze.

I clear my throat and try again. "Um, this is Murphy. He's massive, isn't he? We think he's part Irish Wolfhound, part Great Dane. He belongs to Millie."

Zach gestures in Millie's direction. "You're in my maths set, aren't you?"

Millie nods her head, opens her mouth, then shuts it again.

I've never seen her so quiet before. It's kind of freaky.

"Do you never speak?" Zach says. "So what's the deal with this dog? Why's he got two leads on?"

Millie finally remembers how her voice works. "He's strong."

And then there's a long, awkward pause.

Maybe we should talk about something other than dogs. But what?

I'm frantically trying to come up with something when a huge gust of wind whips through the park, sending my hair in all directions. I grab my head and try to smooth it back down.

Aargh! I must look a complete moose! It's not like I'm looking my best as it is, having been chasing a crazy canine around for the past forty-five minutes.

"I'm such a mess," I say. Then immediately hope Zach hasn't heard me.

"Why do you care all of a sudden?" Millie asks, a smile twitching at the corner of her mouth.

I'm still deciding how to answer when Murphy starts barking.

And it's then I realise that while I was fussing with my hair, I've let go of his lead.

"Murphy, sit down," Millie says in alarm. "Murphy, I said, sit. Sit, Murphy. Muuurrrrpppphhy! Noooo!"

But Murphy's spotted his beloved Pansy mincing by some trees a short distance away. Barking furiously, he sets off at top speed, dragging Millie after him. She tilts backwards at an alarming angle, like a water-skier.

"Argggh!" Millie screams. "Suzy, what are you doing? You weren't supposed to let go. Help meeeeeeeeeeeeeeee!"

The Yorkie freezes in shock when she sees Murphy heading for her, then scampers out of the way with only seconds to spare.

"My baby!" Mrs Pepper shrieks. "Get that beast away from my baby!"

Zach's bent over with laughter, so doesn't see the Yorkie running to hide behind his legs. But there's no way Zach can miss Murphy, who doubles back and leaps up onto him.

Zach thumps down awkwardly to the ground as Millie finally releases the lead, barrels into Zach and also goes flying. Murphy, happy now he's snared his true love, is lying on the ground, nuzzling Pansy's head as the smaller dog trembles between his paws.

I'm absolutely horrified. "I'm so sorry. Are you guys all right?"

"My ankle," Zach says, as he struggles to sit up. "It really kills. I think... I think it might be broken."

CHAPTER SEVEN

Dring ting ting!

The bell above the door of Bojangles café announces the fact I'm late — again. I was supposed to meet my friends here after school fifteen minutes ago. But that's the least of my problems right now.

Stressed does not even begin to cover it.

Although I do love the smell in here. Mmm. It's a scrummy mix of cinnamon, coffee and freshly baked cakes. It's so delish my tummy growls and I relax slightly.

But only a smidgen.

I've been worrying non-stop about what happened in the park yesterday. Zach wasn't at school today and I'm completely freaking out. What if his ankle really is broken? I mean, way to make a good impression. I've done some dumb things in my life, but I've never *maimed* anyone before.

"Suzy!"

Over in the corner, Danny's waving. I squeeze my way through the chairs to where he, Millie and Jamie have taken over a table, and collapse into the spare seat.

Bojangles is one of our favourite places in the world. It's a bit scruffy, but it's dead cosy, and the staff are always friendly to everyone. Even to people like us who make a drink last hours and can't afford to tip much. The four walls are painted different colours, none of the chairs or tables match and cool music's always playing – the kind that's not in the charts and you wouldn't listen to at home, but sounds perfect somewhere like here.

"All right?" Danny says, twanging one of my ringlets.

I squirm away. I *hate* it when he does that.

As I reach out for Danny's cola, he slaps at my hand. "Oi, get off. I ordered you a hot chocolate."

"With cream and marshmallows?"

"Course. Like I'd dare forget."

"So where've you been all day, Suze?" Millie asks. "We've hardly seen you since break."

"Around," I reply vaguely.

"Seen Zach yet?"

"Nope," I say, giving her a shut-up-now-before-I-kill-you glare.

"What was that face for?" Millie says, sounding hurt. "I only wondered."

"What's going on with this Zach?" asks Danny. "Millie's mentioned him a few times today."

Ever since we arrived at school this morning, Millie's been dropping non-too subtle hints about what happened in the park. So far I've managed to avoid discussing it with Danny, but I think my luck may have run out.

"Millie and Suze ran into a bit of trouble walking Murphy yesterday," Jamie tells him, smirking at me.

I scowl back.

"Really?" Danny says. "What happened?"

"Murphy's besotted with some Yorkshire terrier and chased it halfway round the park before knocking over this guy," I say quickly, before anyone else can speak.

"Oh, c'mon, Suze," Millie says, "it's a much better story than that."

"Two hot chocolates?" With perfect timing, the waitress arrives at our table. The drinks she's carrying are enormous, stacked high with whipped cream and miniature marshmallows. My mouth waters in anticipation.

"Yumalicious, yes please," Millie says.

I reach out for my mug, but the waitress eyes me with alarm and, avoiding my hands, puts the cup carefully down on the table. Honestly. Just because there was a *teensy* spill a couple of weeks ago.

I spoon a large helping of cream into my mouth and sigh with pleasure. "Mmm. This is the best. So, um, what's everyone been up to?"

"Don't you go changing the subject again," Danny says, poking my side. "Tell me what happened in the park."

"I already did," I say, defensively.

"Liar," Danny says. "Millie?"

Millie's only too happy to oblige. "Well, Murphy ran wild because Suze let go of her lead. And what made you let go of the lead, Suzy?" There's a mischievous glint in Millie's eye.

"I was getting a leaf out of my hair," I improvise. "And let's not forget I was doing you a favour by helping walk *your* dog," I add meaningfully.

"So it was nothing to do with the fact you were trying to impress Zach, then?" Millie teases.

I nearly choke on my hot chocolate. "What? That's such a lie, I was not!"

"Who *is* Zach?" Danny asks again.

"A new boy in my maths class," Millie tells him.

What am I supposed to say now? Talk about busted!

If Danny had been caught flirting with some other girl, I'd be gutted. I pluck up the guts to peep at him out of the corner of my eye.

Huh?

He's grinning. He actually thinks this is funny.

"If that was your best attempt to impress someone, you'd best stick with me," Danny says. "That poor guy probably didn't know what hit him."

"I do, it was Murphy," Millie says, and the three of them start to laugh.

I don't believe this. How can Danny be *laughing*? This is so typical of him. Sometimes I wonder if he cares about me *at all*.

"Aren't you bothered?" I ask.

"Course not," Danny scoffs. "Millie's only joking and you wouldn't go off with anyone else. C'mon, Suze, lighten up. What happened sounds hilarious."

"It wasn't," I protest, but that makes them snigger harder. "And how do you know I wouldn't go off with someone else?"

"Because you wouldn't," Danny says. The way he says it, dead confidently, makes me so mad that something inside snaps.

"Is it because you think nobody else could like me?" I ask sharply.

Danny stops laughing. "Huh?"

"Do you think nobody else would fancy me?"

Suddenly the atmosphere around the table has changed, and nobody's smiling any more. Millie and

Jamie are staring at each other awkwardly, while Danny just seems confused.

"What are you going on about, Suze?" Danny leans forwards, reaching for my hand, but I jerk it away. "Hey, what's wrong?"

"Nothing. Just leave me alone." I stand up and storm out of the café. As I rush past the window, out of the corner of my eye I can see my friends staring after me in disbelief.

Later that evening I'm grumpily pushing a piece of chicken round my plate and listening half-heartedly as Mum witters on about her mother-of-the-bride outfit.

"The choice is between a hat and a fascinator," she tells Dad and Aunt Lou, who clearly couldn't care less. "What do you think? A hat is more traditional, of course, but a fascinator might be fun."

"A what-inator?" Dad asks. "It sounds like a robot."

"A *fascinator*," Mum says, exasperated. "You know, a headpiece with feathers or flowers on it."

"What do you want to wear feathers on your head for?" Dad says, looking baffled. "Won't you look like a cockerel?"

"No, of course not," Mum huffs. "And actually, I'm starting to wonder why I bother. You're showing no interest in this wedding, all you do is make dismissive comments. It's—"

"What did you say you wanted to wear?" Aunt Loon interrupts.

"A fascinator," Mum repeats.

"A what?"

"A FASCINATOR," Mum shouts, losing patience.

"What's that when it's at home?" says Aunt Loon.

Aaargh, make them stop! Why did Mum have to ask the Loon over for dinner? This conversation's enough to make a person ram a skewer into their ears for some peace.

Luckily for us all, Aunt Loon's drowned out by the phone ringing.

"Would you get that, Suzy?" Mum asks.

"Why?"

"Because you haven't eaten anything and the rest of us are enjoying our meal. It's probably for you anyway."

"It could be Millie with an international fashion disaster," Dad jokes. "Shock, horror – she's realised that her shoes don't match her necklace, what should she do? Her life may as well be over."

I ignore him.

"Suzy?" Mum says again.

"*What?*"

"Will you answer that phone?"

"I'll get it," Harry says, jumping up.

"Where's she going?" Aunt Loon demands.

"Phone, Aunt Lou," Mum tells her.

"Where?" Aunt Lou cups her hand around her ear.

"The PHONE," Mum yells.

Aunt Loon looks disapproving. "Young ladies shouldn't leave the dining table. We're eating."

A few minutes later, Harry's back.

"It's Danny," she says to me, wiggling onto her chair. "He didn't want to talk to me, just to you. He sounds weird."

Even though part of me wants to run as fast as I can towards that handset to sort things out, I will not budge from this table.

"Have you gone deaf?" Dad asks. "What's going on? Usually you and the phone are tighter than two coats of paint. You do realise something life-changing may have happened in the mere seconds that have passed since you last saw your friends?"

"Chris," Mum says, shaking her head slightly. "Is everything all right, Suzy?"

"Uh-huh." I stab at a piece of broccoli.

"He said it was important," Harry adds.

"Tell him I'm busy."

"Tell him yourself."

"Harry, don't be rude," Mum tells her. "Go on, Suzy. Don't keep Danny waiting."

I still don't move.

"Suzy," Mum says warningly.

"Okay, okay! I'm going."

I close the door firmly behind me, because this is one conversation I don't want overheard, and pick up the handset Harry's abandoned. I've not got a clue what I'm supposed to say. Danny and I have never had a fight this big before.

Luckily Danny speaks first. "Suzy, are you there? I can hear breathing."

I lean against the wall and slide down it until I'm sitting on the floor. "Hi. Why didn't you ring my mobile?"

"I did. About eight times. You weren't answering."

Oh. Right. I guess my phone's still abandoned at the bottom of my bag.

"Are you going to tell me what that was all that about earlier?" Danny doesn't sound angry, but Harry was right, he doesn't sound his usual self.

Mum bustles past taking plates to the kitchen.

"Are you still there?" Danny asks.

"It's difficult to talk right now," I say. "There are people around."

Harry appears and starts leaping around in front of me. "Hey, is Danny coming over soon? Ask him, Suzy. Ask him."

"Get lost," I say furiously.

"What?" Danny says.

"Not you. I'm talking to Harry."

"Let me speak, let me speak," Harry whines.

Mum races out of the kitchen and drags my sister away. "Sorry, Suzy."

"Suzy, what's going on?" Danny asks.

"Nothing."

"Did I do something wrong?"

"No. Not really."

There's a painful silence, then I hear him sigh heavily.

"Look, this is hopeless," he says. "I'm coming over. I'll be with you in a minute."

"Danny, wait—"

But it's too late. He's gone.

The second I replace the handset the phone rings again.

"Hello?"

"Hi, Suze, ohmigod I've been dying to speak to you."

"Hey, Millie," I say wearily.

"Are you all right? I've been trying for ages to get through on your mobile but you weren't answering. I thought you weren't talking to me. I'm sooooo sorry for what happened. I didn't mean to start a fight or anything. Have you talked to Danny?"

"Yeah, just now. He's coming over."

"Do you hate me?" Millie asks worriedly.

"Of course I don't hate you," I tell her, "but why did you think it would be a good idea to tell Danny I'd been flirting with another guy?"

"I know," Millie says, sounding subdued. "It was just a dumb joke, I didn't mean it. I really am sorry."

"Yeah, me too," I say. "I completely overreacted."

"What was that about? You went kind of mental back there."

"I don't know," I tell her. "I was a complete cowbag, but I'll sort everything out with Danny when he gets here."

"All right," says Millie, although she sounds doubtful. "Text me later and let me know what happens. I'll talk to you properly at school tomorrow, but it'll be fine. I just know it."

"I know," I say, although I'm starting to wonder.

What if Danny thinks I'm the most horrible person in the world? What if he wants to break up? What if—

The doorbell rings.

I can't stress about it any more.

Danny's here.

CHAPTER EIGHT

Danny's standing on our doorstep, shifting his weight from foot to foot and fiddling with the zip on his coat. His hair's all bushy from the wind and his cheeks are pink. Though he's been here a million times, Danny's acting like he doesn't quite know where to put himself. Normally he'd be inside and rummaging through the fridge faster than you could say 'free food'.

"Come in," I say awkwardly.

"Thanks," Danny replies, stepping inside.

I hear the back door close and Amber and Mark's voices greet Mum in the kitchen. There's some chatting, then Amber's indignant voice says, "Mum, don't listen to them, a fascinator would be perfect. I'm sure Conni G would approve, don't you, Markymoo?"

Gnargh, enough already with the stupid fascinator.

"Did I hear the doorbell?" Dad sticks his head round the lounge door. "Oh, hello, Danny, how's things?"

"Hi, Mr Puttock," Danny says. He's known my parents forever, but he still can't call them by their first names. Apparently it's way too weird.

"We're going to my room," I say.

Dad peers over the top of his glasses. "Well, you know the rule."

Oh yes. The rule that dictates I must keep the door open at all times whenever Danny's in my bedroom, to stop what Mum and Dad call 'funny business' going on.

Exactly what they think we're going to get up to, I don't know. How can a person feel like doing anything even vaguely romantic with their entire family of crazies only millimetres away? Ick.

"We need some privacy," I say, without really thinking.

Dad's eyebrows threaten to shoot off the top of his head.

"Um, we're only going to talk," Danny says quickly, his ears blushing bright red.

Dad looks mightily relieved, but doesn't back down. "You know the rule," he repeats. "It's door open, or downstairs. Your choice."

"It's so unfair," I mutter as I head upstairs, Danny following behind.

"Life's unfair," Dad calls after us.

Making sure the bedroom door's open a crack,

Danny and I settle ourselves at opposite ends of my bed. My room's a tip. There's a load of school books strewn over the floor, necklaces hanging from the desk lamp and discarded magazines chucked everywhere. Avoiding Danny's gaze, I hug my old teddy, Wilbur, to my chest, and rest my chin on his head as I stare at the duvet, tracing the spiral pattern with my finger. I can tell Danny's watching me.

All of a sudden I think I might puke. I hate arguing. And I hate how I've been feeling lately. Why did I have to get all weirded out about Zach? I just want everything back the way it was.

"I bet you're kissing," Harry says, outside my room.

"Go away," I shout.

From behind the door there are retching noises. "Bleurgh, you are. I can hear you."

"Harry, shut up and leave us alone." I leap up, slam the door shut and return to the bed.

"Do you want to put on some music?" I ask.

"No, I want to know what's wrong," Danny replies.

"You sure? I downloaded this great new album yesterday and—"

"Suzy, I don't want to listen to music. I want to know what's up. Spill."

"I told you," I say, trying to sound cheerful. "I'm fine."

"So you often flip out in the middle of coffee shops,

do you?" Danny replies, sarcastically. "You didn't look fine earlier."

I blink in surprise. Danny's usually so easy-going.

"I'm sorry," I say.

"I don't understand where all that stuff came from." Danny gazes at me intently.

I shift uneasily. "I'm not sure. I guess it was just the way you were acting, making out like nobody else could ever fancy me."

Danny gazes at the floor for a moment, then leans back on his elbows. "I didn't mean nobody would want to go out with you," he says sadly.

"I know," I say. "I was being mad. It just... bugged me you weren't jealous. Like you didn't care or something."

"How do you know I wasn't jealous?"

"Were you?" I'm genuinely surprised.

"Well, only about this much." Danny holds his thumb and index finger a tiny distance apart. "But it still counts, right?"

"I guess," I admit, trying not to feel too disappointed. "I wasn't trying to impress Zach, though," I add.

It's only a teeny-weeny fib, so it doesn't *really* matter.

"Course you weren't. Why would you when you've got a boyfriend as amazing as me?" Danny grins, and squishes me in a huge hug.

"Exactly. So can we forget about this now?" I plead, my voice muffled against Danny's shoulder.

"Forget about what?"

"Dunno," I say, smiling to myself. Phewey.

I must have been totally insane to think I had feelings for someone else. Danny's the only guy that I want. The whole Zach thing was a blip. Nothing more. Talk about a relief.

Danny clambers off the bed and I try not to feel too gutted as he grabs my iPod and starts scrolling through the songs until he finds one he likes.

Er, hello, what about the kissing and making up? Shouldn't that be happening round about now? I swallow down my frustration.

"Hey, you got your ticket for the party," Danny says, spotting the blue piece of paper lying on my desk.

"Yeah, Dad finally gave me the money. It should be a laugh," I say. And actually, I mean it. It'll be fun to go out for the night with my friends, even if the party is going to be the lamest thing ever.

There was a bit of a hoo-ha when it emerged that our year wouldn't be allowed at the senior prom, so the party is a budget compromise, just for us. The PTA is way too tight to hire a nightclub, so it's going to be held in the gym, probably with naff streamers and cheesy music, just like the ones we had at infant school.

Now Danny and I have got everything sorted out, we'll have a great time, I tell myself. For the first time in days, I feel properly happy and lean over to give Danny a kiss. If he's not going to make a move, I flipping will.

"I told you to keep this door open," Dad says, bursting in. Danny and I leap apart, and I don't know which of the three of us is more embarrassed.

Dad turns crimson and starts coughing and spluttering. "What's going on in here? What did I say to you? Get down, er, get yourselves, ahem, downstairs. Right now," he blusters, then in his hurry to leave, walks into the doorframe.

Danny and I crease up laughing.

"So are you *sure* everything's all right with you and Danny?" Millie asks for the millionth time as we wait on the hockey field. Miss Lewis has picked Kara and Jade as captains and now they're choosing their teams. Surprise, surprise, neither Millie or I have been picked yet.

"Yes," I tell her, yet again. I've already had to send Millie about twenty texts to tell her we're okay, and sit through an in-depth conversation in registration this morning going over everything. Millie needs a lot of reassurance as she's stressing so much about what she did, but it's starting to get a bit annoying.

"I'll have Lucy," Jade says.

"And I'll take Kate," Kara says, quick as a flash.

Ugh, I hate waiting to be picked. I'm never chosen until right at the very end. I'll be left with the three other non-sporting pariahs: Rachel (science nerd), Claire (severely asthmatic) and April the Goth (doesn't believe in team sports and refuses to participate in anything apart from looking moody). Happens every time.

"I promise, Mill, everything's fine," I say, shivering as it starts to drizzle with rain.

"Phew. Because I was really worried there for a minute, you know. It would be too, too freaky if you guys broke up. I'd have felt terrible if—"

"I'll have Millie," Jade says, interrupting us.

"See ya, fingers crossed you're on our team," Millie says, as she goes over to join the huddle surrounding Jade.

As I predicted, now it's just me and the other three rejects.

Kara sighs heavily. "I guess I'll have... Suzy."

Once the teams are sorted and the bibs are handed out, I'm relieved to see I'm playing right half. This is a billion times better than being goalie, which wheezy Claire's stuck with, because then she doesn't have to run around. She looks terrified, and I genuinely feel for her. Last time I was goalkeeper I spent the whole match leaping out of the way of the ball. It properly hurts when it whacks you.

My relief at the position I've been given only lasts until I see who I'm marking.

Jade.

"So. Suzy. I heard what happened in the park," she whispers, bashing her hockey stick into the ground and smiling wolfishly.

My heart stops. Oh *God*.

"Hmmm?" I say, as if I have no idea what she's talking about.

"With Zach and the dog? Zach couldn't stop talking about it. Or you, for that matter."

What's Zach been saying? Although I've seen him around school today, I've been so mortified I've cunningly managed to avoid contact by running away whenever I've seen him coming. Subtle, no? I was totally relieved to see he's walking, which made me feel a bit better about things. He's not crippled for life after all.

The whistle blows, and Jade dashes off, leaving me trailing along after her. It's literally only about a minute before she scores (turns out Claire ducks from the balls as well).

"Suzy, you need to mark Jade, for God's sake," Kara yells. "Don't just waft around pathetically, expecting her to wait for you."

Yeah, yeah, whatever.

We return to our original positions and wait as Miss Lewis goes to sort out Claire's protective padding and offer what seems to be a motivational speech.

"I think Zach really likes you," Jade says, while we wait.

Huh? Did she just say what I thought she said? After what I did to him, is she for *real*?

"You what?"

"Zach. I think he really likes you," Jade repeats.

A warm fluttery glow starts to spread through me. "I've got a boyfriend," I say, trying to feign cool.

"So?" Jade says. "Doesn't stop someone else fancying you, does it?"

I shrug.

I can hardly believe it.

Zach likes me.

Zach likes *me*!

Someone other than my boyfriend *does* think I'm worth going out with. Someone super-hot, at that. Shows how wrong Danny was.

But as I think of Danny, the happy excitement is replaced with queasiness and I come down to earth with a bump. The Zach thing was meant to be a blip, I remind myself firmly.

I have to stop thinking about Zach. In fact, from now

on I'll be completely indifferent if I see Zach, or hear his name mentioned. Won't feel a thing.

"Hey," Jade says. "Are you going red?"

"No," I mumble, starting to blush. I stare down at the grass.

"You are. You like Zach, don't you?"

"I don't. I told you, I'm going out with Danny."

"So?"

"Shut up, Jade," I say. "I don't like Zach. Leave it."

"Whatever," smirks Jade, and as the whistle finally blows, she whacks at my shin with her stick.

Oh dear God and mother of all that's holy. It's pain like I've never felt before. My eyes are watering, and I'm still hopping up and down on the spot howling as Jade tackles Kara, gains control of the ball then weaves her way up the field, and scores again.

"Suzy!" Kara says furiously. "What the hell are you doing, you idiot? I told you to mark her."

As the game continues, even the pain in my leg can't distract me from thinking about Zach. No matter how hard I try to focus on Danny, Zach keeps shoving him out of the way.

Many goals and much more abuse from Kara later, the whistle blows and the lesson is finally over. Miss Lewis gives the captains the jobs of collecting up the bibs, and as Kara and Jade walk past, I hear Kara say to Jade, "He's never going to go for you."

"We'll see," Jade retorts, angrily throwing the bibs into the box. "It's only been a couple of weeks."

My ears prick up, but I can't hear any more.

Oooh, I'd love to know who they were talking about. Has Jade, she of the I-can-get-anyone-I-want smugness, actually got boy trouble?

What a lovely, lovely thought.

CHAPTER NINE

This is a nightmare.

Exactly what *do* you do when you appear to fancy someone who isn't your boyfriend, he seems to like you back, there's absolutely nobody in the world you can talk to about it and your head is on the verge of exploding trying to process it all?

You go along to the canteen for lunch and pretend like nothing's happening, of course.

Well, that's what I'm doing, anyway.

I spot Danny ahead, waiting for me like he does every lunchtime. We don't share any classes this year, so it's the only time we see each other.

My breath catches in my throat at the sight of him. What if he knows something's wrong? Maybe he'll be able to tell. And then what will I say?

Just compose yourself, Suze. Get it together. He hasn't

even *noticed* you yet, he's talking away to someone.

Hey, it's Jade he's chatting to. I didn't realise they were on speaking terms. She's standing *reeeeally* close to him as well, but that's probably because of the crush of people fighting to get through the doors. And now she's walking off at top speed.

"Hi." Danny grins when I get nearer, pushing himself up from the Year Nine poetry display he's leaned against. A group of girls from the year below bundle past and one girl gets shoved by her friend into Danny.

"Ohmigod, I'm so sorry," she mutters, turning scarlet as her friends screech with laughter.

As they scuttle off, still giggling, several of them turn to stare at my boyfriend with weird dreamy expressions.

Girls can be so strange sometimes. How old are they anyway, five?

"Hiya," I say. "Was that Jade you were talking to just now?"

"Um, yeah."

"How come?"

"No reason," Danny says. He's kind of flushed. It is boiling in here. "We're doing a project together in art and she wanted to talk to me about it, that's all."

"Oh. That's weird. I've just had PE with her and she didn't say anything about it."

"Nothing to say, that's why." Danny prods me gently towards the canteen. "C'mon, shift it, Puttock, I'm starving. Mills and Jamie are saving us seats."

The dining room's buzzing with people everywhere and the deafening sound of chairs constantly being scraped across lino. I wrinkle up my nose as the stink of grease and disinfectant assaults my nostrils. No matter what's on the menu, the smell's always the same.

"There they are." Danny points. Millie and Jamie are leering at unsuspecting passers-by with carrot-stick fangs.

"What do you two look like?" I ask, when we reach them.

"I vant to suck your blooood," Jamie replies.

"Not vith those teeth, you don't," I tell him, rummaging in my bag for a drink. "I think you vant to see a dentist."

"We're heading round Jamie's after school," Millie says. One of her fangs falls out and orange dribble rolls down her chin.

"Sounds good," I say, twisting open a bottle of water and chugging it down thirstily. "Meet you by the lockers later, then?"

Millie nods, and sticks in a new fang.

"What have you got for lunch?" Danny asks me.

"I've got a tuna mayo sarnie, wanna swap?" He waves it in front of my face.

Vom. There is nothing I hate in the world more than tuna, and Danny knows it. In my opinion, fish is the food of the devil.

"No way." I gag at the smell, pushing his hand away. "I ate my sandwiches earlier, I was starving. I'm going to go and get something else. Anybody want anything?"

"Can you get me a flapjack?" Jamie asks.

"Ooh yeah, get me one while you're there," Millie adds. "And a banana."

"And me," Danny says. "Can I get a carton of milk, as well?"

"Everyone's going to think I'm a right chubster ordering all that stuff," I grumble. I leave to a chorus of piggy grunts.

Grabbing a tray, I join the back of a queue that's way too long for the stuff they try to pass off as food in our canteen. Ironic really, considering the healthy-eating posters plastered all over the walls. You take your life in your hands every time you eat anything cooked here. Salmonella? E-coli? All in a day's work for our dinner ladies.

"Oi." Someone prods me gently on the arm. When I see who it is I nearly drop my tray in alarm.

"Wow, what a reaction," Zach says.

"Yeah, well, you made me jump," I splutter.

Zach eyes me appraisingly. "So. I've finally tracked you down. Are you going to tell me why you've been legging it every time I've come anywhere remotely near you the last couple of days?"

Oh nads. He noticed? I suppose the textbooks I sent flying when I was hiding from him in the French room might have been a *bit* of a giveaway.

"I... I haven't," I say.

"Really? Doesn't seem that way to me."

I stare at him guiltily.

"I'm guessing it's because of what happened in the park?" Zach says.

All of a sudden I find a blob of black chewing gum on the floor terribly interesting. I scuff at it with the toe of my shoe. "Um, yeah. About that. I'm really sorry."

"I'm not going to lie, it has been a bit of a nightmare," he says, hitching up his trouser leg to show me the bandage on his ankle. "I won't be able to play football for ages."

I wince. "I'm really, really sorry."

"Well, dropping that lead could have happened to anyone," Zach says. "That's one strong dog."

"Yeah, but... I feel awful. Really, really bad," I say, trying to ease my guilty conscience. Because dropping the lead wasn't exactly the accident Zach thinks it was.

My hair has a *lot* to answer for. "Did I say I was sorry?"

"You did. But if you're as sorry as you claim, you'll want to make it up to me," Zach says.

My cheeks start to burn and I clear my throat loudly. We shuffle along as the line moves. I glance over at Danny, but my friends are busy trying to balance spoons on the end of their noses.

"Er, make it up to you?" I echo, dumbly. "How?"

"I'll think of something," Zach says, winking cheekily. "But you can start by not avoiding me any more."

"I—"

"What do you want?" a dinner lady interrupts, wiping her nose with the back of her hand.

Barf. Why do I bother with this place? More to the point, I hadn't even noticed we'd reached the front of the queue. What did I want again?

My brain is utterly scrambled, and I'm sure the reason is the person standing only millimetres away from me. What did my friends want, again?

I grab a jacket potato with cheese, two bananas, a flapjack and an orange juice. It's only when I've paid that I realise I've got my order completely wrong. "Oh no, that's not what I wanted. Can I change these?"

"Nope. Who's next?" says the cashier.

Zach grabs his tray of dry-looking lasagne with some

shrivelled carrots on the side. "Where do you want to sit?" he asks. "It's packed in here."

"Er, I'm actually already sitting with my friends," I say, awkwardly. "I'd ask you over, but there's no spare chairs and—"

"Whatever," Zach says, shrugging. "Guess I'll see you around."

As he walks away I feel a small twinge of disappointment. And I realise it's because there's a part of me that wishes I was going with him instead of back to my mates.

Outside the school gates, I can see Danny and Jamie waiting for me and Mill. They're taking turns to give each other dead legs and are hopping around yelling with pain. God, they look like they're really hurting each other, the crazy fools. Even if I live to be a hundred, I don't think I'll *ever* understand boys.

"Hi," Millie and I greet them. Jamie wraps his arms round Millie and they start kissing.

"Hi, Suze," Danny says, waving at me goofily.

No kisses for me, then.

When I compare Danny and I to Millie and Jamie… well, there is no comparison. It's like we're still thirteen, and stuck in some kind of freakish time warp.

Danny could at least *try* and make me feel special.

Sure, he doesn't know what's been going on inside my head, but he's sure as heck not helping me get over it.

"Come on, guys, let's get going," Jamie says, eventually prising his face away from Millie's.

"We were waiting for you, mate," Danny says.

In an effort to make us look like a proper couple, I grab hold of Danny's hand. He manages to keep hold for almost a minute, but lets go to tell some joke with accompanying animated gestures.

It doesn't take long to get to Jamie's; it's round the corner on the fancy estate and is our favourite place to hang after school. Because Jamie's parents work late a lot – they run their own design business and are never around – the four of us often go to their massive house on the premise of doing 'homework'. It would be the truth, too, if homework ever involved watching the world's largest TV and eating our own body weight in junk food. Jamie's parents always have in the best snacks.

"I'll grab some drinks," Jamie says, heading into the kitchen. He grabs Millie's wrist and pulls her after him. "You're coming with me."

"You're so bossy," says Millie, but follows after him happily enough.

As Danny and I make our way through to the lounge we can hear Millie screeching, "Don't you dare! Not the ice…"

followed by a loud shriek. Then there's lots of laughing before it goes quiet. No prizes for guessing what they're up to.

Again.

Danny flicks on the TV and comes to sit next to me on the sofa. He immediately becomes engrossed in some dumb cartoon. My mind drifts off and I'm back in the dinner queue talking to Zach.

Those long eyelashes. His dazzling smile. That adorable floppy hair.

No! What I am doing? I give myself an annoyed shake. I have *got* to stop thinking about Zach.

Danny taps me on the leg. "Hey, are you okay? You've got a weird expression on your face. Like you're constipated or something."

Well, that's charming. Thanks a bundle, Danny. Way to make a girl feel good about herself.

"I'm fine," I tell him.

But Danny's not listening. He's staring at the screen, where a pretty TV presenter in a tight T-shirt is talking excitedly and bouncing all over the studio. My boyfriend's tongue is practically hanging out. Why doesn't he ever look at me like that?

"Er, do you want to be any more obvious?" I say.

"Shhh," Danny says, flapping his hand in my direction.

"Now the moment all you fans of The Drifting have been waiting for," the girl squeaks. "We've got four tickets for their upcoming tour in London to give away to one lucky viewer, plus an extra ticket for a parent or guardian. The prize includes travel costs from anywhere in the UK. Lines close at the end of the week, so get texting the number at the bottom of the screen if you want to win this amazing prize."

"Remember the number, remember the number," Danny yells, diving across me for his rucksack. He roots around for his mobile. As Danny pulls the phone from his bag, he frowns at the screen and presses a couple of buttons.

"What's up?" I ask.

"Huh? Oh, nothing," Danny says. "Just a text." His thumb stabs the delete button.

"Who from?" I ask, curious.

"Nobody," Danny says hurriedly. "Um, I mean not nobody, obviously. It was just Dad, asking what time I'm coming home for dinner. What was that number for the Drifting comp again?"

"I don't know why you're bothering," I grumble. "Those things are a complete rip-off. It costs loads to enter."

"But someone's got to get the prize," Danny says. "And it might as well be me. Besides, you'll be grovelling when I get those tickets. Wouldn't it be cool to see The Drifting live in a massive stadium?"

"Yes it would, but you're not going to win."

"I might," Danny says, keying in his text and pressing the send button several times.

"Except you won't." Ugh, he's being so annoying. Those things are such a waste of money.

Jamie and Millie interrupt our bickering, handing out chocolate milk and dumping bowls of nachos and dips onto the floor.

"So is everyone excited about the party at the weekend?" Millie asks after she's cosied up with Jamie in one of the big, comfy armchairs.

"Hadn't thought about it much," I lie, reaching out for some corn chips. I've only spent the last week rummaging through my wardrobe, trying to figure out what I should wear.

"Here's hoping Barnes and Lewis stay off the dance floor this year," Jamie says.

We all shudder. The memory of those two tangoing traumatised everyone for months.

"If there's a repeat performance, I'll hurl," Danny says.

"You're talking with your mouth full and nobody wants to see your half-chewed food," I say narkily. For some reason, I'm finding him really irritating today. In fact, everything's annoying me. I'm just so *prickly* at the moment.

Danny swallows with a loud gulp.

"That's seriously gross," I tell him.

"Wrong. *This* is gross," Jamie says, opening his mouth wide and sticking out his tongue, revealing a pile of chewed nachos.

"Ewwww!" Millie and I scream together. Millie thumps Jamie's arm, but she's giggling hysterically.

I smile weakly, trying to fight the urge I have to walk out of the room, out of the house, and not come back. What's wrong with me? Since when did I become the Queen of Flouncy Over-Dramatic Exits?

I'm trying my hardest, but I'm just not having fun. For the first time in my life, I don't want to be here.

Millie squeaks as Jamie wrestles her onto the floor, threatening to drop stringy cheese over her face.

"You've got salsa by your mouth," I tell Danny.

"Huh? Oh. Where?"

I don't attempt to wipe it off for him. "It's there. On your chin."

Mille and Jamie have now moved on from play fighting and are snogging again.

"Oh, get a room, you two," Danny says, throwing a cushion at Jamie's head. They don't pay any attention.

I watch them together and chew at the inside of my cheek miserably. Where's that passion in my life? Sure,

Danny and I kiss and stuff, but it never seems to be, well, all that sexy.

"Hey," Danny says, poking me in the side with an odd expression on his face. It's then I realise I must look a right perv gawking at my mates getting off with each other.

"Guys," I say loudly, "do you want to watch a film or not?"

Millie sits up quickly, looking startled.

Oops. Maybe I sounded narkier than I intended.

As Jamie grabs the remote and flips on the movie channel, Millie snuggles up to him. He drops an arm around her shoulder, kissing the side of her head.

I can't help comparing them with me and Danny again. The differences couldn't be more obvious. Danny's moved to one end of the sofa, staring intently at the screen, and I'm curled up at the other. All of a sudden it feels as though there's miles of space between us.

CHAPTER TEN

I've still not found an outfit for the party. Since I got home from school, I've managed to scatter the entire contents of my wardrobe over every available surface in my bedroom. There are clothes I've tried on and discarded all over the floor, my desk, my bed, hanging from the lamp, thrown over the iPod dock... and still nothing feels right.

I'm getting seriously stressed, because I've promised myself I'm going to wear something stunning, go to the party where I will ignore Zach all night and have an utterly amazing time with Danny.

Unfortunately, there's *no* way I'm wearing any of these clothes, so my plan has crashed and burned at the very first hurdle.

"Suzy, phone!" Dad yells up the stairs.

"Coming," I shout back.

Slight problem. Exactly how am I going to get to the door?

"Suzy!" Dad bellows again.

"All right, all right, I'm coming!"

Dad's leaving the hall as I get to the phone.

"That girl is mad," he grunts, as I pass.

"Huh?"

"Millie," he says. "She's yabbering on about some clothes thing. I don't know what she expects me to do about it. And where's your mobile? After all the moaning and wailing you did to have one, you never seem to use the damn thing."

I rack my brains. It's probably buried somewhere in my bedroom underneath all those clothes. Dad thrusts the receiver at me and stalks off. At the other end of the phone, I can hear the tinny sound of Millie talking.

"And you see, Mr Puttock, *that's* why the top won't work with that skirt. So I thought maybe I could wear the electric blue one, but then I'll have to rethink my accessories—"

"Mil?"

"And I haven't got any other shoes so it's a total nightmare. What do you think I should do?"

Millie finally pauses for breath.

"Hey, Mil, it's me."

"Oh, Suze, hi. Where did your dad go?"

"He left. You scared him off."

"Really? Oh well, never mind. You've got to help me. I have absolutely nothing to wear to this stupid party. At the moment, I'm seriously considering that naked might be the way to go." Millie sighs dramatically.

"Yeah, I hate all my clothes too," I say.

There's a long pause, then Millie gasps.

"I know," she says. "Bring your stuff round and we can have a kind of mix and match fashion show. Bring make-up too."

"Brilliant idea," I say. "See you in five."

Upstairs, I grab the suitcase from the top of Mum and Dad's wardrobe before racing back to my room and haphazardly stuffing my clothes into it. There's quite a lot of them, and after I've added accessories, jewellery and make-up, I've got a bulging suitcase I have to sit on to close, plus four overflowing carrier bags.

Once I've dragged it all downstairs, which takes ages, I realise with dismay I'm never going to be able to carry everything to Millie's. It's not all that far, but even pro weightlifters would get a hernia.

"Harry, the monster truck mega marathon is about to start!" calls Dad, walking into the hall. "Are you leaving home?" he asks when he sees me, a little too hopefully for my liking.

"Oh, ha ha, you're hilarious. Will you give me a lift?"

"Where to? What's all this?"

"Clothes. I need to get to Millie's. Please, Dad."

"Not a chance. I'm about to watch something on TV."

"But how am I supposed to get all these bags there?"

"Why on earth would you need to?" Dad says, looking bewildered. "Actually, don't answer that. I'll never understand you females. You're all bonkers."

"I'll take her," Amber says, wafting down the stairs in a long skirt and floaty peach top, "if you'll let me borrow the car. I can drop her off on the way to pick Mark up from work. We're meeting the wedding photographer tonight."

The blood drains from Dad's face and he gulps.

He does have quite the dilemma.

If he lends Amber the car, I'll leave him alone and he gets to watch his monster trucks.

On the other hand, it's highly likely he'll never see the car in one piece again, because Amber is the worst driver in the history of the world. In the year since she got her licence, she's already had six accidents – the most memorable being when she drove into a wall trying to avoid an already squashed squirrel. Mum and Dad have resorted to hiding the keys from her.

Part of me hopes that Dad will refuse. Driving with Amber is way scarier than any roller coaster, but there's no other way of getting this stuff to Millie's. Desperate times, and all that.

"Please, Dad," Amber says.

"Pleeeeease, Dad," I join in.

"Pleeeeeeeease," we chorus.

"Oh, all right then," Dad says reluctantly. "The keys are hidden under the potatoes. Just *be careful*."

"I always am," says Amber, kissing Dad on the cheek and heading towards the kitchen.

"Ready?" Amber says, jamming the keys into the ignition. She reverses backwards at speed, and then there's a huge crash.

I make an instinctive grab for the door handle.

"Oopsy," Amber says, leaping out of the car. "Who left that wheelbarrow there?"

"You're halfway across the lawn," I say, but Amber ignores me, heaving the wheelbarrow out of the way.

"Let's try again," Amber says. This time she makes it out of the drive and onto the road.

"Mind that cyclist!"

"Calm down, Suze, I'm miles away."

Amber misses the bike by millimetres. In the wing mirror, I watch the cyclist wobble into the kerb and fall off. He leaps to his feet and angrily gives us the finger.

"Watch out!" I cry, as a car stops abruptly in front of us. I fly forwards as Amber hits the brakes. Good job our car's ancient, or I'd be getting intimate with an airbag right now.

"Gosh, Suze, you really need to chill. You're so tense."

Anyone would be tense in my situation, faced with their imminent death. Keep talking, Suze. Distract yourself. "So, how's the wedding planning going?"

"Fine," Amber says, but her voice sounds flat.

That's weird. Usually Amber's bouncier than Tigger when she's asked about wedding stuff and will waffle on about it for *hours*.

"Got much left to do?"

"Not much." Amber shrugs. "Everything's booked. Dad's nearly convinced it doesn't mean he's gay if he wears a cerise cravat. We've just got to find a pink suit for Mark now. In fact, most things are nearly organised, but I'm wondering…" Amber's voice wobbles.

"Wondering what?" I ask.

"Nothing," Amber says, shaking her head violently. "I'm fine. No problems at all." She smiles brightly. "Shall we put on some music?" Amber leans over for her handbag, which is down by my feet. "I know I've got some CDs around somewhere…"

"I'll find them," I say hastily, trying not to panic.

Fortunately Amber straightens up and beams her thanks. I'm the one who should be grateful. At least now she can see the road.

"Could you pass me the crisps from my bag, please?" Amber asks.

I pull out and open a family-sized bag of Kettle Chips, which Amber grabs from me. She tucks them between her legs and starts munching with gusto.

"These would be so much better with some coleslaw," she says.

"I thought you were on your pre-wedding diet, Amber?" I ask. After she got engaged, she started exercising like crazy and existed pretty much on fruit and vegetables, determined to be as thin as Conni G on her big day. Although, come to think of it, I've not seen her doing her workouts in the lounge for a while.

"I am, but I'm starving and it's ages until tea," Amber says, screeching to a very delayed halt at a red light.

By the time we arrive at Millie's, my knuckles are white from gripping the seat. We've narrowly avoided collisions with a moped, a pensioner and a double-decker bus, mainly caused by Amber's inability to eat, talk and drive all at once.

"Thanks for the lift," I say shakily, unpeeling my fingers and gathering my things together.

"No probs," Amber says. She waves out of the window

as she zooms off, then swerves wildly and nearly hits a parked car.

As I drag the bags towards Millie's, I can hear shouting coming from an open window in their house. When I get nearer I can see Millie's big sister, Sophie, and her dad having a row. Murphy seems to be joining in, howling loudly at the top of his doggy voice.

"Young lady, what do you look like?" Millie's dad is shouting. "You're not going out wearing that. You'll catch your death of cold and you look like a... well, I'm not going to say what you look like."

"What do you know about fashion? Your idea of an on-trend outfit is making sure your shirt's not tucked into your pants," Sophie screams back.

"Don't you *dare* speak to me like that! You're grounded. Where are you going? Come back here. I said, you're *grounded...*"

Sophie charges out of the house wearing tiny black hot pants and a skimpy fuscia halter-neck that shows off her naval. She slams the door and barges past without saying a word. Within seconds the door flies open again. Millie's dad stands in front of me, red-faced with fury and hanging onto Murphy's collar for dear life.

"I swear I'll kill that girl... Oh, er, hello, Suzy." He focuses on my bags. "What's all this? Millie didn't mention you were coming to stay."

"Erm, I'm not. These are just a few things Millie wanted me to bring over."

"Really? That's a lot of bags. Well, she's upstairs. Go on up. You didn't see which way Sophie went, did you?"

"Er, not exactly," I say as I stagger inside. "Maybe in that direction?" I gesture vaguely. I'm staying well out of it.

As I approach Millie's room, I can hear her singing very loudly – and very, very badly – to the newest Drifting song.

"Girls walk past me on the street,

But all I can think about is you,

All I can think about is yoooooooooooooooou…"

Her voice cracks as she attempts – and fails – to hit the high note.

I knock and stick my head round the door. Millie's leaping around on her bed, singing into her hairbrush. Millie's room is just as messy as mine is, but much cooler because it's decorated in this amazing deep purple colour, and is like a twinkle palace, with fluffy fairy lights draped over every surface. The walls are covered in posters of The Drifting, especially ones of the lead singer, Nate Devlin, who Millie *adores*.

"You're finally here!" Millie squeals. "I've been waiting *forever*. Did you bring the clothes?"

"Course," I say, dragging my suitcase and collection of

carrier bags into the room. "Your hair looks great, by the way. Love the colour." The original purple streak now has a bright pink one next to it.

Millie dives right in, throwing clothes out behind her like Murphy digging a hole in a sandpit. "This could work... This is a definite no... How do you still have *this*?... Oooh, this is gorge!"

Millie straightens up, holding a turquoise lacy vest top out in front of her.

"This would go perfectly with my red skirt, and I could stick that pink corsage on the front," she mutters. On anyone else all those colours would look terrible, but Millie has a way of making crazy outfits work. "You weren't going to wear these were you?" Millie asks.

"Nope, they're all yours," I tell her, emerging from her wardrobe. "Do you think this would suit me?"

Millie glances at the pretty black and white top I've found which has sequins around the neckline. "That doesn't work on me, but I bet it'll look fantastic on you." Millie walks over to where I'm gazing at myself in the mirror. "Danny won't be able to keep his hands off you."

Danny.

Right.

I smile half-heartedly at Millie and slump down onto the bed.

"What about other accessories?" Millie muses. "Heels, obv, but I wonder what else would go... did you bring that chunky black belt?"

"Yeah, it's in there somewhere."

I lie down onto the bed, fold my hands behind my head and stare up at the ceiling.

"Oh, I so love this song," Millie says happily, as The Drifting's last number one blasts from her speakers. *"What you doing, what you saying, you know I can't believe it...* C'mon, Suze, join in!" She takes hold of my hand and tries to pull me onto my feet. "Hey, what's up?"

"Nothing."

"Liar." Millie collapses down onto the end of the bed and stares at me with hawk-like intensity. "You *always* dance to this song. What's up?"

"Nothing," I repeat.

"I know you're fibbing."

"Mill..."

"If you don't tell me I'm going to tickle it out of you." Millie menacingly waggles her fingers.

"Don't you dare!" I say, scrambling to sit up as she starts to crawl along the bed. I'm the most ticklish person in the world and Millie knows it. She's got tons of information out of me over the years just by threatening to ambush my feet.

"You've got five seconds to spill."

"Um…"

"Five."

"It's nothing."

"Four."

"Really, it's not that big a deal…"

"Three."

"… and I'm probably overreacting."

"Two."

"Millie, stop…"

"One. That's it." Millie leaps towards me.

"Okay, okay! I'm not sure about things with me and Danny." As soon as I blurt the words out I wish I could swallow them back down again. Millie's eyes widen in surprise.

"Wha…?" Her brow furrows. "I thought you sorted everything out?"

"We did. But I don't know, lately I've been feeling a bit, um, strange about some stuff."

"Has Jade been talking rubbish again? Suze, you really shouldn't listen to her."

"It's not that."

"Then what? You're great together. What's wrong?"

"I don't exactly know," I try to explain. "I'm wondering if…"

"What?"

"I've kind of been thinking about someone else," I mumble.

"You what?" Millie screeches so loud I'm surprised the windows don't shatter. "You fancy someone else? *Who?*"

"Shhh," I beg, terrified someone will hear.

"Is it Henry? Oli? George? Josh? Rob? Or what about that guy in your geography class? It's not Freaky Hugh, is it?"

"Would you shut up? It's none of those people."

"Then who?" Millie stops and takes a big gasp. "Ohmigod, is it a girl?"

"No!"

Good grief, Millie's imagination is way too wild.

"So who is it?"

I've come this far. I might as well tell her.

"Zach," I say quietly.

"Zach?"

"Zach," I confirm.

There's a long silence while Millie digests what I've told her. I can't read her expression. I should have kept my big mouth shut.

"You can't," she eventually says. "Suze, this must be a mistake. Sure, he's hot, but you don't even know him."

"It's just... oh, I don't know. Lately my brain's been feeling so messed up and arrrrrgh!" I grab Millie's pillow and jam it over my head.

"You can't hide under there for ever," Millie says.

"Can too," I reply.

Millie tugs the pillow away and I pull my knees up to my chest. Millie puts her arm around me and gives me a reassuring squeeze.

"How do I figure this out?" I say quietly.

"You're not unhappy with Danny are you?" Millie asks.

"Not exactly," I say.

"Then there is no problem," Millie says firmly. "Suzy, we're a foursome. You, me, Jamie and Danny. It's always been that way. You can't break that up."

"I don't want to, but—"

"You just have to keep away from Zach," Millie interrupts. "I'm sure the feelings will go if you ignore them."

"Do you think?"

"I know."

"Okay." I nod decisively. Millie's advice sounds sensible. Ignore my feelings. Easy peasy.

Millie plants a big sloppy kiss on my face with a loud, "Mwah!" and laughs as I wipe her lip gloss and slobber off my cheek. "Suze, you're such a silly, you know that? Everything's going to be fine. You and Danny are rock solid."

Feeling reassured, I beam happily. "Thanks, Mil. I feel loads better now. And now that's sorted, can you help me find something to wear with that top?"

CHAPTER ELEVEN

When other schools have parties, they hire out nightclubs. And in those American movies, their gyms get transformed into magical wonderlands. What do we get at Collinsbrooke? A few paperchains hanging limply off the wall bars and trestle tables stacked high with cheap pop and balloon animals. Is this a children's party? No. Honestly, the teachers and PTA have absolutely *no* idea.

Sure, everyone suspected the party was going to be a cringe-fest. But this is cheaper and tackier than anything even my imagination could conjure up.

"Seen Barnes?" Danny points across the dark room.

The single disco ball on the ceiling is sending pathetic reflections across the dance floor. It's empty apart from Mr Barnes, who, in honour of tonight's chosen charity – the RSPCA – has donned a full-on dog costume and is attempting to pull off what he clearly thinks are 'trendy moves'.

"Oh good Lord," I groan.

I lean into Danny and in an unusual moment of affection, he slings his arm around my shoulder. I must have caught him off guard, but for the first time in a while, I feel like everything's going to be fine.

"Hey, have you seen what Jade's wearing?" Jamie nudges Danny and gestures to where Jade is perched up on a pommel horse. Their eyes go out on stalks.

Jade's squeezed herself into a tiny denim mini and skin-tight silver top that leaves little – no, scratch that, nothing – to the imagination.

Only Jade could get away with an outfit like that. She looks like a pop star. On anyone else at this school those clothes would look so ridiculous people would laugh in their face. Jade, however, has every boy dribbling and quivering uncontrollably.

All of a sudden the top and skinny jeans I borrowed from Millie seem really boring and childish.

Someone taps Jade on the shoulder, and as she turns, I realise it's Zach. While he nods away at something Jade's saying, I notice that his hair's been carefully styled to frame his face. He looks amazing, and I could totally melt at how cool he is in his yellow T-shirt and short-sleeved checked shirt, teamed with jeans and trainers.

But I won't.

Although I'd love to know what he and Jade are talking about. And why they keep turning in our direction.

Zach's eyes connect with mine and he grins suggestively. I turn away and pretend I haven't seen. Ignore your feelings, Suze.

"Coming to dance?" Danny asks.

"Er, not yet. I'm going to get a drink," I say, stepping out from under his arm.

"Get me one while you're there," Danny calls after me.

I'm pouring lemonade into flimsy plastic cups when I feel a hand on my waist.

"'Scuse us," Zach says, leaning past to grab the cherry cola bottle.

How does he always have such an effect on me? I'm trying to ignore my feelings, but that's impossible when I'm fizzing more than the lemonade I'm holding. I'm betrayed by my own body.

"Want some?" Zach asks, taking a long slurp of drink and smacking his lips.

I hold up my cups. "I'm good, thanks."

"So," Zach says. "I was hoping you'd be here."

"Oh yeah?" I reply, trying not to sound bothered. "Why's that?"

"I thought of a way you can make things up to me."

"Eh?"

Zach gestures towards his foot. "For the ankle, remember?"

Oh. That. I hoped he'd forgotten.

"Dance with me later," Zach says, taking a step forwards, so we're standing tantalisingly close.

"I can't," I say, shaking my head and forcing myself to move away.

A cute crinkle appears at the top of Zach's nose as he frowns slightly. "Can't? Or won't?"

"Well, both, I guess. Danny's right over there."

"Right. Your boyfriend," Zach says. He grabs a handful of popcorn and begins to eat it slowly.

"Yes, my boyfriend," I say firmly. "And I need to take him this drink."

"Sure," Zach says, stepping aside.

But as I pass, he gently grabs my wrist. Lemonade slops all over his trainers, and the popcorn goes everywhere, but he doesn't seem to care.

Zach leans in so close the smell of his citrus-spiciness makes me go all wobbly. My eyes shut for a split second as I inhale deeply.

"Come and find me if you change your mind," Zach says softly.

It takes every iota of strength I have to walk back to my friends.

"Cheers, Suze," Danny says, taking a cup. He seems slightly tense. "Who was that you were you talking to?"

"What? When? Nobody," I say defensively.

"Yeah, you were," Danny says. He tilts his head curiously, and a flicker of suspicion crosses his face. "I saw you. Wasn't it Zach?"

Behind Danny's back, Millie's scowling fiercely.

"Oh, yeah," I say hurriedly. "It was. He was just asking who sings this song."

"What?"

"Yeah, dumb, huh? Shall we go and dance?"

I ignore Danny's disbelief, and drag him off onto the dance floor. But all I can think about is Zach. It doesn't help that he's constantly staring at me, even after one of Jade's friends coaxes him onto the dance floor, where he dances very gingerly on his dodgy ankle. Despite that, he's actually moving to the music's rhythm, unlike Danny who's flailing in all directions.

"Suzy?" Danny waves his hand in front of my face.

"Hmmm?"

"I said, are you staying here with Millie? I'll be back in a minute."

"Oh. Yes. Sure. I'll stay," I say distractedly.

"Are you okay?" Danny shouts over the music. "You've been acting kind of strange."

"No, no, I'm good," I reassure him.

Once Danny's gone, Millie grabs me. "What was all that with Zach earlier?" she asks. "He looked like he was making a move on you. Even Danny noticed."

Good grief, do these people have nothing better to do than watch every single tiny thing I'm up to? "Nothing," I say.

"Are you sure? It didn't look like nothing." Millie sounds sceptical. "What's going on?"

"Millie, will you drop it? He asked me to dance and I said no," I explain. "I'm doing exactly what we said. Ignoring him, and focusing on Danny."

Millie seems relieved. "Well, that's all right, then. Just stick to the plan. Hey, I love this song! Woooooohhh!"

"I don't. I'm going to go and sit down for a bit," I say.

"You can't leave me all on my own," she says, mock-pouting.

"I'll get Jamie to come over," I tell her, and Millie agrees to let me go.

Jamie's standing at the side of the room, stuffing his face. "Hey, Suze. I got ten sausage rolls in my mouth at once!"

"Your mother will be proud," I tell him, relieving him of his plate and pushing him towards the dance floor. "Millie wants you. Did you see where Danny went?"

Jamie shakes his head. "He was heading in the direction of the toilets last time I saw him." He disappears into the crowd, shouting over his shoulder, "See you later. And guard those mini pizzas, I'm coming back for them."

Putting Jamie's plate down on a nearby table, I search the crowd for Danny.

"Hello," says a voice close to my ear.

Zach again.

Tingles run down my spine I feel his warm breath on my neck. I wonder what it would be like if he kissed me there?

No, no, no! I am not supposed to be thinking about that.

"I'm looking for Danny, have you seen him?" I say pointedly.

"Nope. Had a fight?"

"Absolutely not," I say. "We're having a great night."

"Me too," he tells me, and then someone barges past us, treading on Zach's injured foot.

"Aaargh!" Zach yowls, his face turning pale.

"Hey, are you okay?" I ask.

Zach doesn't speak for a minute, his eyes are screwed up and he's swearing under his breath.

"Sheesh, that hurt. Whew. Actually... I think I should rest it for a bit. People keep making me dance in here. Give us a hand outside, would you? Then I can find somewhere quiet to sit down."

I should really carry on hunting for Danny. "I can't," I tell Zach firmly.

"Please?"

"I've got to find my boyfriend."

"Suzy, please. My ankle really kills. It'll only take a minute, then you can go back."

I'm weakening. Zach really seems to need my help. And the reason his ankle's bad is because of me anyway. So it's not like I have much of a choice.

"Okay," I reluctantly agree.

Zach leans his hand on my shoulder and we walk towards the door. Well, I'm walking, Zach's hopping.

It's super cold outside, and neither of us have coats. Zach collapses onto one of the picnic tables in the courtyard and I stand awkwardly, wrapping my arms around myself, trying not to shiver in Millie's sleeveless top. Zach stretches out his long legs, and I can see our foggy breath mingling in the air.

"I can't believe how much that hurt," he says, rubbing his foot and grimacing.

"I'd better go," I tell him.

"Wait a sec," Zach says, grabbing my hand and pulling me down next to him. I wait for him to release me, but instead he starts rubbing his thumb in tantalising circles over my palm, making me shiver.

"Cold?" he asks.

"Freezing."

"I could warm you up if you like," Zach says, a cheeky glint in his eye.

"No, you're all right, thanks," I tell him, with a smile I can't help.

It might be my imagination, but Zach seems to be inching closer to me.

All of a sudden I'm not entirely sure where this is heading and it's feeling all kinds of weird. I'm scared and excited and nervous all at once.

"So, can I ask you something?" Zach says.

"Um, depends what it is," I reply.

"What's the deal with you and this guy you're seeing?"

"Danny?" I ask stupidly, like there might be some other guy he's referring to.

"Jade says you've been together ages."

"Yeah. We've hung around with each other since Infants, but got together when we were about thirteen."

"Thirteen? Are you for real?" I can't work out if Zach's laughing, or horrified, or stunned, or a combination of all three.

"Yup," I say.

"And you've never fancied anybody else?" he asks.

I shake my head.

"Nobody? Not even me?" He squeezes my fingers gently as he gazes intently into my eyes, and I instantly turn to slush.

Please, someone make this stop. Make it not be happening.

"Zach... this isn't..."

"Isn't what?" He tilts his head and I know he's about to kiss me. It's exactly like a scene from one of those cheesy rom-coms Amber's always watching.

Zach leans in, closer... closer... and I feel myself moving in towards him.

Then I come to my senses.

What am I doing? This isn't right. This is bad.

Really, *really* bad.

Just in time I whisk my face around, and Zach crashes into my ear.

"Hey!"

"Zach, I can't do this."

"But you like me." He says it as a statement, not as a question.

"I'm going out with someone."

"I don't care."

"I... I... this isn't right. What about Danny?"

"But isn't that him over there?" Zach says, nodding his head in the direction of the main building.

And it is. My boyfriend's standing at the corner of the courtyard. And I think he's seen us. I'm about to run over, to desperately try to explain, when I notice there's someone with him.

A someone wearing a silver top.

Jade.

As I watch, everything flips into slow motion as Jade leans forwards and they start to kiss.

My boyfriend is kissing another girl.

Danny is kissing another girl.

How *could* he?

I wrench my hand free from Zach's, and stagger to my feet.

I have to get out of here.

I hear Zach calling after me, but don't turn back. Somehow I make it to the school gates, and numbly, like I'm in a trance, stagger down the street. I'm not sure where I'm going. I just need to get away.

I try and block out the image of what I've just seen, but it keeps battering and bashing its way back.

Danny kissed Jade, Danny kissed Jade…

I replay the whole horrific scene over and over, refusing to believe it. Refusing to admit that it's true. But the evidence is impossible to ignore and although it takes a while to sink in, eventually it does.

And then I crumple down onto a seat at the bus stop, drop my head into my hands, and burst into tears.

CHAPTER TWELVE

"**Why won't** you talk to me?"

The duvet, pulled tightly over my head, muffles Millie's voice. It smells icky and sour under here. Mum needs to wash my bedding.

No, wait a minute. The smell isn't coming from my bed. It's me.

Pheeewwwey. After all that dancing last night, I *really* need a shower.

But I suppose being smelly is only appropriate, seeing as how everything in my life stinks at the moment.

How could Danny do that to me?

I grab my phone, which is under the covers next to me, and check the time. It's 4.07 p.m., exactly three minutes since I last looked.

Fifteen missed calls from Millie, but no new messages. Danny hasn't bothered getting in touch.

Maybe I should text him. Perhaps there's an explanation.

Wait. No. What am I thinking? He's been a git of the most gargantuan proportions, and the fact he hasn't bothered texting to beg and plead for my forgiveness just makes things a zillion times worse. It's like he doesn't even care. He's forgotten about me overnight.

I've been curled into a tiny ball all day, and can't remember ever feeling this bad before, not even when I got food poisoning from one of Dad's barbecued chicken legs.

My family don't know what's up, but they've all been in and out of here all day, trying to figure it out and discussing me in loud whispers outside my room.

Dad only poked and prodded me a couple of times to make sure I was still alive before he went away. Amber tried to make me taste-test some canapés to help me feel better, but there was no way a spinach and ricotta vol-au-vent was passing my lips. Harry was the most inventive, and fired silly string at my head. But even that didn't get any kind of reaction.

I just feel dead inside.

It was when Mum failed to lure me downstairs with a jumbo slice of chocolate cake that she realised the situation was serious and summoned reinforcements.

So now Millie is attempting to get me to emerge from my pit of despair.

"C'mon, Suzy, please, please talk to me. Where did you go last night?"

"I'm not coming out," I mumble.

"What? I can't hear you."

I squeeze my eyes tightly shut.

Go away, go away...

Millie prods me through the bedding. "Suzy, I'm really worried about you. Where did you and Danny disappear to last night? And why won't you answer your phone?"

So many questions, and I don't want to answer any of them. I roll over, away from Millie.

Millie moves to sit on the other side of the bed. "Suze, I'm not budging," she says.

"I'm not coming out," I mumble again.

"I still can't hear you," Millie says, sounding frustrated. "Stop talking through the duvet."

"I'm not coming out, ever," I say, loudly. "Just leave me alone."

There's no reply. I hold my breath, but I can't hear Millie leaving. I'm not falling for this. I'm staying put.

My phone buzzes loudly and my heart leaps.

Danny! It's Danny!

I grab my mobile, but when I read the screen my heart sinks back down again.

It's not Danny. It's Millie.

**Not going anywhere. Come out NOW
and talk 2 me.**

Millie is the most persistent person in the world. It's no good resisting, I'm going to have to admit defeat.

Reluctantly I tug the covers down a smidge.

Millie grimaces. "Ohmigod. You look terrible."

"Cheers, *mate*," I say, attempting to pull the covers back over my head.

Millie grabs the duvet just in time. "I'm sorry. It's just… your make-up's a little scary."

Oh, right. I didn't take my mascara off last night. I probably look like a psychopathic panda.

"So, what's up?" Millie asks gently. "I'm guessing it's something to do with you and Danny. Did you have another fight?"

"I don't want to talk about it."

"Sorry, no can do. Your mum's forbidden me to leave until she knows you're okay. And she's way scarier than you are."

"Hmph."

"Suzy, I'm supposed to be your best friend." Millie sounds hurt. "You can tell me anything. Why won't you speak to me?"

"Have you talked to Danny?" I ask.

Mille shakes her head.

"Has Jamie?"

"Yes," Millie says quietly. "But Danny wouldn't say anything either. What the chuffing heck happened?"

I'm not sure I can say the words out loud. Saying it will make it real, and I don't know if I can handle that. Of all the disasters I've ever had in my life, this is the worst by miles. And I didn't think *anything* would trump the Ryan underpants trauma.

"Suzy... what did you do?" Millie presses. "Did something happen between you and Zach?"

"What? No! How could you think that?"

"I figure it has to be something bad, and, you know, after what we talked about the other day..." Millie shrugs apologetically. "Zach was obviously trying it on last night."

"It wasn't *my* fault," I say indignantly. "I saw Danny..." My voice falters.

"You saw Danny what?"

"I saw Danny kissing Jade," I blurt out, hugging the duvet tightly round me as yet more tears tip down my cheeks.

The colour drains from Millie's face and she shakes her head furiously. "You what? No. No! Suzy, you're wrong. You must have made a mistake."

"Mil, I wasn't. I saw him."

Millie's mouth opens into a silent 'o'. "But, but... he wouldn't."

"Yes he would. Because he totally did," I say miserably.

"If that's what really happened, I'm going to kill him," Millie says angrily. "But it doesn't sound right. I mean, he's so into you... and *Jade* of all people? She's not his type."

"But she's gorgeous," I wail. "You saw the way Danny and Jamie were looking at her last night. Who wouldn't fancy her? Millie, what am I going to do?"

"Try and chill," Millie says. Her face is ashen and she looks majorly stressed. "I'll give Jamie a call and get him to talk to Danny, see what he can find out."

"I know what I saw."

"There's got to be an explanation," Millie says forcefully. "We'll get this sorted. I can't get any decent reception in here though, I'll have go outside."

"Okay," I mutter. I know the real reason she's going outside has nothing to do with her reception. It's because she doesn't want to speak to Jamie in front of me.

"Back in a sec," Millie says, as I huddle into the bedclothes.

The next few minutes are the longest I've ever experienced in my entire life. When I manage to peel myself away from the bed, I can see Millie through the window, pacing up and down the footpath outside the house. She's waving her hands about, and shaking her head lots. When she finally flips the phone shut, I leap back under the covers.

"Well?" I ask when Millie returns.

She shifts uncomfortably. "Danny was there when I rang. He says he saw you in the courtyard with Zach and you were holding hands."

My heart skips a beat. Oh God. So he *did* see.

"Is that true?"

"No. Well, sort of. But not like that. And anyway, what's that got to do with anything? It was nothing. Zach and I were just talking. Danny had a full-on snog with Jade Taylor."

Millie bites her lip. "He says that he saw you two just before Jade kissed him, and he was so shocked he let it happen."

"He *let* it happen? What a liar! He certainly wasn't moving away in a hurry."

"But you were with Zach, though, right?"

"Yes, I was, but *nothing* happened," I say impatiently.

"Are you sure?"

"Of course I'm flipping sure. Don't you believe me?"

She doesn't need to know we nearly kissed. After all, I moved out of the way, didn't I?

Unlike *some* people.

Millie's distraught. "I'm sorry. I did double-check.

But apparently Danny said he thought it was pretty obvious what was going on."

"But... but... no! He's wrong! Nothing happened!" I shout at the top of my voice and slump onto the bed, trying to keep back yet more tears.

This isn't my fault, I try and convince myself.

I'm not the one who kissed someone else, even if I did kind of want to.

"I'm sorry, Suze," Millie says, coming over and putting her arm round me.

I collapse onto her shoulder, and sob like I've never sobbed before.

"Suzy, you need to get up or you're going to be late," Mum says firmly on Monday morning.

"I can't," I whimper. "I'm ill. And probably infectious."

As if the whole thing with Danny wasn't bad enough, the thought of having to face everyone at school today – including Zach and Jade – is heaps worse.

"Oh, love," Mum says, sitting down on the bed and stroking the hair away from my forehead like she used to when I was little. I told her Danny and I had fallen out, but refused to elaborate further.

"Can't I have today off?" I ask. "One day. It won't matter. We never do anything important on Mondays."

"I know you're having a tough time, but it's not going to be any better tomorrow. You might as well get it over with. Putting it off will only make things worse."

How does she know? I might have thought of a way to fix everything in the next twenty-four hours. Okay, so it's a long shot, but it's a possibility, and I'm desperate here.

"Suzy, I'm sorry, but you have to go to school."

"I don't think I can," I tell her.

"You can," Mum says, standing up. She means business.

"You can't make me."

Mum bends down and heaves up the mattress. I tip out of bed with a thump.

"Ooof!"

Evil. The woman is stronger than she looks.

"You're going to school," Mum repeats. "It's for your own good, so I'm calling Millie to come and meet you in ten minutes. I want you up, dressed and eating breakfast before she gets here. And don't forget to shower. There's no way of putting this politely, so I'll just tell you: you reek."

Charming. It's impossible to get any sympathy in this place. Can't she tell my life is over?

A short time later I'm looking slightly more presentable, although it would be easy to assume

I'd been dragged through a hedge several times before being given a firm shake for good measure.

I trudge downstairs into the kitchen where Amber and Mark are in their PJs, swaying back and forth, gazing into each other's eyes and humming 'The Bridal March'. My vicious death-stare puts an end to that. I slump wordlessly into a chair and ignore the Cheerios Harry starts flicking at me.

When the doorbell rings, I don't move.

"Morning, Millie, come in. Suzy's in the kitchen," I hear Mum say.

"Hi, Suze," Millie says, as she walks in. "God, you look awful." She clamps her hand over her mouth. "Sorry. I didn't mean..."

"That's the second time you've said that to me in two days," I say darkly.

"It's just your hair—"

"You girls need to get moving," Mum interrupts, ushering us out of the door. She shoves a piece of toast and jam at me as I pass. "Eat!" she says firmly.

I dump the toast in next-door's bin.

"So how are you doing?" Millie asks cautiously, as we head off down the road.

"How do you think?" I say moodily.

"Did you speak to Danny yesterday?"

"No. He didn't bother ringing.'

"Suze, people fight all the time," Millie says. "It doesn't mean anything. You'll sort this out."

I stop walking and stare at her disbelievingly. "I don't know how."

"You will," Millie insists. "You have to."

"I'm not convinced."

"C'mon," Millie says, grabbing my arm and pulling me along. "It'll be fine, I promise."

We've got as far as the corner shop when I spot the backs of two familiar heads.

Wait a minute. Isn't that... ?

"Hey, it's Jamie," Millie chirps. "And Danny's with him. Jamie? Hi!" Millie blinks innocently and I realise exactly what's happening.

"You did this, didn't you?" I say, starting to feel dizzy. I should have eaten that toast. "You set this up. That's it, I'm going home."

Millie seizes my bag strap. "You're not going anywhere. You and Danny have to sort this out. The sooner the better."

Up ahead, I think Danny and Jamie are having the same conversation.

"We only want you to talk to each other," Millie says, as she continues to drag me along.

And then, all of a sudden, Danny's right in front of me, glowering fiercely.

"What do you want?" he demands.

My breath escapes in a big, cross whoosh. How dare *he* be angry with *me*!

"What do *I* want?" I snap. "I want to know why you got off with Jade, you cheating bag of—"

"I didn't!"

"Er, I *saw* you? God, you're such a liar."

"Me? You were with Zach!" Danny shouts. "And I didn't kiss Jade, *she* kissed *me*."

"Oh, like that makes a difference," I fire back sarcastically.

"Suzy, don't you think—" Millie says, but we ignore her.

"Actually, yeah, it does," Danny says. "I didn't want to kiss Jade, but somehow I get the impression that's not the case with you and Zach, given the way you were cosying up together out there. How long's it been going on?"

"How long has what been going on? *Nothing's* going on, you idiot."

"Guys…" Jamie steps up beside us, but we ignore him too. "This is hopeless," I hear him say to Millie.

"Yeah, sure," Danny says. "You've fancied him for ages, haven't you? It explains everything, including why you've been such a moody cow lately."

"What? How dare you? Don't blame me for this," I shriek. "When you, you—"

"Don't shout at me." Danny's voice cracks and unless

I'm very much mistaken his eyes have gone all watery.

Which kind of stops me in my tracks.

Is Danny crying?

The last time I saw him cry was when Ben Croft stole his Scooby-Doo pencil on our school trip to St Albans. We were seven.

Danny doesn't *do* tears.

And while part of me is thinking he totally deserves it, another part wants to give him a big hug and say it's going to be all right.

Messed up or what?

I'm given a sharp reality check when the image of him and Jade together invades my brain space again. *Danny's* in the wrong. And no matter how painful this is, there's no way in hell I'm apologising first.

"I'm going." Danny scowls before storming off down the road.

"You okay, Suze?" Jamie asks, giving me a quick hug.

I shake my head, avoiding meeting his gaze.

"I'd best go after him." Jamie hitches his backpack over his shoulder and runs off down the road.

Tears are flooding down my cheeks and I hate Mum for tipping me out of bed this morning. I knew I should have stayed put.

CHAPTER THIRTEEN

At lunchtime, I'm walking down the path that leads towards the library with Millie. My feet are dragging along the floor and I'm utterly depressed.

"Are you sure you don't mind me going? I don't want to leave you but I really need to get in some practice before the test," Millie says for the billionth time.

"No, go" I sigh. "I've got stuff to do anyway. This book needs returning and my history homework needs finishing. It's due this afternoon."

"Okay then, if you're sure. I'll see you later," Millie says as she heads off towards the languages building. She's got German club today. Millie's freakishly good at languages, and absolutely *relishes* any opportunity where she's actively encouraged to talk. Plus it doesn't hurt that there's a hot tutor visiting at the moment. Millie's not really interested in improving her language skills, she just wants to flirt with Dieter. Although how sentences like '*Ich habe meine*

Bratwurst verloren' can be sexy is beyond me.

I'm reaching for the door when it flies open and I have to leap out of the way to avoid getting walloped in the face.

"Hey!" I yell as a couple of boys race past, but they completely blank me.

Are all males total knuckleheads, or just the ones at this school?

I take a deep breath and try to compose myself. This situation with Danny is such a mess, and it's making me feel terrible. He's one of my best friends. It's majorly wrong that we were shouting and screaming at each other this morning. And the day hasn't got any better since then.

I got stuck in goal during the first period hockey match and, after being distracted by the world's biggest seagull landing on the goalpost, I got whacked on the head with the ball (courtesy of Jade, who else?) so now I have a thumping headache and possible brain damage.

Then I had to listen to Jade in the changing rooms, talking extra loudly to Kara for my benefit, going on and on about what a fantastic time she'd had on Saturday night. I only just resisted strangling her with Millie's tights.

After that, I collided with some kid in the corridor,

and he spilled a can of Irn Bru all over me. Despite trying to get it off, I'm still soaked, sticky and orange.

All in all, the sooner this day's over, the better.

I slowly make my way into the library and head to the returns desk.

"This is six weeks overdue," the librarian says, snapping my book shut and tapping so officiously on her keyboard, I'm surprised it doesn't snap in half. She peers over the top of her glasses. "What do you have to say for yourself?"

I shrug.

"Honestly, I don't know why I bother," the librarian says, sighing heavily. She moves away from her computer to bash away at a calculator. "The fine will be five pounds and twenty-four pence."

I stare at her, horrified. "What? You're kidding. I don't have that much."

"Then you should bring your books back when they're due."

I fumble around in my purse and locate two pound coins and a load of silver. There goes that new magazine I was going to buy. "That's all I've got," I say.

Painfully the librarian counts all the cash out, and fixes me with a steely gaze. "You're two pounds short. I'll let you off the twenty-four pence."

"Cheers," I say sarcastically, sticking my head back in

my bag and returning with a coin that's seen better days. It's a bit green now, with something mouldy stuck to it. The librarian flinches in disgust when I pass it to her.

"And the rest?" she says.

"I haven't got it," I tell her.

"Here you go," someone says behind me. Danny reaches past and drops a coin into the librarian's outstretched hand.

"Huh?" I'm so shocked my mouth falls open. I only realise when my saliva dries up and I almost start choking.

"I've been looking for you. We need to talk," Danny says.

Oh, so *now* he wants to speak to me.

"I thought you'd already said everything," I tell him, injecting as much ice into my voice as I can manage.

The librarian is hardly even bothering to hide the fact she's ear-wigging, so Danny steers me over to the bookshelves.

"Don't you think we should try and sort this out?" he says.

"You didn't want to know earlier."

"Suzy... don't be like that."

"I'm just struggling to understand why you get to call the shots when you're the one who got off with someone else," I hiss.

The librarian has followed us over to the shelves, where she's making a terrible job of pretending to categorise the books. Her ears are flapping so hard I'm surprised she hasn't taken off.

"I didn't..." Danny protests.

"I *saw* you!" I say, a little louder than I meant to.

Everyone in the library turns around to gawp. The librarian shushes in our direction, but I know she doesn't really mean it. She's enjoying this more than an episode of *Corrie*.

"I'm not doing this here." Danny drags me out into the corridor.

"Get off!" I yank my arm away from Danny's grasp. "Don't touch me, you two-timing git."

"Why won't you listen? Jade kissed me," Danny says crossly. "Anyway, you can talk, you were about to get off with Zach."

"That's so not true," I snap.

"Don't treat me like I'm stupid," Danny says.

"Why not? You were the one who got off with the school slapper, weren't you? And there's nothing going on with Zach and me."

"Sure," Danny says.

"There *isn't*. I was about to go inside when I saw you."

"Mmm-hmm."

"It's true!" I yell in exasperation. "And stop shifting this onto me. How exactly *do* you have a one-way kiss?"

"It was a... mistake."

I snort. "Did she slip and her mouth fell on yours or something?"

"Look, Jade likes me." Danny stops when he sees my expression of stunned amazement. "What? Why's that so unbelievable?"

" I... er..."

Actually, I don't know why I find that so strange. I suppose Danny's never seemed like Jade's type. This is the boy who named his hamster Chewbacca and applied for Junior Mastermind five years in a row (specialist subject: the original *Star Wars* trilogy).

He's just... *Danny*.

I mean, I can't see Jade settling down to watch sci-fi movies when there are clothes to buy and parties to be at instead.

"You really don't believe me, do you?" Danny says. He rubs the back of his neck and frowns. "You don't think someone like Jade would fancy me."

"That's not true, it's just—"

"Suzy, I know things haven't been right with us lately," Danny mumbles, refusing to meet my eye and playing with a drawing pin on the noticeboard.

Hearing him speak that out loud is like being kicked in the chest. All of a sudden I can't breathe properly. This is not a conversation I want to be having in the middle of a school corridor. Or anywhere, in fact.

"Don't say that," I protest.

"Why not? It's true, isn't it? You've been all weird and snappy."

"I'm not—"

"Yeah, you are," Danny interrupts, his face tight with tension. There's no sign of the friendly, happy Danny I'm used to. "I'm not psychic, Suzy. Lately it seems like I'm supposed to know what you're thinking, but you've stopped talking to me. It's like I don't know you any more."

I swallow. Hard.

What's happening here? I was the one who was having problems with Danny. I never once thought he might have a problem with *me*.

Oh God. Are we *breaking up*?

We can't. I don't know if this is what I want, and my head's all messed up. Everything's moving too fast. I need time to think.

"Danny, I—"

"Hiya, Suzy," a voice calls.

I groan inwardly when I see Zach emerging from the library. Could his timing be *any* worse?

"How's it going?" he says, oblivious to the tension crackling in the air. He flings his arm casually over my shoulder. "Saturday was a good laugh, wasn't it?"

Danny's gaze darts from Zach to me and his eyes narrow.

"Am I interrupting something?" Zach asks.

I'm frozen to the floor, too stunned to move.

"Yes," Danny says shortly.

"Oh right. Sorry," Zach says. "Catch up with you later, Suze..." he adds meaningfully as he wanders off.

"Are you still going to tell me there's nothing going on with you two?" Danny snaps.

"No, you're wrong, honestly," I say, starting to panic. "Danny, I—"

"I'd almost come round to believing you. How dumb am I?" Danny says.

"I'm telling you the truth," I plead. "You're being ridiculous!"

"I'm not," Danny says, sounding wobbly and unfamiliar. As he bends to pick up his bag, I notice his hands are shaking.

"Danny, please. Don't go. Can't we talk about this?"

"No," Danny says, his voice cracking. "And by the way, we're over."

CHAPTER FOURTEEN

IT's official. Being dumped is poo.

Exactly when am I going to start feeling better? It's been days, and I still feel as though my heart's been ripped out, trampled on, then whizzed in a blender for good measure. And I have no estimated date of recovery.

So much for wondering if it would be exciting to be single and what I was missing out on having been with Danny for so long. Turns out, *nada*.

Far from being a whirlwind of non-stop flirtation and excitement, it's just boring and lonely. And the whole flippin' world seems to know Danny and I have split. Everywhere I go, people in school are whispering and pointing at me. It seems the Danny/Suzy/Jade love triangle is even hotter gossip than the news that Abi Parker in Year Eleven has got through to the quarter-finals of some reality TV talent show with her dancing ferrets. Talk about humiliating. Everyone knows that Danny dumped me for Jade.

It's been ages since the bell went and Millie's waiting for me. I summon the energy to speed up a little and squeeze past some irritatingly shouty kids in the year below, who are blocking the stairs with their PE kits and violin cases.

Millie's been amazing since Danny and I broke up, making sure I'm okay, feeding me vast quantities of chocolate and handing me tissues whenever I start blubbing.

Which has been often.

Because it's hard not to think about Danny pretty much twenty-four hours a day. And I feel sick about what nearly happened with Zach and me, and how I was so utterly stupid. But that always disappears in a flash when I realise what Danny did was much, much worse. Then I get so angry, I can feel it bubbling throughout my body.

All right, so perhaps I was a *teensy-weensy* bit at fault, and I hadn't been the best girlfriend over the last few weeks we were together, but at least *I* didn't swap saliva with anyone else.

Not that he seems to care, though.

If he sees me in school, he just stares straight through me. It's like I don't exist.

And as much as I don't want to admit it, it makes me really, really miserable.

Because I miss hanging out with him. I miss my mates, and our group of four. Everything's fallen apart, and I don't know how to fix it.

Or if it's even fixable.

Millie smiles when I finally join her. "Hey, Suze." She offers me the bag of jelly babies she's munching her way through.

I shake my head and gesture towards the double doors. "You want to go and sit out somewhere?"

"Sure," Millie agrees, and we head towards the netball courts. Miracle of miracles the sun's actually shining and almost warm, so we find a dry bit of path to sit on.

"How're you doing?" Millie asks cautiously, loosening her tie.

"Same old," I say, shrugging my shoulders.

"Oh, mate," she sympathises. "I don't know what to say. This is pants."

"That's the understatement of the year."

We sit in silence for a while, watching the netball practice, and then I realise I'm going to have to ask the question that's been eating away at me. I can't torture myself any more.

"So, um, how's Danny?" I ask, trying to sound casual. The more evil part of me wants to hear he's utterly consumed by misery and devastated beyond belief.

"Um, okay, I guess," Millie mumbles.

He's *okay*? My life's falling apart. How can he be okay?

"Has he, um, said anything about me?"

"Not really," Millie says, uncomfortably. "I think he's trying to focus on other stuff."

Oh. Right. Not planning a way to win me back, then.

Well, I didn't want to be won back anyway. Perhaps I should try his tactic and focus on other stuff too.

"Do you fancy coming over on Friday night?" I ask. "Mum and Dad are going to watch some magician Amber and Mark want to book for their wedding, so we could have a girlie night at mine."

"Friday? Oh… I, er, can't." Millie shifts uneasily and pulls some sunglasses out of her bag.

"How come? Are you with Jamie?"

"I'm free on Saturday night, let's do it then instead."

"But my parents are out on Friday. What are you doing?"

"Nothing. I'd just rather go out on Saturday, that's all."

Millie's the world's worst liar. But why's she fibbing to me? Unless…

Suddenly I feel all wibbly as I realise what's going on. My fingers pluck angrily at a blade of grass. "You're doing something with Jamie and Danny aren't you?"

Millie doesn't answer and offers me a jelly baby.

I shake my head. "You are, aren't you?"

"Um, yeah," Millie says guiltily. "Sorry."

I try not to look bothered. "Oh. Well, no worries. What are you up to?"

Millie wriggles. "Um... nothing special. Are you sure you don't want a sweet?"

I push the bag away. "Why does it look like you're lying, Mil?"

Millie stays quiet.

"Millie?"

"Um. Okay. Right. Um. You know how Danny entered that competition for those tickets for The Drifting?"

I nod slowly. An icy dread is slowly seeping through me. Surely he can't have?

"Well, he kind of... won," Millie continues, leaning forwards to hug her knees and refusing to meet my eye. "Danny's got tickets for the concert on Friday. He's taking Jamie and me with him to London. I'm sorry."

Is this for real?

"You *what?*" I splutter. "You're going to see The Drifting? Without... without me?"

"Suzy, please don't. I feel terrible, but Danny made me promise not to tell you. And this is a once-in-a-lifetime opportunity to see Nate Devlin in the flesh. I'd never be able to afford to go normally. I'm so, so, so, so, super sorry I didn't say anything, but what was I supposed to do?"

I'm so angry I can't speak. This is outrageous! How could my friends do this to me?

"I can't believe Danny didn't say anything," I mutter, squinting crossly in the sun.

"You're not exactly with Danny now," Millie says awkwardly.

"Yeah, but... but... I *love* The Drifting! This is so unfair. Danny only got into them in the first place after I gave him the album for his birthday last year."

"I know."

"Anyway, wasn't the prize for four tickets plus one for a guardian?" I remember. "So if there's just three of you going, isn't there a spare ticket?" I know it's pathetic, practically begging to go along, but this is The Drifting we're talking about. The Drifting, who I've loved since *forever*.

"Suzy, please don't drop me in the middle of this," Millie says. "It wasn't my ticket to give away..."

"He's given the ticket away?" I pounce on the snippet of information. "Who to?"

Millie physically flinches.

"Who's Danny given the ticket to?" I repeat.

"Um…"

"Millie," I say warningly.

"Oh rats. I really didn't want to have to tell you this. It's, um, well, it's Jade." Millie says the last part so quietly I'm not sure I hear her right.

"He gave the ticket to *Jade*?" I screech. Half the netball team stops playing and crane their necks in our direction, trying to see what's going on.

"What are you looking at?" I snap.

"Suzy, don't be like this…"

"But don't you think that's low?" I demand. I'm so mad I could actually pop.

Millie swallows hard. "It's not the best, but he's allowed to give the ticket to whoever he wants."

"Don't think I'm impressed with you, either. You're supposed to be my best friend," I say. "I can't believe you're going to see The Drifting with Jade, of all people."

"Look, Suze, I know this is tough, but don't forget that Danny's my friend too," Millie says. She picks at her neon green nail varnish. "Not to mention he's my boyfriend's best mate. I know it totally sucks for you, but I can't take sides. And Jamie and me did try to help you sort it out."

That is *so* not the point.

"I suppose at least this proves I was right," I say bitterly as I fiddle with my bag strap and try not to cry. "He was lying all along. Danny did fancy Jade."

"Suzy, I'm really, really, really sorry," Millie says. I can tell she's feeling bad. Well, good. She should. "We'll do something great on Saturday to make up for it, okay?"

Exactly what's going to make up for The Drifting, though? Seeing them would be the best thing in the *world*. Hanging out at the shopping centre or going to see a movie isn't even going to come close to matching it. I've never been to a gig before, and I'm The Drifting's biggest fan *ever*.

And then there's the idea of Danny going with Jade. I'd never have thought she was his type.

This is too, too horrible.

"What does he see in her?" I ask, swallowing hard past the lump in my throat.

"See in who?"

"What does Danny see in Jade?"

Millie's taken aback. "Um. I'm not sure. I think she's the one who's made all the moves, to be honest."

"Really?" I say, in disbelief. "But what does Jade see in Danny?"

"Suzy, I can't believe you're even asking me that," Millie says, sounding shocked. "I know you wouldn't automatically put the two of them together, but Danny's a great guy. He's kind, he's a laugh, and he's just nice to hang out with. Plus, he's really cute."

I guess I knew that. Sort of. I mean, I always had lots of fun with him. I just didn't think *Jade* would.

"C'mon, that's the bell. We'd better go." Millie gathers up her things and pulls me to my feet.

Although Millie threads her arm through mine, I feel a horrible mix of hurt and anger and sadness.

My boyfriend's dumped me for the school bitch.

My best friends don't want to hang out with me.

And now I've missed the chance to see my best-ever-favourite band in the whole wide world.

Sucks to be me, all right.

CHAPTER FIFTEEN

I've hardly slept since I heard Millie's news and so have been up for hours. But then I've had a lot to get done this morning, and don't think I've ever achieved as much by 8 a.m. before. For a girl who stays in bed until the last possible millisecond, especially on a school day, this is a pretty big deal.

I'm still completely gutted that I'm missing out on the concert. I mean, this is not just any band we're talking about here. It's *The Drifting*.

The Drifting, who I've dreamed about seeing play live practically since I was born. The Drifting, whose albums I listen to constantly on my iPod, and in my bedroom, and force my parents to play in the car.

In fact, to say I'm gutted would be the understatement of the century. But during my night of raging insomnia, I had time to do a lot of thinking, and I realised I have two choices: I can either curl myself into a tiny ball, refuse to get out of bed, and sulk for weeks – or I can get revenge.

After much deliberation, I went with revenge. The sulking in bed was tempting, but not entirely practical. Plus Mum would never let me get away with it.

So... I decided I'm going to get Zach to be my boyfriend. That'll show Danny. He's not the only one that can start seeing someone new within five seconds of us breaking up. And I'm sure Zach will have loads of cool things for us to do together. Okay, so nothing like the Drifting concert, but fun, jealousy-inducing stuff nonetheless.

Now all I have to do to get my plan to work is ask Zach out. Yep, that's all. Even though the thought makes me want to vomit with fear. I've never asked anyone out before. And there's always the possibility Zach could say no. Which would be so humiliating I'd either die on the spot or have to leave school. Neither of which seem great options.

I'm trying to stay positive, though. After all, he tried to kiss me at the party, which is a pretty clear indication of liking someone, isn't it? Even so, as much as I try and tell myself everything's going to be all right, I'm really, really, *really* nervous. My hand is shaking trying to apply mascara.

It's taken several hours of hard work, but I look pretty damn good, even if I do say so myself. It was worth getting up early this morning, even if the beautification has taken slightly longer than planned.

There's a loud banging on the door, and I jump out of my skin. The mascara brush flies across my face, leaving a thick, dark streak.

"Suzy, what are you doing?" Mum says. "I didn't realise you were still here. I thought you'd left for school ages ago. You're late. Shift."

"Okay, okay, I'm going," I say, grabbing a tissue, and swiping at the black smear. Once it's gone, I stand back, check my reflection one last time and smooth down my uniform.

Deep breath. It's time to do this.

Although I run as fast as I can to school (not easy in Amber's borrowed heels), I'm super-late for registration, which means I can't speak to Zach before lessons start.

And then at first break, I have to see my tutor for a massive lecture about my lateness, as well as my lack of commitment and effort lately. Obviously I can't tell her it's because my entire life is in meltdown.

By the time lunch rolls round, I can't eat anything because my stomach's churning so hard with nerves, and I'm still no closer to finding Zach.

Having given Millie the slip by pretending I had

a meeting with Mr Patterson about my English essay, I'm skulking round the school corridors hunting for him.

Where *is* he?

I'm retreating in despair from the music rooms – not that Zach plays an instrument as far as I know – when a voice coos at me from over by the lockers.

"Well, if it isn't Suzy Puttock, all on her lonesome," Jade says sarcastically. "Where's your boyfriend? Oh, wait a minute. Silly me. Danny dumped you for... who was it again? Oh, yes. Me."

I try to walk past, but Jade steps out and blocks my path. "I was wondering if you'd seen Danny anywhere?" she asks with false innocence. "I wanted to find out when we're leaving for the Drifting concert tonight. You heard Danny won tickets for us, didn't you? We're getting the train to London after school."

I glare fiercely and manage to spit out, "Haven't seen him."

"Oooh, is wittle Suzy upset? Are you missing your boyfwend?" Jade says in a stupid baby voice, faking concern.

"Leave me alone."

"Aww, are you upset because Danny likes me now? Is ickle Suzy jealous?"

Behind Jade I can see Danny coming down the corridor. The sight of him, and Jade's stupid simpering face, flips me over the edge. I shove Jade out of the way, but push a little harder than I'd intended.

Crying out, Jade flings herself dramatically against the wall. From the expression on her face, she's trying really hard for tears.

"Danny, I'm so glad you're here," Jade whimpers.

"What did you do?" Danny asks me, sounding shocked.

"Nothing," I say. "She's faking."

"You have to help, Danny," Jade says, sniffing and making her voice sound shaky. "Did you see Suzy attack me?"

"You don't honestly believe this, do you?" I ask.

"You did shove her," Danny says awkwardly.

"She's a lunatic," Jade chips in.

"She's not..." Danny says. "Look, I'm sure Suzy didn't mean it."

"Ow, my arm really hurts," Jade says, fake tears beginning to glisten in her eyes. You have to give the girl credit; she's putting on an Oscar-worthy performance.

"I didn't even push you that hard," I start, then realise I'm fighting a losing battle. "Oh, why am I even bothering?" I hiss, tossing my head and storming off down the hall.

A quick glance over my shoulder shows Danny's

comforting Jade, who's milking her 'injuries' for all she's worth. His eyes meet briefly with mine before they flick away, his attention fixed firmly on Jade.

What a numpty. Why can't Danny see she's making it all up? I'm so tempted to go back and say something... but no. Even though I'm so angry my head's on the verge of exploding, I can't dwell on this right now. There are other things I need to focus on.

Like finding Zach.

Breathe and stay calm, Suze. Breathe and stay calm.

I repeat my mantra as I return to the footie field, which was actually the first place I checked, but there's still no sign of him. Nor is he in the library, the common room, the canteen or the assembly hall. I've been rushing around so much my face feels bright red, and a quick visit to the toilets confirms my worst fears.

My hair has gone static like I've been zapped with a cattle prod, my carefully applied make-up has smeared itself down my now shiny cheeks and there are sweat marks under my armpits.

Ewww! Definitely not foxy.

I nick some deodorant from a Year Seven, smooth my hair as much as possible and wipe away most of the mascara. It's the best I can do, because I really don't have long left to complete my mission.

I'm on the verge of admitting defeat, when, as I emerge from the toilets, I spot a herd of boys slouching their way towards me. And unless I'm much mistaken, I recognise one of those boys as being Zach.

Result! I've finally found him.

Only... why did he have to be with so many people? And why did it have to be when I look so utterly minging? I really don't need an audience for this... and oh *no*! Zach's talking to *Ryan* of all people.

A less positive person would think this was doomed to failure and admit defeat, but as I remember Danny and Jade, I get all fired up. I'm not going to quit.

"Hi, Zach," I say, slipping alongside him.

Only I kind of mumble it, and I don't think he hears. He's deep in conversation with Ryan about some defence strategy Man U has started using or something.

"Hi, Zach," I repeat, but my voice still doesn't seem to be working, and my greeting comes out as a high-pitched squeak.

Ryan glares in my direction. "What do you want?"

"Hey, Suzy," Zach says. "What's up?"

"Um, you know, not much," I manage to reply, my voice cracking. I can't read his face. Is he pleased to see me, or not?

"Cool. Did you want me?" Zach asks.

Do I want him? Well... yes. Who wouldn't? He's so deliciously sexy, and that white T-shirt he's got underneath his open shirt and school tie shows off his chest and mmmm...

Oh, wait a minute. He didn't mean 'do you want me' in that sense, did he? He's only asking what I need him for. My cheeks turn red.

"So... ?" Zach prompts.

"Um, well, it's kind of private..." I glare meaningfully over at Ryan, who scowls back.

"Can you leave us to it, mate?" Zach says.

"Watch out for her. She's a headcase," Ryan warns Zach, twirling his finger by his temple. He says something when he catches up with the rest of the lads and there's a huge roar of laughter.

"Ignore him," Zach says. "So, how's it going? I heard you and Danny broke up."

"Um, yeah._ The fact that he got off with Jade was kind of hard to ignore."

"I get that," Zach says.

In my head, the image of Danny and Jade kissing flashes into my head so vividly it's like looking at a photograph.

I blink hard, and try to ignore how shaken it still makes me feel. I need to compose myself. I'm not here to discuss Danny. I'm here to ask Zach out.

"Um, I was, er, wondering if you'd like to—"

"Hey, Zach, you playing after school?" one of his friends yells.

NYARRRGGGGGGGH! This is *impossible*!

"Sure, I'll see you then," Zach shouts back. "Sorry, Suzy. What were you saying?"

"Oh, um, I was, um, wondering if, maybe, you'd, you know, like to go out with me sometime?" I finally blurt so fast the words are a jumble.

"Would I like to go out with you?" Zach repeats slowly.

Oh rats. He doesn't want to. This is bad. Really bad. I hope I manage not to collapse with shame before he's out of eyeshot.

"Uh, don't worry," I say, still speaking at a hundred miles an hour. "Didn't mean it. I've got to go—"

"I'd be up for that," he says.

Huh? Did he just say yes? I think he did! I'd just better make extra, extra sure.

"You would?" I say cautiously.

"Yup. We'll grab some food, okay? Stick your address and mobile number into my locker, number 324, and I'll call for you tomorrow night at seven."

Zach jogs off before I've got time to reply. He didn't even ask if I was free tomorrow. Of course I *am*, but he wasn't to know that. Does that mean he thinks I don't have a life? Because I *could* be going out with friends or something. Does it mean—

No! I am not going to obsess about this. It doesn't matter. Because I, Suzy Puttock, have a date with Zach!

CHAPTER SIXTEEN

Five hours, twenty-three minutes and twelve seconds later, it still hasn't sunk in that Zach has agreed to go out with me. I'm pretending to do my homework but am still so stunned that Zach said yes I couldn't concentrate on anything if I had a gun to my head.

I just can't believe it's actually going to happen.

I grab my mobile, in case he might have texted me when I wasn't paying attention.

Nothing.

Oh well. Maybe I'm expecting too much. It's not been that long since I saw him. I'm sure he'll text tomorrow to let me know where we're going. Not that I'm paranoid or anything, it's just it would be nice to have some concrete proof we agreed to go out.

It seems even more unreal as nothing else has changed. Everything is going on around me as normal. Well, as normal as things get in the Puttock household.

Like right now I'm sitting in the lounge with Dad and Harry, who are watching some programme on the kids' channel, and Mum's stitching names on eighty rose-scented bags for wedding favours. She's been sewing for a week, and isn't even halfway through yet.

If only they knew what happened to me today.

Although they probably wouldn't care, or even get how momentous this is. I'm really excited, and it's the only thing keeping me from dwelling on the thing-that-must-not-be-thought-about.

Which obviously I think about every five seconds. Because tonight's the night of the concert.

So while I'm hip-hop-happy about Zach, I also feel hugely sucky about the fact my so-called friends have a hot date of their own, with The Drifting, and will have arrived in London by now.

Talk about mixed emotions.

I chew on my pen as I ponder exactly how I'm going to ask my parents about going out with a boy who – gasp – isn't Danny. In this house, that's going to warrant front-page news and a full-scale investigation.

"Hahahah!" Dad chortles loudly at a puppet panda on the screen. "Look at this! He's catching custard pies in his mouth. Classic!"

"Is it all right if I go out tomorrow night?" I ask casually.

"Of course it is," Mum says, dragging her attention away from her sewing. "As long as you're back by ten. Are you going somewhere with Millie?"

"Um, not exactly." I tap the pen against my teeth uneasily.

"Oh, are you and Danny doing something? It's about time you made up," says Mum.

"Er, no. We haven't."

Mum's brow furrows. "That's a shame. I'd have thought you'd have sorted things out by now."

"Actually, Mum…"

"Wahahahaha!" roars Dad again. "Jen, have you seen this? You really must watch. It's hilarious. Funniest thing I've seen in ages."

Mum turns obligingly to the screen for a few moments, laughs weakly to humour my father, and then turns back to me.

"Actually, I've got a date," I tell her.

"A date?" I've never seen Mum so shocked. "With who?"

"A guy from school."

"Do I know him?"

"No you don't, he hasn't lived here that long," I say, with exaggerated patience. Honestly, what's with the interrogation? It's only a date!

"I'm not sure I'm happy about this... What do you think, Chris?"

"Anything you say, Jen," Dad agrees, not really listening.

"Oh, you're hopeless," Mum says. "Suzy, what happened with Danny? You've been together so long – do you really want to throw all that away? "

"I'm not throwing it away."

"But have you really tried to make up with him?" Mum persists.

"Mum, can you please let it go?"

"It's such a shame. After all, you're childhood sweethearts, and he's such a lovely boy."

"So lovely he got off with someone else," I finally snap.

Okay, I was wrong. *Now* I've never seen Mum look so shocked.

"Oh. Oh, Suzy. I'm so sorry. Are you sure? That doesn't sound like something Danny would do."

"Of course I'm sure," I say. "I *saw* him. With my very own eyes. And now I've got a date with Zach and—"

"Would you two keep it down?" Dad says. "I'm trying to watch this."

"I've got a date with Zach and I really want to go," I continue, slapping my folder shut and ignoring Dad. "He said he'd call for me, so you could meet him – quickly – if you really have to, as long as you don't let Dad anywhere near him."

"I suppose it's all right," Mum frowns. "But I still think it's a shame…"

She's interrupted by Amber bounding excitedly into the room. "When Mark's back from work he's going to give me a hand finishing off the menus and place cards – does anyone else want to help?"

"I'm busy," Dad says, shooting out of his seat so fast someone could have shoved a firework up his bum. "I'm going to see Joe down the road about a, er, car thingy. Very important man stuff," he calls as he darts from the room.

"And I can't either," Mum says, looking genuinely distraught. "There's a concert on at Aunt Lou's home that I promised I'd go and watch with her."

"Oh no," Amber wails. "According to my planning schedule, it all has to be done by tonight. Harry, you'll help, won't you?"

"Bog off," Harry says, crunching her crisps loudly.

"Suzy?" Amber says hopefully.

"Sure, what the heck," I tell her. "It's not like I have anything else to do on a Friday night. Not like I have a life. Not like I could be at the concert of my favourite band watching them perform or…"

"Excellent!" Amber chirps. "Mark'll be back

about eight. I'll give you a shout when we're getting started."

It's only after she's gone that I realise what I've signed myself up to. An evening of wedding mush with the smoochiest couple in living history.

While my friends are rocking out with The Drifting, I'm going to be helping Amber and Mark make wedding stationery.

As if I have no control over them, my eyes swivel towards the clock on the mantelpiece. I have *got* to stop watching the time, otherwise I'm going to spend the whole evening obsessing over when they'll be arriving and queuing and finding their seats and—

No. That is not what I want. I must busy my mind with other things.

So, in a never-before-seen fit of organisation, for the first time ever my homework's finished on Friday rather than being forgotten about until Monday morning and copied from whoever's nearest in registration.

Then I go upstairs and sort out my underwear drawer.

Then I arrange the clothes in my wardrobe by colour.

And then I tidy my desk.

By the time I've finished, my bedroom has never been so organised.

It's freaky. I'd almost forgotten that the carpet was blue in here. It's actually quite nice.

192

And I've found the H&M voucher Amber gave me for my birthday, which I thought I'd lost.

So that's something, I guess.

But it's nothing compared to seeing The Drifting. I'd surrender my voucher in a heartbeat if I got to go to the gig instead.

With nothing else left to sort, tidy or clean, I try and read through a magazine but throw it at the wall when I come across a five-page interview special with – you guessed it – The Drifting. I put on some music instead, but Radio One has a special broadcast from the concert, with a reporter talking to fans about how excited they are. I hit the power button so hard it falls off.

I slump onto my bed and stare up at the ceiling while my imagination tortures me with how much fun Danny, Millie and Jamie are having with Jade.

With The Drifting.

Without me.

It's almost a relief when Amber calls me downstairs, where she's set up a wedding craft station in the dining room.

"Hi there, Suzy." Mark beams at me from his seat at the table. "Thanks for helping with all this. I never knew there was so much planning involved in weddings. Good job Amber's got it all under control, eh?"

"Mmm," I say, trying to sound convincing. In my opinion, Amber's got less control than knickers with broken elastic.

"Here are the menus…" Amber says, spreading a pile of cards and shaking open a bag of pink marabou feathers across the table. "And look at these amazing chihuahua stickers I managed to find. These need to be stuck on, as well as the feathers, and then onto all of the place cards, which also need writing."

"What's with the chihuahuas, Ambs?" I ask, trying not to sound too alarmed. Which I clearly am.

"An addition to the theme." Amber beams. "Aren't they the cutest? I read in a magazine they're Conni G's favourite dog, and I thought they'd go well with the pink."

My sister gets weirder by the day. I mean, when have you ever seen a pink chihuahua? But it's her wedding, she can do what she wants. As long as I don't have to take a mutt down the aisle on a lead or anything. Actually, I'd better keep my mouth shut about that. I wouldn't want to give Amber any ideas.

"They're beautiful, princess," Mark says, squeezing Amber's hand, nearly crumpling a menu in the process. "Although nowhere near as beautiful as you."

"Watch out, Mark," says Amber, saving the menu and whisking her hand away as he moves to sit at the other end of the table.

Eh? That's not like her. Usually these two act like someone needs to throw a bucket of cold water over them.

"So, Suzy, what are you doing at home on a Friday night?" Mark asks, picking up a different menu.

"Mark, *watch out!*" Amber screeches, leaning down the table to snatch the card away. "See what you've done? You've got grubby fingerprints all over it."

"Sorry, Ambypamby," Mark says, shamefaced.

Amber huffs before launching into a lengthy and detailed set of instructions on what we're both supposed to be doing.

It basically involves sticking a feather under a chihuahua.

"Got that?" Amber says. She eyes me warily. "Suzy, please be extra careful. You know what you're like."

I pull a face as Mark laughs.

"Muffin, calm down, she'll be fine." He picks up a handful of feathers. "Suzy, I was listening to the radio on the way home – they were coming live from the Drifting concert. Did you hear it?"

"Nope," I say tightly.

"They're very popular, aren't they? Tickets must have sold out quickly."

"Yup."

"It's such a different experience seeing a band play live. I remember when I was your age, I went to my first concert. I went to see—"

"Mark, nobody cares," Amber interrupts. "Suzy doesn't want to hear what you did a million years ago. Please focus on the sticking. That feather's all wonky."

"Looks straight to me," Mark says.

Amber whips out a tape measure from her bra. "See! It's exactly one millimetre higher at this end. Concentrate, Mark, for goodness' sake."

I soon get into a routine of grab card, stick feather under chihuahua, push away card, and repeat. It's strangely soothing, in a funny sort of way.

Things move on, and change is good, I tell myself as I go through the pile, parroting an article I read in some magazine.

And let's not forget about Zach!

An involuntary grin crosses my face and instantly I feel a bit better. Tomorrow can't get here fast enough.

CHAPTER SEVENTEEN

The next morning, I'm woken by the sound of cats yowling outside. I try and see what time it is, but I'm half-asleep, and my eyes don't seem to be working.

Help! I can't see anything! Nothing at all!

Oh my God, oh my God, what happened in the night? Have I gone *blind*?

I sit up in alarm and a magazine falls off my face. I must have fallen asleep reading it last night. All of a sudden, although it's still dark, I can see stuff again.

Well, phew. Talk about a relief.

And now my sight's returned, I can see what time it is. Although I kind of wish I couldn't. Because it's 5.03 a.m. On a *Saturday*. That's practically the middle of the night. Those blooming cats have a lot to answer for.

I yawn widely, and as the skin on my face stretches, it feels dead strange. When I run my hands over it, it feels all bumpy. And really sore.

Uh oh. I hope I haven't had a bad reaction to that face pack I stole from Amber's room last night. The one that promised spa-like results and deep skin cleansing. The instructions said to leave it on for twenty minutes, but I got distracted and it was on for over an hour. My face was kind of burny by the time I took it off.

I'd better check it out.

I flick on the light, blinking as the brightness hurts my eyes, then stumble over to the mirror.

"Aaaarrrrrrghhhhhhhhhhhhhhhh!" I scream.

I have never, ever, *ever* in my whole life had as many pimples as I've got right now. They're huge, and to make things worse, most of them are those really nasty painful red bumps that stay for ages and shine like beacons. Plus I've got about six white-heads.

What am I going to do? They'll *never* be gone by tonight.

"Aaaarrrrrrghhhhhhhhhhhhhhhh!" I scream again as my door bursts open. Dad leaps in, brandishing Harry's foam cricket bat and swinging it around manically.

"What are you doing?" I yelp.

"You screamed. We thought there was a burglar," Dad explains breathlessly. "Where is he? Is he hiding?" He flings open the wardrobe door.

Okay. It's way too early for this level of lunacy.

"What are you on about? There is no burglar."

"Then what was all the noise for?" Dad asks, the bat dropping down from above his head. He peers at me. "And what's wrong with you? Are you ill? It's not chicken pox, is it?" Dad starts edging away.

"No, I used a face pack last night and now I'm covered in spots..."

"I don't understand," Dad says, ominously.

"I screamed when I saw myself," I explain.

"Suzy, let me get this straight. You wake up the whole house screeching like a banshee because you've got a spot?"

"It's not just one. Look at them!" I point at my chin.

"Get back to bed," Dad says. He's turned a kind of purple colour. "Am I the only sane one in this bloody asylum? I'd be better off living in the shed," I hear him grumble as he stamps off down the corridor.

I stick my tongue out behind his back as I skulk back to the mirror. There's no way I'm going to get back to sleep now. Oh well. At least I've got plenty of time to try and figure out how to get rid of these spots.

Considering how long I've been up, I should have had more than long enough to sort myself out and get myself looking vaguely normal. So why is it that with only half an hour before Zach's due, my face still looks like the Himalayas and I'm nowhere near ready?

The temptation to cancel was overwhelming, but I didn't have his number. And I'm starting to think he's lost mine.

I check my phone for what must be the six-hundredth time today. Nothing. Why hasn't he texted? I have no idea where we're going. If we're still going anywhere.

I practically jump out of my skin when there's a knock at my door.

Eek! That can't be Zach already, can it? I grab my dressing gown and throw it on over my less-than-attractive spotty knickers and bra.

"Who is it?" I call, panicking.

"Me," Millie replies, walking in.

"Oh thank goodness. Hi," I say, so relieved it's not Zach I forget for a moment I'm still annoyed with Millie.

Millie eyes widen when she sees me. "What happened to you?" she asks, poking a finger at my chin.

"Long story." I twist my face away. "What do you want?"

I'm not going to be overly friendly. I'm still not willing to forgive and forget that my so-called best friend went to see The Drifting without me.

"Don't be like that, Suze," Millie says, her face falling. "I came to see how you were."

"Fine, thanks." I turn my back on her to flick through the hangers in my wardrobe.

Millie bites her lip. "Suze, I know you're bummed about missing The Drifting. And the fact that I went. And the fact that Jade was there. But I'm sorry. I bought you a present, if that helps," she says, shaking a carrier bag at me.

I can't resist the temptation. I do love a present. "Jelly babies?" I say in disgust, when I peer inside the bag.

"Oops, no, they're mine," Millie says, grabbing them. "Under those. It's a The Drifting vest top and programme from the concert," she explains.

I hold the top out in front of me and smile unenthusiastically. "Thanks."

"Hey, a smidge more excitement, please," Millie says, poking her fingers into the corners of my mouth and forcing it into a smile. "I know it's not as good as the actual concert, but you've wanted one for ages. Dad gave me money to get a tee for myself, but I've made the ultimate sacrifice and given it to you instead."

"Sorry, Mil," I say, pushing her off and starting to laugh. "It's great. Thanks. It's just, you know, with missing out on The Drifting and the whole Danny thing..."

"I know," Millie says as she flops down onto my beanbag. "It's rough. I get that."

"So, how was it?" I ask. I have to be mature about this. I can cope with hearing the details.

"You really want to know?"

"I really want to know."

"They were fantastic!" Millie raves, her eyes lighting up. "They did an amazing entrance with these massive explosions and the band came up through the floor."

"Wow," I say, impressed despite myself.

"They did all of the songs from their new album, and had these crazy dancing holograms," Millie continues. She holds out her mobile, and I scroll through a load of blurry photos, then a short video where I can just about make out The Drifting over the noise of the crowd.

"God, it looks incredible," I say enviously, sneaking a glance at my own phone.

Still nothing from Zach.

"It was," Millie says. "Their encore was 'All I Think Of Is You,' but by then you could hardly hear the music because the girls were screaming so loud. It was awesome. I wish you'd been there."

I smile wryly. "Yeah, me too. It sounds mind-blowing. So, er, did Jamie have fun?"

"Yeah, he loved it."

"How about, um, Danny?"

"I guess," Millie says vaguely.

"Was he... was he really coupley with Jade?"

"No. His dad was there, so it would have been a bit weird.

Jade kept trying to get him to kiss her, but you know Danny isn't really into that," Millie replies tactfully.

The idea of Jade pawing Danny sends a stab of hurt through me. I turn away to rummage through the clothes in my wardrobe again. Anything to avoid picturing Danny and Jade together.

Think about something else, quick… like the outfit I'm going to wear tonight.

It took ages to decide — most of the day, in fact — mainly because I don't know where we're going. I've finally decided on dark blue skinny jeans, a red satin top and my new jacket. With a big belt, a chunky bangle and the gorgeous silver necklace I found in Amber's jewellery box, I should look pretty good. If only my pimpletastic face wasn't going to let me down.

As I wiggle into my trousers, Millie frowns. "What are you getting all dressed up for?"

"I've got a date," I say casually, slipping on my jewellery. I can see Millie's reflection and her face is a stunner.

"A *date*?" Millie shrieks. "For real? With who? When did this happen? Tell me everything, immediately."

I know as soon as I tell her she's going to blab to Jamie — which means it won't be long before Danny knows too.

"Zach," I tell her.

"*Zach?*" Millie's eyes widen. "When did that happen?"

"He asked me out yesterday," I say.

Well, he probably would have done if I hadn't got in there first, so it's not *exactly* a lie.

Millie looks dismayed. "But I was really hoping you and Danny would sort things out."

"You're not serious?"

"Course. Why wouldn't I be? You guys are my best mates. I hate things being like this," Millie says miserably. "I hate having to hang around with Jade, too."

"Yeah, well, it's a bit late for Danny and me now."

"But you've been together for so long. Are you sure you can't just talk to him and—"

"Millie, we're over," I tell her firmly, even though I get a pang saying it. "Danny's seeing Jade now. What am I supposed to say to him?"

"I don't know. But I don't like it," Millie replies in a small, sad voice. "I've got to get back. Let's go to Bojangles tomorrow and you can tell me all about it then. I'll text you when I wake up." She pushes herself up onto her feet. "Have a good time tonight," she says on the way out, although she doesn't sound like she means it.

As I listen to Millie clatter down the stairs, I'm half-tempted to race after her and beg her to help me get things back to the way they were.

Then I shake my head. I'm going out with Zach now.

Which means I need to focus on looking fabulous and, more importantly, on hiding these spots. Someone, somewhere, must have a solution.

I dash downstairs, bribe Harry away from the computer with the jelly babies Millie's left behind, and hit Dr Internet for answers.

Okay, that's a little bizarre. Is it some kind of joke? Because lots of the sites are saying you can use a green cover-up stick to neutralise red blotches, and then put ordinary concealer on top.

For real? Well, I'm desperate enough to give anything a go. I don't have any green cover-up stick, and I can't find any in Amber's mammoth cosmetics bag, but I do manage to locate some green eye-shadow. It has to have the same kind of effect, right? Carefully I dab it all over my face, trying not to notice the resemblance between me and the Incredible Hulk.

Ding dong!

Argh, that's the doorbell!

No, no, no.

Zach *can't* be here already.

What on earth possessed him to be early? Danny always used to arrive half an hour after any time we'd agreed because he knew I'd never be ready when I was supposed to be.

"Danny's here, Danny's here!" Harry yells, bursting out of her room and stampeding down the stairs.

"Harry, don't," I shout, throwing down the make-up and chasing after her. But it's too late. She's already pulled the front door open.

"You're not Danny," Harry says accusingly.

"Clearly," Zach says.

"I'm not allowed to talk to strangers," Harry says, then slams the door in Zach's face.

"Harry, what are you doing?" I say in horror, racing up behind her.

"Where's Danny?" Harry demands.

"I'm not going out with Danny any more," I say through gritted teeth. "Now scram."

I fling the door open again. "Zach, hi. I'm so sorry... what's wrong?"

"Your... face..." he murmurs.

Oh *no!*

I can't believe Zach's seen me like this. My face is green. *Green!*

"Ha ha," I laugh manically. "I was messing around with my little sister and dressing up. I'm pretending to be an alien from Planet Zingba. We're all about the fun in this house! I forgot I still had all this on. Er, wait here a minute, I'll be out in a sec."

And with that I shut the door on him again.

I rush back upstairs to try and sort out my face, but even after my best efforts I still look suspiciously lumpy, as well as slightly crusty. But I'll just have to hope wherever we're going has dimmed lighting. I slip in my lucky star earrings, then run downstairs so fast I nearly break my neck.

Skidding into the hall, I groan when I see my nightmare just keeps getting worse.

Mum and Amber have invited Zach inside and he's backed up against the wall, looking like he'd rather be jabbed at with hot pokers than facing this particular interrogation squad.

"So which do you think, Zach?" Mum's asking, shoving a magazine in his face. "Do you prefer the traditional fruit cake, or this heart-shaped chocolate one?"

"It's important to get another male opinion on these things," Amber adds, waving bits of pink material at him. "I'd also like to know what you think about this pink ribbon. It's not exactly the same shade as this swatch, which is the colour of the bridesmaid's dress, but would you have noticed?"

"Um…"

"What are you two doing?" I ask in alarm.

Mum swivels around to glare at me. "Suzy, what are you doing, leaving Zach outside?"

"Could you be any more embarrassing?" I ask, through clenched teeth, opening the front door.

"Could you?" Mum counters. "Where are your manners? What's Zach going to think?"

"I didn't think anything," Zach says, shrugging and spitting his chewing gum into the flowerbed.

Mum's face darkens, and I sense it's time for a speedy exit.

"We're going now. I'll be back by ten," I say.

"Wait," Amber calls after us. "Zach, you haven't told us what you think about the cake yet..."

Well, *this* hasn't been the best start.

CHAPTER EIGHTEEN

"So what's the plan?" I ask. "I wasn't sure you were coming. You didn't text me." I giggle, to show I'm messing around, but I'm so nervous that instead of coming out all casual, I sound hysterical.

Fortunately Zach doesn't seem to notice. He seems loads more relaxed now we're walking away from the house and his hand keeps brushing temptingly close to mine. Not that I have the guts to reach out and take it or anything. No *way* am I that brave. Plus, my palms are a tad sweaty.

"Text you? Why would I?" Zach asks. "I said I'd be round at seven."

"I know, I just thought..." My voice trails off lamely. Exactly what did I think? I guess I'd hoped he might text to say hi, or to let me know where we were going, or at the very least to confirm that everything was still on. Perhaps I was expecting too much. I can be such a muppet sometimes.

"It did make me realise I don't have your number though," I say.

"Huh? Oh, right, I'll give it to you later," Zach says.

"Okay, great. So, where are we going?" I ask.

"Thought we'd grab some food," Zach says, shoving his hands into his jeans pockets. They're sitting so low that I can see pants peeping over the top. I quickly avert my eyes.

"Where?" I ask cautiously, expecting him to say a pizza place, or the cheap noodle shack, which is where I went with Danny once.

"Miller Street," Zach says.

"Oooh, yeah!" I say excitedly.

Blimey, this is actually going to be a real date. Miller Street is where the decent restaurants are, and I've never been to a proper restaurant without my parents before.

This is the best!

Although... if he expects me to split the bill, I hope I've got enough money. I only brought a tenner.

"Erm, it's not too expensive, is it?" I say awkwardly.

"Nah," Zach says.

In that case, I refuse to focus on niggly worries. Instead I'm going to ignore my nerves and enjoy the happy, excited feeling I've got from knowing someone's finally taking me somewhere decent.

Ten minutes later, the excitement has evaporated. Because we're not going to a restaurant. It's a little café, which isn't even on Miller Street – it's on one of the little side roads leading off it. And outside it, there's a faded banner which reads, *Seafood Speciality Evenings*.

Yep, the place specialises in *seafood*. And I'm the girl who hates fish with a passion. Oooooh, this is not good. Even the smell wafting out of the open kitchen door is enough to make me queasy.

Maybe I should say something. But what if that puts him off me? I don't want to ruin our date before it's begun. I can't do it. I'm sure there'll be *something* for me to eat.

My heart starts to thump as I follow Zach, my stomach churning every step of the way. Inside, the café is lit only by candles, I'm guessing to conceal the fact it's actually pretty tatty, and immediately makes me worry that my spots will cast crazy shadows all over my face, making them seem even bigger. The floor is sticky underfoot, and there are stinky fishing nets hanging from the ceiling.

We head to a seat by the window, and as I sit down, the chair wobbles terrifyingly. I grab onto the table for support. The last thing I need is to end up sprawled on the floor. God knows what I'd catch down there. Besides, I need to make Zach think that I'm sophisticated and elegant. Someone sophisticated and elegant who enjoys seafood, and isn't in danger of hurling their dinner all over him.

Which is a very real possibility.

Taking the menu (actually a laminated piece of A4 paper) from a waitress, I scan it nervously. Then I nearly have a meltdown. Partly because of the food – unsurprisingly, there's not a lot of choice for a girl who doesn't eat anything remotely fishy – but also because of the prices! This place costs way more than the noodle shack.

"Um, Zach?"

Zach's gorgeous eyes peep over the top of his menu, and the floaty feeling I get shuts me right up. I can't give myself away now. If I do he'll never want to want to see me again, let alone want to be my boyfriend.

"What are you going to have?" I say.

"Not sure, it all sounds great."

"Mmm, it really does," I enthuse fakely.

"Are you ready to order?" a waitress asks, appearing at the side of the table.

"Seafood platter," Zach says, shoving the plastic menu back at the girl. "Suzy? What are you having?"

"I'm not actually that hungry, so I think I'll have the soup of the day, please," I reply, forcing a smile. It was the cheapest thing I could find on the menu.

But it turns out to be a big mistake.

A big, big, *big* mistake.

When the soup arrives, it's a kind of grey colour, with horrible rubbery things floating around on the surface. My insides clench as I stare down at it.

"Everything all right?" Zach says.

"Yes... fine. Just, um... it smells so good. Looks yummy."

Zach takes a huge bite of crabstick and chews happily.

I lift my spoon and prod gingerly at my dinner. Maybe I can distract myself by getting Zach chatting.

"So, whereabouts in Collinsbrooke do you live?"

Jeez, was that seriously the best I could come up with? What a lame-o.

Zach wipes his mouth with the back of his hand. "Clarendon Street."

Clarendon Street? That's not far from where Jamie lives, although it's a lot less posh.

"My friend lives near there," I tell him. "Jamie Turner. Do you know him?"

"Yeah, I'm on the football team with him. Not as good as he thinks he is," Zach says dismissively.

I decide it's probably best to pretend Zach didn't just say that.

"So do you like living there?"

"S'all right," Zach says, spearing a prawn. Ugh. It still has eyes.

"I'm surprised I haven't seen you round there," I say, trying not to shudder. "I hang out with Jamie a lot. Well, I did. Not any more, I suppose. Jamie's best mates with Danny, you know, the boy I used to go out with and..."

Stoptalkingstoptalkingstoptalking! Even I'm not daft enough to not realise talking about your ex on a date with someone else is a bad idea.

My voice melts away. I wait for Zach to say something, but he just keeps shovelling food into his mouth like he's not eaten all week.

I'm so busy trying to work out what to do next that I inadvertently lift my spoon up to my mouth and take a mouthful of soup. And nearly spit it straight back out again. It's disgusting. And because I've left it so long, it's gone all cold. Don't be sick. Swallow quickly and breathe... breathe.

Only... oh dear God – I can't breathe. I actually *can't breathe*! There's something stuck in my throat. I'm going to die! I'm going to die!

I grab out blindly for my glass of water and take a huge glug.

It only makes things worse. Now I'm choking.

My face has gone red and tears are streaming down my cheeks.

Why isn't Zach *doing* something instead of sitting there, staring at me with that horrified look on his face?

Out of the corner of my watery eye, I see a waitress sprint up to our table. "Are you okay?" she asks, sounding panicked.

Wordlessly, I shake my head. Of course I'm not flipping okay! I'm *dying* here!

The waitress moves behind my chair, and delivers a sharp karate chop to my upper back. It's then a fish bone flies out of my mouth. Gasping a grateful, heaving breath, I watch helplessly as it tumbles in mid-air, almost in slow motion, heading towards Zach's face.

Oh. Please. No.

The bone hits Zach smack on the side of the nose, where it bounces off with a *poooiiinng* and lands on top of the buttered roll he's just about to take a bite of.

Oh my God. Oh my God. *Please* tell me that didn't just happen.

Zach drops his bread in disgust.

"Well, that was a close one," the waitress jokes, smiling as she fusses around us. "Feeling better now? We'll give you a discount on that, as an apology, all right?" She pats me on the shoulder sympathetically.

It's nice that she's so concerned. At least someone cares about me. Zach's more interested in getting another bread roll.

I put my spoon on the table and try to compose myself.

No way am I eating any more of that soup. It's lethal. And now not only is Zach going to remember me as the girl who tried to cripple him, I've become the girl who tried to cripple him and then spat fish in his face.

Maybe I should just pretend that everything's normal. Maybe he'll forget... or something.

"So, um, have you always been a big football fan? Which team do you support?" I say, my voice still all croaky.

It seems football is the magic button to press. Zach's face brightens, and that's it, he's off. He talks and talks and talks.

Well, that's a relief. The fish bone has been forgotten. Hurrah! But is he ever going to stop? He's been going on for ages.

I've now heard all about his favourite club, each of the players there and what kind of season they're having, followed by the entire history of Zach's footballing career and how he's hoping to be scouted by one of the top clubs any day soon. "Did I tell you about the cup match I won for my last school?"

"No, I don't think so," I say, doing my best to appear interested.

"Yeah, I was amazing," Zach brags. "It was three all, with only two minutes to go, and this school was our biggest rival, right, so I won the ball from this guy who must have been at least twice the size of me..."

I tune him out.

"Suzy?"

"Huh?" I jerk myself back to the room. "What did you say?"

"We'll split the bill, okay?" Zach says.

"But..."

How can I say my meal cost nowhere near as much as his dinner? Plus he's not allowing for the fact my soup was discounted due to the fact it nearly killed me. I don't want to sound tight, but Zach had three colas, and ended up eating everything – including the cold soup. *And* he didn't even ask if I wanted pudding. It's the one bit I was looking forward to as it wouldn't be fishy. Danny knows I like pudding best, and I'd sell my soul for double-chocolate fudge cake.

Zach works out the amount down to the nearest penny, and tells me how much I owe.

"I'm really sorry, but I haven't got that much with me," I say, throwing my tenner down onto the table. It's still more than my meal cost.

Zach counts out some cash, doesn't leave a tip, and we stand up to go.

"Um, are you going to walk me home?" I say nervously. I'm expressly forbidden from walking around at night on my own so I'll have to call my parents to come and get me if Zach's not coming back with me, which will please Dad no end.

"All right," Zach says. "I have to go past your road to get home anyway."

As we start walking, I peep out of the corner of my eye at Zach. He's so much better looking than anyone I've ever known in real life before. Is the lack of interesting conversation such a big deal? So he's obsessed with football. Big whoop. Because how many girls are lucky enough to have someone this gorgeous be interested in them?

Zach sees me peeking at him, and as our fingers brush together, he grabs my hand with his.

He's holding my hand.

He's holding my hand!

All too soon, we're pushing open my garden gate and arriving at the front door.

Now what happens? What if Zach wants to kiss me? What if he *doesn't*? Oh, I'm just so rubbish at all of this.

I grab my keys out of my bag and jangle them apprehensively.

Zach ducks his head slightly to check his reflection in the porch window. He tweaks a few strands of hair, and then turns to me. "Right then, I'm going to head off."

"Sure. Encountering my family once in an evening is

usually more than enough for most people," I say.

"Yeah, too right," Zach says.

We stand in an awkward silence.

"So..." I say, meaningfully.

We stare at each other for a few moments, then, without any warning, Zach lunges forwards and lands a smacker hard on my lips.

Flipping heck! He certainly doesn't mess around.

Relax, Suzy. Cherish this moment. It's your first kiss with a boy who isn't Danny.

Hmmm, it's certainly different to what I'm used to. For starters, Zach tastes a bit fishy. And I'm not sure I like that nippy thing he's doing with his teeth to my bottom lip. Not to mention he's a bit... well... *licky*. Kind of like being lapped by a dog.

But maybe this is how other people kiss. I wouldn't really know.

I do like the way Zach's running his hands up and down my back though, bringing them to rest on the top of my bum. I'll just concentrate on that.

We kiss until Zach pulls away, making a big squelchy noise.

"See you," he says, wiping his mouth with the back of his hand. He vaults over our garden gate and swaggers away.

CHAPTER NINETEEN

"**Good morning**, Puttocks," Millie says cheerily, as she walks into the kitchen the next morning. "Whatcha up to?"

"Table plan," I explain, picking up my bowl of cereal from the work surface.

Mum, Amber and Mark are all sitting at the kitchen table, staring intently at the large piece of paper laid out in front of them. Every so often they move around Harry's Lego Minifigures, which each have a guest's name stuck on them.

"Can't Aunt Lou sit with Mark's uncle and aunt?" Mum asks, moving the Poison Ivy Minifigure next to a cowboy and a pirate.

"She'd be better off at a table by herself, if you ask me," I mutter, rolling my eyes at Millie. "Ideally in different room to the rest of us. This is what, day five of this process now? You've still not managed to agree on who should sit where."

"Well, it's a very tricky business," Mum says. "So many family politics to take into account. So many people won't get on. Now, what about putting Clara there with Rose?"

"No, Mum, that's not going to work," Amber says. "They don't speak since the incident with the Christmas pudding, remember?"

"What about putting Clara over here, then, with Jenny," Mark offers.

"Mark!" Amber shouts crossly, slapping her hand down on the table and sending all the Minifigures flying. "You *know* that's not going to work. You *know*. You suggested it yesterday and we had to go through the whole history of how at Cousin Sara's wedding they attacked each other with their cake forks. You just don't *listen*, do you? Sometimes I feel like you don't care about this wedding *at all*!"

And with that, Amber storms out of the room. Mark just stares after her, blinking in astonishment.

"Um, I'd better go and make sure she's all right," he says awkwardly.

"Wedding jitters, Mark, that's all it is," Mum says, patting him reassuringly on the shoulder. "Happens to the best of us. She'll be fine."

"See what I have to put up with?" I say to Millie,

as I wash up my bowl at the sink. "Wedding insanity from morning until night."

"Yeah, seems fun," Millie says, wrinkling up her nose. "Are you ready to go?"

"Yep, I'll just grab my coat."

As we leave, we trip over a pile of wedding catalogues stacked by the gate. Over the last few months, Mum and Amber have signed up for every vaguely wedding-related magazine in the world. We average about twelve a day, which must weigh a ton to lug around our neighbourhood. Poor Mr Postie now visibly snarls whenever he sees any of us.

"So, how was the date then?" Millie says, as we leave the cul-de-sac.

"Yeah, good," I say evasively.

All night long, I dreamed about the fish bone hitting Zach in the face. Over and over and over again. I want to curl up and die every time I remember.

But I *think* Zach forgave me. After all, he kissed me, didn't he?

"Come on, I need more than that," Millie says.

"What do you want to know?" I ask. I've been dreading Millie's many, many questions.

"Everything," Millie says. "Like, where did you go?"

"That café just off Miller Street," I reply.

"Which one? Not that place that does fish in the evenings? He wasn't daft enough to take you there, was he?"

"That's where we went."

"Seriously?" Millie starts laughing. "No way. He took you, a girl who won't even have a goldfish in her bedroom, to a fish restaurant?"

"Actually it was great," I snap.

"Are you sure?" Millie says dubiously.

"Yes!"

"Well, exactly what was so great about it?" Millie says, as we cross the road. "Come on, Suzy, I know I said last night I thought this was weird, talking to you about someone other than Danny, but I'm trying here. Tell me all about it. "

"Um, okay, well, Zach didn't stop complimenting me all night," I fib, figuring it's time to get creative. "He told me how much he liked my outfit, and how pretty he thought I was. Danny never used to say anything like that."

"And did you, y'know, kiss?"

"Mmmm," I reply dreamily, though the kissing wasn't exactly what you'd call dreamy.

"You did? So soon? I didn't think you would have. Isn't that a bit quick?" Millie sounds gutted.

"It was dead romantic. He walked me home and kissed me at my front door under the stars…" Stars, street lamps, same difference.

"Is he a good kisser?" Millie asks.

"What do you expect from someone that fit?" I reply, dodging the question.

"Wow." Millie still seems to be grimacing slightly, but manages to compose herself. "So. What was the kiss like, then?"

"Um…"

"Oh, look, there's Miss Pepper. Hi, Miss Pepper," Millie calls over the road, where Miss Pepper and Pansy are walking.

Miss Pepper picks up Pansy protectively and scowls. "Where's that vile beast of yours?" she says. "Got loose again, I expect."

"Er, no, he's at home with my dad," Millie replies. "And he's not a vile beast, he's a sweetheart. He's just enthusiastic, that's all."

"Wild and out of control, I think you mean," Miss Pepper sniffs. "You'd better keep him away from my Pansy in the future, otherwise I'm contacting the council."

"Wow. Talk about bitter," Millie says, as Miss Pepper stalks off. "Just because Murphy jumped her fence again. It's not like he actually hurt Pansy, he just wants to be friends… Anyway, where were we? Ah yes. The kiss."

"It was fine," I say. "Nice. You know."

"Suze, are you sure everything was all right?" Millie says suspiciously, as we wait for the traffic lights to change. "You can tell me, you know."

"I know, but there's nothing to tell. It was great, what more do you want?" I say, willing Millie to believe me. I frown in concentration, trying to transplant positive thoughts into her head. *You will tell Danny it was all fab. You will tell Danny it was all fab…*

Millie shrugs. "Okay, then. Whatever you say."

As we reach Bojangles a few minutes later, I glance through the window of the café, just to make sure they've got enough space for us. This place gets heaving on the weekends. Inside, I can see a couple sitting at the table where we always sit.

When I look closer, I realise it's Danny.

With Jade.

I can't believe he brought her *here*. To our place. In our seats.

Silently I watch the waitress put the drinks down on the table in front of them. Danny's got his usual Coke, but Jade is drinking hot chocolate. With cream and marshmallows. Exactly like the one I've been dreaming of all morning.

That's my drink. That should be me.

"What's wro— Ohhhh," Millie says, spotting what I've seen. "Are you okay?"

"Yep, course," I say brightly. It's a shame I couldn't stop my voice shaking, otherwise I could've almost sounded convincing.

Jade glances up and sees us staring in the window. She smiles slyly, and shuffles closer to Danny, draping her arm round him as she tries to feed him a marshmallow.

Danny pushes her hand away.

Serves you right, I think meanly. If you knew Danny like I do, you'd know full well he hates marshmallows.

Undeterred, Jade pops the marshmallow into her own mouth and strokes Danny's hair, leaning over to kiss his cheek.

The thought of charging through the café, tearing her away and shouting, "Get your hands off him!" is very, very appealing. But I have to remember Danny's not my boyfriend any more. He chose Jade over me.

It does make me feel a tiny bit better when I notice how uncomfortable Danny seems. I mean, he's not kissing her back or anything. In fact, he seems kind of, well, squirmy.

"Shall we go somewhere else?" Millie says awkwardly.

I shake my head and heft my bag higher onto my shoulder. "I think I'll go home."

"Oh, Suzy, no, come on – there's that other coffee shop we can go to instead if you like…"

"I'm sorry, I just want to go," I tell Millie. "See you at school tomorrow, yeah?"

"See you," Millie replies, looking concerned. "I'll text you later, okay?"

When I get home, the first place I head is the fridge. I need calories, and I need them fast. Which is a shame, because all that can be found in the kitchen is half a lettuce, a bag of carrot sticks and an out-of-date tub of hummus. Yueurch. Hardly the comfort food I was after.

I slump down onto one of the kitchen chairs, and pull out my mobile, scrolling through my list of contacts until I get to Danny's name. I open up a blank screen and my thumb hovers over the keypad, ready to text.

What am I doing? I don't know what to say to him. I can't exactly tell him I wish he wasn't with Jade, can I? Or that I'm annoyed he took her to Bojangles. It's a public place, and I'll just sound pathetic.

"Suzy, there you are!" Mum says, hurtling into the kitchen. I quickly press the cancel button, and shove my phone away.

"Do we have anything decent to eat?" I ask, walking over to the cupboard. When I fling it open I see it's full of jars and jars of pickled onions and mayonnaise.

"I can't remember when we last had biscuits in this house," I grumble, shutting the door in disgust. "It'll be a relief when this wedding's over and you've all stopped these weird diets. I'm a growing girl, I need my nutrients."

"Suzy, stop that and listen, something terrible's happened," Mum says dramatically.

I spin around in alarm.

Oh no. Her face is all pale and she looks dead shaky. My imagination shoots into overdrive. "What's happened? Is something wrong with Dad? Or Amber? Has Harry had an accident?"

"No, no, it's much worse than that," Mum says, flapping her hand. "It's the dresses for the wedding. The shop rang just after you left to say that the adjustments still haven't been made on yours and they've made a mistake with Amber's and ordered the wrong one in!"

"Oh thank God." I sag with relief. "I thought something terrible had happened."

"Suzy, it *is* terrible," Mum says, sounding shocked. "Everything has to be perfect. Amber's been in her room crying ever since. Mark's up there now, trying to calm her down. I don't know what's got into you lately. I know you've had a difficult time with Danny but that's no excuse to take it out on everyone else. Stop being so self-obsessed."

"*Me* self-obsessed?" If I wasn't so angry, I'd laugh.

Does she have any idea what she sounds like?

"Yes, you. Your attitude lately has been shocking. Your sister's getting married and—"

"I *know* she's getting married. It's not like I can forget when it's being shoved in my face twenty-four hours a day, is it?" I shout. "All you care about is Amber and this stupid wedding."

Mum's stunned. "Suzy, you can't mean that?"

"I can. For once, I'd like someone to actually care about *me*. I just… oh, forget it. I'm going to my room," I say, walking off.

And that's where I stay for the rest of the day, feeling properly sorry for myself. Everything sucks. It sucks at home, it sucks at school, it sucks with my friends, it sucks everywhere.

Even after Mum comes up and apologises to me, I refuse to budge.

Every time I leave my bedroom something awful seems to happen.

So I figure maybe it's best if, for now, I just stay put.

CHAPTER TWENTY

"**Hand in** your essays on the way out," Mr Patterson says at school next day when finally, *finally*, English is over and it's lunch. Mr Patterson's classes are usually my favourites, but today I just can't concentrate.

I roll my eyes at Millie. "It's lunch. Praise the saint of all foodstuffs."

"Tell me about it," she agrees.

"I'm really thirsty; I need a drink. Then do you want to go and find somewhere to sit down?" I ask, glancing out of the corridor window. "It's stopped raining, though I bet it's still flipping freezing."

"I can't," Millie says. "I'm really sorry, but I said I'd meet up with Jamie. I haven't seen him since Friday night, so…"

"Okay, no probs. I'll grab a bottle of water and come with you."

"Well, you see the thing is Danny's going to be there too." Millie's voice trails off.

Oh. I can see why she thinks that would be awkward. Especially if Jade is with him.

"Right." I nod quickly. "I'll see you later, then."

"You're not going to be on your own, are you?"

"No," I scoff. "Course not. Do you think I'm a total loser?"

But after Millie's gone, I gaze wistfully around the corridors at the groups of friends, talking and laughing together.

Because I *am* on my own.

For as long as I can remember I've hung out with Danny, Millie and Jamie. And although Millie has been super supportive since Danny and I broke up and spent lots of time with me, it's only natural that she's going to want to see her boyfriend too.

But that leaves me as a total Norma No-Mates with no idea of what to do with myself.

I get my drink, then go and sit behind the humanities block, where I busy myself for a bit painting my nails radioactive orange.

Then I wander over to the IT block, where I surf the internet for a while. I can never get on the PC at home much — Harry or Dad's always hogging it, or Amber's on the wedding forums. But after updating my Facebook page and checking a couple of gossip websites,

I'm getting bored and a bit fed up of being alone.

What to do, what to do... Oooooh, I know – Zach. I'll go and find him and see if he wants to spend the rest of lunch with me.

Down on the field, Zach's playing a game of football.

"Whoooo, good shot!" I cheer loudly, as Zach scores.

Several heads swivel towards me and then the boys start laughing.

"Ooh, Zachky baby, is that your girlfriend?"

"Ooh, Zach, you are wonderful," one boy coos in a high-pitched voice, blowing kisses. They're all shoving at him, and Zach swears at them crossly.

"What are you doing here, Suzy?" Zach says, pushing the lads out of the way and jogging over to the sideline.

"Came to see you. Wondered if you fancied hanging out," I say nonchalantly.

"Er, no? I'm in the middle of a match."

I try to hide my disappointment. "Oh. Okay, then. Do you fancy doing something after school instead?"

Zach's gaze flicks past my shoulder, then he grabs my shoulders and abruptly pulls me forwards. Before I know what's happening, he's landed a heavy kiss on my mouth.

Crikey. Clearly 'subtle' is not in Zach's vocabulary. And he's going with the nippy, licky kissing technique again. Which I'm still finding kind of ick.

I can hear all of Zach's mates wolf-whistling and shouting. Someone (I suspect Ryan, but I can't see because my eyes are shut) bellows something totally x-rated. Which is kind of embarrassing. Everyone's watching us!

And then I realise how daft I'm being. I always moaned at Danny for not showing me any affection in public. This kind of attention is just what I wanted from a boyfriend.

Isn't it?

As Zach pulls away, I discreetly wipe my mouth.

"What were you saying?" he asks.

"Um, I just wondered if you wanted to do something after school?"

"Yeah, sure," Zach says, but he's distracted now, watching the ball as it flies down the other end of the field.

"Where do you fancy going?"

"Wherever you— Oh come on, Gibbo, what are you doing? Pass it here... pass it!"

"I'll meet you by the gates later, then," I shout after Zach, as he runs off and slides into a tackle.

"Sure," he yells back distractedly.

As I turn to walk away from the football field, I see Jade standing on the path behind me, not too far away.

Hah! I bet she's jealous and starting to realise Danny's totally emotionally stunted. Not like my new boyfriend.

I grin triumphantly to myself. I'm moving on from Danny and things with Zach are going to be great. I just know it.

Okay. It's 4.15 p.m. Zach was supposed to meet me half an hour ago and there's still no sign of him. It's drizzling and it's cold, and I suspect my hair is clinging to my head like a squid on a rock.

Maybe he's been held up somewhere. I'm sure he'll be here any second. And it's not like I'm never late for anything, is it?

I suppose it makes a change that I'm the one waiting for once. It is pretty annoying. Now I know why Danny always got so irritated with me.

The crush of people streaming through the main gates has trickled away. Everyone, teachers and students alike, usually vacate Collinsbrooke at home-time like there's been a bomb scare, leaving it deserted in three seconds or less. My phone is clutched in my hand, ready to receive the text from Zach which I'm sure must be arriving any minute now, explaining where he is. This would be a lot easier if I had his number... then I could just ring and find out what he's up to.

Actually, why hasn't he hasn't he given me his number yet?

234

Uh oh. The paranoia's kicking in again.

I check my watch for the squillionth time, then open up my bag and rummage through, trying to appear important and busy, like I've got every reason to still be here.

I'll just give it a few more minutes.

"Why are you loitering, Suzy Puttock?" Miss Lewis asks suspiciously as she walks past, clutching her briefcase tightly and sporting a particularly ugly purple and yellow tracksuit.

"I'm waiting for someone," I tell her, smiling sweetly.

"Hmmm," Miss Lewis says, flaring her nostrils. "If you say so."

Of course that's what I'm doing! I wouldn't *lie* about it. Does she think I have nothing better to do with myself than hang around this dump? That there aren't a billion and one other places I'd rather be? Honestly, teachers are insane.

I wait for a few more minutes and the rain starts coming down harder. When I look up, a particularly large drop splats into my eye.

I swallow down my disappointment. It's time to admit he's not coming.

He must have got held up or something. I'm sure there's a good reason, because he wouldn't just leave me standing out here, freezing my tush off.

Hitching my bag over my shoulder, I stick my coat over my head, and am about to make a run for home when I hear loud voices talking behind me. Zach's walking down the school steps with a bunch of his mates.

I smile prettily and wave. "Hi, Zach."

"Suzy? What are you doing here?"

What does he mean, what am I doing here? Did he… did he *forget* about me?

"Um, waiting for you?" I reply, apprehensively.

Ryan, standing nearby, coughs something that sounds suspiciously like, "Stalker!"

I ignore him. "We were supposed to meet after school?"

"Oh yeah… right. Sorry, Suze. We had a game to finish off and I kind of forgot." Zach runs his hand through his hair. It's wet and flops back sexily onto his forehead.

Wow.

He's the only boy who could get caught in a rainstorm and end up resembling a male model instead of a drowned rat. My insides are doing faster flips than a Russian gymnast.

"So do you want to go somewhere now?" I ask.

"I can't. I'm going round Stevo's to play on his new console," Zach says.

Say *what* now?

"You know, I'm so pleased I waited around in the rain,

only to find out that you forgot all about me, and now you *have* actually bothered to turn up, you're blowing me out again. Cheers very much, Zach," I say furiously.

I regret the words the second they're out of my mouth when I see Zach's startled expression. What am I *thinking*?

"Whooooooo," Ryan sings mockingly. "Get you!"

Oh, would you *shut up*, dodgy-pants boy.

My teeth are starting to chatter. "Fine. You know what, I'm going home. I'm freezing."

"No... wait." Zach huffs, then says something to his mates. There's a chorus of jeers and loads of boys jab their thumbs to their foreheads as Zach heads towards me.

Haha! He picked me!

"Where are we heading, then?" Zach says, as we huddle under my coat. "Please don't tell me we're going to yours."

The only place I can think of right now is Bojangles. Which is kind of a special place for me and my friends. But I guess if Danny can take Jade, there's no reason why I can't take Zach.

"There's a cool café round the corner," I say.

"Oh yeah, Starbucks?" Zach says, perking up a bit. "Cool. They do the best Frappucinos in there."

"No, not Starbucks," I tell him. "The one a bit further down, Bojangles?"

"That hippy place?" Zach wrinkles up his nose.

"It's quirky. And cool. And they do the best hot chocolate."

"Whatever," Zach says tetchily. "I'd still rather go to Starbucks."

Why's he in such a grump? It's not like I forced him out with me or anything. It's probably because we're cold. That has to be it. Please, let that be it. It'll be okay when we're inside drying off, and a bit warmer.

"Are you sure you want to go to this place?" Zach says, as we finally arrive at Bojangles's door.

"Behave, you'll love it," I say, pushing him playfully. Unfortunately I catch Zach off balance. He stumbles and falls into a puddle that comes nearly up to his ankles.

"Argh!" Zach yells. "This water's freezing. What did you do that for?"

"I'm sorry... I was only messing about."

Zach shakes his head. "Let's just go in, okay?"

Inside I try to relax. It's busy – seems like everyone had the same idea of escaping the rain – but there's a table for two over in the corner that's perfect.

"God, it's crowded," Zach grumbles as we push our way through the tables. "There's no room in here. And it's full of kids."

"It's cosy," I correct him.

Zach gingerly sits down on a seat that's really old and scruffy. He squirms as I dump my dripping coat and bag onto the floor.

"What's wrong?"

"There's a spring poking out of the cushion and going up my bum," Zach says, feeling the seat pad and scowling.

"Oh, have you got *that* chair? Danny and I always joke about it when we come in..." My voice trails off. Zach doesn't look like he thinks it's very funny.

"Can you swap it?" I say. But all the other chairs are taken.

"Hi, guys," the waitress greets us, hurrying up and looking frazzled. "What can I get you?"

"Hot chocolate with cream and marshmallows for me, please," I say.

"Do you do Frappucinos?" Zach asks.

The waitress is confused for a moment, and then laughs. "Er, no. Sorry. We could do you a coffee milkshake?"

Zach pulls a face. "I don't want a milkshake. I'll have a Coke float."

"Coming right up," the waitress says cheerfully. "It might be a couple of minutes, we're very busy at the moment."

"Whatever," Zach says, dismissively.

Ugh, he's being *so* rude. But it must just be because he's cold and wet. I'm sure he'll snap out of it soon enough.

After the waitress leaves, we sit in awkward silence. Zach picks up a coaster and starts trying to spin it on its corner.

"I think the rain's stopped," I say, staring out of the window.

Zach just grunts.

This is a disaster. He's not even talking now.

I know. He loves football. I'll try that. "Did you win your match?"

"Nah."

"Oh. Never mind. What have you been up to since Saturday?"

"Nothing much."

It would be easier trying to get blood out of a stone. Who knew someone this gorgeous could be so freaking *dull*?

Whoa. I'm shocked I just thought that. I didn't mean it. Of course Zach's not dull. I just need to find the right thing to talk to him about. Think, Suze, think.

It was never this hard with Danny.

I wasn't supposed to think *that*. But it's true. I miss hanging out with him. I miss having a laugh with him, mucking around, the fact that we used to be able to talk and talk and talk. And the way he'd go along with my stupid games, like when I wanted to know who could hold their breath the longest, or when I wondered if we could still do shoulder stands. (We both could, only I collapsed sideways, my knee collided with Danny's nose and there was an awful lot of blood.)

I can't image doing any of that stuff with Zach.

I miss the fact Danny and I could sit in silence without feeling twitchy and uncomfortable – or feeling the need to say stupid things to fill the silence, like I do right now.

But then, Zach has his good points too. Like not getting off with someone under my nose, for a start.

Zach checks his watch, sighs quietly, and turns towards the kitchen. "Where are our drinks? She's been ages."

"I think they're coming now," I say, wishing Zach would stop being such a stresshead. It's making me uneasy.

"Here we go," the waitress says, carefully balancing her tray. "One hot chocolate and one lemonade float."

"That's not what I ordered," Zach says.

The waitress consults her notepad. "I'm sorry, I—"

"How hard is it to remember a Coke float?" Zach says. "God, how stupid are you?"

"Zach!" I stare at him in disbelief.

"No problem, I'll change it," the waitress says with a forced smile.

"Don't bother, we've been waiting ages already," Zach says, grabbing the drink out of her hands. It slops all over his trousers, and Zach curses.

"I'm sorry," I mutter under my breath as the waitress scuttles off to get some napkins. But I'm not sure who I'm apologising to.

We drink in silence, angry waves radiating from Zach, while I'm caught up in a mixture of embarrassment and confusion.

I am majorly, majorly weirded out.

This is the sexiest guy in our year. I fancy the pants off him, and out of everyone he could have gone out with, he picked *me*. So why is this just not working? How is it possible we have nothing, absolutely *nothing* to talk about?

I don't get it. Zach must be having a bad day or something.

Our drinks disappear in record time, and then we're hovering awkwardly on the pavement outside Bojangles.

"Right… see you, then," I say, willing Zach to offer to walk me home. As painful as this last hour has been, I still want to try to fix things.

Zach checks his watch. "Hey, if I run, I might still be able to make it over to Stevo's. See you around," he calls over his shoulder as he races off down the road.

"Bye..." I call weakly.

Earlier he was snogging my face off on the football field. Now he can't get away fast enough. Talk about blowing hot and cold.

What am I doing wrong here?

CHAPTER TWENTY-ONE

"Suzy!"

I've been trying to skulk home alone, so I didn't really want to see Millie racing at top speed down the corridor towards me right now. People are scattering like wildebeest as she charges through the crowds.

"Suzy! Hey!"

I smile weakly and wave. For days, Millie, Queen of Interrogation, has been asking about my relationship with Zach. And I'm struggling to find things to tell her. Because Zach and I haven't spoken all week and we don't have any more dates lined up. So how can I explain what's going on when I don't even know myself?

Which is why I was trying to skulk home alone. Question avoidance. But clearly resistance is futile.

"Hi, Mil. What's up?"

"Wondered if you fancied coming into town?"

"Nah, thanks. Think I'm gonna head off."

244

"Oh come on," Millie says. "I haven't seen you properly for ages."

"I'm not really in the mood."

"Don't give me that, Miss Stroppy Bum. You've been acting weird for days. C'mon. Please? I'll buy you some sweets," Millie barters.

Actually, thinking about it, some chocolate would go down pretty well right now. And what would I do at home anyway? Lie in bed wondering what's going on with Zach?

"Hmmm," I say, pretending I'm still unconvinced.

"Anything you want," Millie says.

"Anything?"

"Anything."

"Even the biggest bar of Dairy Milk they sell in the shop?"

"All right, it's a deal," Millie says. "But only if you share."

"Then let's go," I say.

I wonder how long it'll be before Millie asks me about Zach. Sure enough, she doesn't disappoint.

"So how's it going with you and Zach?" Millie says, as we leave the newsagent's, laden down with sweets.

"Fine," I reply vaguely.

"Seen him again recently?"

"Um, no, not really. He's been busy."

"You know, it still feels bizarre to be talking to you about someone other than Danny," Millie tells me.

"Yeah, well... things change."

"I guess," Millie sighs heavily. "So are you and Zach officially an item now?"

"I—"

From behind us, there's the sound of footsteps pounding on the pavement.

"Why hello, ladies," Jamie says, in a mock suave voice, barging between us and dropping an arm over each of our shoulders. "And where are you off to on this glorious afternoon?"

"Town," Millie says. "Wanna come?"

"Sure." Jamie shrugs. "I've nothing better to do."

"Such a charmer," Millie says, as Jamie wraps his arm round her waist and plants a big smacker on her cheek.

I can't help feeling envious. Their relationship is just so... easy.

I wish it was like that with me and Zach. But maybe I'm expecting too much, too soon. Millie and Jamie have been together for ages. Zach and I will get to that stage eventually. It'll just take time.

And it'll be great to hang out with Jamie again. I've not seen him much lately. Although the thought of being with these guys does make my heart sink just a touch... because only if I was green and hairy could I be more gooseberry-like right now.

A short while later, I'm feeling a bit better.

We're sitting on the steps outside the shopping precinct at the spot where all the boardies and BMXers hang out. There have been three colossal slams since we arrived, which are always insane to see, plus Millie and Jamie are on their best behaviour and not permanently joined at the lip. All that and I've beaten my own personal best for eating chocolate, having hoovered a jumbo-sized bar in less than five minutes. Result!

"Mmmm," I say, leaning back queasily.

"Pass the chocolate," Millie says.

"All gone," I say, opening one eye and grinning sheepishly.

"What? Already? You pig!"

"What can I say? After the week I've had, I needed it," I tell her.

Millie frowns. "Suze, are you okay?"

"Wow, did you see that guy just then?" Jamie interrupts, pointing at a skater who's now lying flat on his face, spreadeagled on the floor.

"Uhhh, my belly hurts," I say, as I rub my hands across my tummy.

"Serves you right," Millie says. "Shouldn't have scoff—
Oh, hey, Danny, I didn't expect to see you here."

"Hi," Danny mumbles as I hurriedly sit up.

Danny's clasping a carrier bag from an expensive clothes
shop, and shuffling uncomfortably in front of us.

"Hi, mate," Jamie says, sounding freakily cheerful and
blatantly trying to lighten the atmosphere. "Sit down, why
don't you? Stop hovering."

"Uh, I'm not staying," Danny says, his gaze flitting in my
direction. "I've got a load of homework to do and…"

"Stop being such a sad git," Jamie says, thumping his
arm.

"Yeah, but…"

"You and Suzy are going to have to talk to each other at
some point," Millie butts in.

She has the tact of a charging bison.

"It's not that…" Danny says feebly. He chews at the
corner of his thumb, something he always does whenever
he's feeling nervous. I notice he's changed his hair. It's
much shorter than before, and makes him seem older. You
can see his blue eyes properly.

To my surprise, my insides flutter. Whoa, what's that
all about?

Millie turns to me. "Suze, you don't mind if Danny stays,
do you?"

"Uh…"

Actually, I don't. Yes, it's going to be strange, but this is Danny. Danny who I've known forever. Danny who, as much as I hate admitting it, I'd like to be friends with again. Not having him around just feels plain wrong. And I really have missed him. I've missed talking to him, hanging out with him, getting his opinion on stuff. Danny wasn't just my boyfriend, he was my best friend. There's been a big hole in my life since we broke up. I hadn't realised until now just how much I'd like to be mates with him again.

"Suzy?" Millie says, her voice sounding tense.

"Sure, stay," I say to Danny, feeling strangely shy.

Millie sighs with relief and gestures to the ground.

Danny sits down in front of me and wiggles around, trying to get comfy. "So… how are you?" he asks after a long pause.

"Fine thanks," I say. "You?"

"Yeah, good."

Millie and Jamie are watching warily.

I tilt my head in their direction. "I don't know what they think we're going to do to each other."

"Sorry, guys," Millie says, guiltily. "It's just a bit weird, that's all. We haven't been together like this for ages."

A faint smile crosses Danny's face. "We could start wrestling if you like, give you something to properly freak over?"

"You sure? You know I can take you," I tease.

"You wish, Puttock," Danny says.

As we grin at each other, the tension begins to fade away. Jamie and Millie start watching a video on Jamie's phone, which gives us some space.

"So what did you buy?" I ask, gesturing to Danny's carrier bag.

"New shirt," Danny says, showing me. It's a blue and yellow checked one from Abercrombie and Fitch. I nod my approval, although I'm surprised. He was never all that interested in clothes before.

"I didn't know you shopped there," I say, as I check the label. "Ouch. Expensive."

"Yeah, well... Jade likes their stuff, I guess," Danny says. "And I'm actually taking the shirt back."

Right. Jade. I should have known she'd have something to do with this. I never managed to get him out of that *Star Wars* T-shirt. She's probably the reason he cut his hair, too. I force myself to ignore a pang of what feels horribly like jealousy.

Danny leans back on his elbows and squints into the sun. "So, how are things with you?"

"You know. Same old."

"How are Amber's wedding plans going? It's this Saturday, right?"

"Yeah. All seems to be sorted. I'll be glad to get it over with, to be honest. At least Mum might go back to normal, then. Well, as normal as she can be."

"And how's Harry doing? She still texts me all the time, you know." Danny's talking quickly, almost like he's nervous. "I saw this chewing gum the other day that turns your mouth bright blue. I knew she'd love it, but didn't get it because, well, now you and me have… I didn't know if…" His voice fades away.

"Harry's fine," I say, rescuing him. "Although she's constantly bugging me about why you don't come over any more."

Danny smiles wryly.

"Anyway, there's no way Harry needs more new jokes," I continue. "She's saving for a remote-controlled fart machine, which I suspect may well make an appearance during the wedding."

Danny chuckles. "I can see that going down really well with your mum."

"Tell me about it. I don't know how I got stuck with such a nightmare for a sister," I say, shaking my head. "Two nightmare sisters, actually."

"Aw, they're not so bad."

"Easy for you to say. You don't have to live with them."

"Oh come on, Amber's all right and Harry's really funny," Danny protests. "Remember that time she planted a dead mouse in your fridge and totally tripped your mum out?"

"Oh yeah," I say, giggling. "I still have *no* idea where she got the mouse from, the little brat. It makes me feel sick to think about it. She'd put it on top of the cheese!"

By the time I finish speaking, we're both cracking up. And I think maybe because it's so good to be relaxed together, and we're chilling for the first time in ages, I get one of those laughing fits where you can't stop for yonks. It feels fantastic. But then for some reason my eyes fill up with tears and I have to blink really fast to get rid of them before Danny notices.

"No matter what you think about your little sister, you can't deny that Harry's entertaining," Danny says, completely oblivious.

"You only say that because you're the same mental age."

"Maybe," Danny concedes. "You know, Suzy, I—"

"Babe, I didn't know you were here!" From nowhere, Jade appears and wraps her arms around Danny's neck. She plants a sloppy kiss onto his cheek, leaving a glossy pink lip-print behind. "Hi, Jamie. Hi, Millie," Jade says, blanking me.

Millie's whispering something urgently to Jamie, but I can't hear what she's saying.

"Hi, Jade," Danny mutters.

"Why didn't you tell me you were coming into town?" she coos, shooting a venomous glare in my direction. "You disappeared really quickly after school. I only knew you were here because Bryony texted to tell me."

"Yeah, I'm sorry," Danny says. "I only came in to take that shirt back we bought the other day. I didn't think I was stopping."

"What are you taking it back for?" Jade demands. "It looked great on you. And besides, you can wear it to Bryony's on Saturday. You haven't forgotten we're going to her party, have you?"

Danny's face falls and I hide a grin. He *so* doesn't want to go to that party. Interesting.

"Well, um, the thing is..." Danny starts.

"Danny!" Jade pouts. "You *promised* you'd come."

"But..."

Jade's eyes narrow ominously. "You're not going to make me go on my own, are you?"

"All right, all right, I'll be there," Danny says.

Next to me, Millie makes a frustrated noise.

"Thanks, babe," Jade says, snuggling close to him. "And you *are* going to keep the shirt, aren't you?"

"Uh huh," Danny says.

Ugh, Jade is so annoying. And so is Danny, giving in to her like that.

Just as I think I can't stand Jade fawning all over Danny a minute longer, for once in my life the Gods smile down on me.

Zach walks past with a group of his mates.

And that's when I realise I have to show Danny I've got someone new. He's busy shoving his new girlfriend in my face, isn't he? Well, two can play at that game.

It's time to set up another date with Zach. Perhaps he's just waiting for me to ask him out. After all, I've asked him the last two times. We can go to the cinema, that's the perfect place. That way, we get to go out, but don't actually have to worry about making conversation. And there's the possibility of some back-row kissing, too.

It's an Einstein-like brainwave that can't possibly fail.

"Zach!" I call.

I don't think he hears me, because he speeds up.

"Zach!" I shout again, scrabbling past Jade and Danny and running to catch up with him.

"Hi," I say. "Didn't you hear me? I was calling you."

"Were you?"

"Yeah. Why don't you come over and hang out with my friends?"

"I can't, I…"

Suddenly I realise what's going on. "Ohhhh… is it because Danny's there?"

"No, it's not that, it's—"

"You don't need to worry. He's with Jade now and we're completely cool. Just come over for a few minutes." I pull Zach away from his friends, who disappear towards the shops, and over to the steps. "Hey, everyone, look who's here."

Danny's face is stony and I feel a small ripple of satisfaction.

I sit down and pat the space next to me. Zach sits down awkwardly, and I snuggle up as close as possible.

"So, Zach, I was wondering if you wanted to see a film tomorrow night?" I coo.

"Tomorrow? Um, I can't," says Zach. "I've got something on. Family stuff. Boring. You know how it is. Sorry."

"Really?" Jade says. "What family stuff? Nobody told me."

"Just something with my parents," Zach says.

"That's okay," I say. "Maybe the day after?"

"Look, Suzy…" Zach runs his hands through his floppy hair. "Can we go somewhere and talk?"

"Talk? What about?"

"How about over there?" Zach asks, pointing to an empty bench on the other side of the precinct.

"Zach," Jade says, tightly. "Can I have a word?"

"Nope," Zach says, scowling at her. "I'm trying to tell Suzy something."

"If you don't want to go to the cinema we don't have to," I tell him. "We can do something else if you like."

"It's not that," Zach snaps.

What's he being so tetchy for?

"Zach," Jade says again. "I want to talk to you, *now*."

"Shut up, Jade," Zach says. "Look, Suzy, I don't think I can do this any more."

"Do what?"

"This. Us. You're too... too... full-on for me," Zach elaborates, not letting me get a word in.

Huh? *Full-on?* What the blinking heck is he talking about?

"And you're way too, well, keen..." Zach continues. "You're always following me around and wanting to do stuff when I'm trying to hang out with my mates. It's just a bit too intense, y'know?"

"But I don't—"

"I'm not looking for anything serious," Zach says. "I need my space."

Beside me I can hear Millie gasp.

"See ya," he says, as he walks off.

Okay. It's taking a while for all this to sink in. But I'm pretty sure I've just been dumped in the worst way possible.

CHAPTER TWENTY-TWO

My life is over.

Later, I'm sitting in Bojangles, sucking hard on an extra-thick strawberry milkshake, and all I can think about is what Zach did to me.

In front of Danny.

In front of Jade.

In front of *everyone*.

NYARRRRRRRRRRRRGH!!!

I collapse down, face first, onto the table.

Ow. That really hurt.

I totally misjudged the distance to the tabletop. Well, isn't that all I need? A head injury on top of everything else.

Fan-flaming-tastic.

"Ohmigod, Suze, are you okay?"

That's a high-pitched, screechy voice which sounds a lot

like Millie's. But right now my head's hurting loads and I feel a bit dizzy so I'm going to need a minute before I move...

"Help, we need an ambulance over here! My friend's collapsed!"

Wait a minute. Is she talking about *me*?

I sit up woozily. "Wha— Millie, what's happening?"

"Don't move!" she says, rushing over.

All the other customers are staring at us, and seem more than slightly bemused by what's going on.

"You've had an emotional trauma and now you've probably got concussion. Lie down here, I'm going to put you in the recovery position."

"No way. These are my new jeans. I'm not lying on the floor."

"But you collapsed. You might be seriously ill," Millie says, trying to wrestle me onto the ground.

"Get off me. I didn't collapse," I say, pushing Millie off with one hand and wincing as I rub my forehead with the other.

"Is everything all right?" asks a waitress, heading towards us with a phone in her hand. "Should I call an ambulance or not? I don't want to get sued."

"I'm fine," I tell her. "Honestly. My friend's a bit of a drama queen, that's all."

"You sure?" The waitress sounds sceptical.

"I'm sure," I say firmly.

The waitress rolls her eyes and heads back to the counter.

"*Me* a drama queen?" Millie says. "I'm not the one passing out in public. Ooh, is that strawberry?" She points at my drink. "Can I have some?"

I push the glass across the table to Millie.

She takes a big slurp and then remembers why she's here. "So, um, are you okay?"

"No."

Millie cringes. "Understandable. You must feel pretty bad."

"Pretty bad? *Pretty bad?*" I shriek, as once more the customers turn to gawk. "That's the understatement of the century. Zach *dumped* me! In front of *everyone*! Everyone including my ex, and his new girlfriend who hates my guts. If I don't die of humiliation in the next hour, I'm moving to Outer Mongolia, and never coming back. My life is one long, embarrassing mess." I wrap my arms around myself and rock backwards and forwards in despair. "Oooooooh, this is hideous."

Millie thinks for a while before she speaks. "Yes, it's bad, but it's not like you wouldn't have realised eventually."

"Realised what?" I say, confused.

Nothing could have prepared me for what Millie says next.

"Zach's a complete dumbass."

"Huh?"

"Suze, how did you not realise sooner? I mean, sure he's great to look at, but he's got the personality of a stick."

I take a moment to absorb what she's said. "But… but… why didn't you say anything?"

"I didn't want to upset you, and you were so hung up on him I knew you wouldn't listen," Millie says, fiddling with the straw. "I figured he'd show his real self sooner or later and you'd ditch him. Can I get one of these strawberry milkshakes, please?" Millie calls to the waitress, now she's polished off most of mine.

"*He* dumped *me*," I point out.

"But you're not still into him, are you?" Millie asks. "Especially after what he's just done."

I shrug half-heartedly.

"Suzy…" Millie pauses for a moment. "Oh, I'm just going to ask. Your dates weren't that great, were they?"

"They were," I say.

Millie watches me intently.

"Oh, all right, they weren't the best," I mumble.

"I so knew you were lying!" Millie says triumphantly. "Sorry," she adds quickly. "Totally inappropriate."

"I did really like him though," I say, as tears start collecting in my eyes.

"Hey, don't cry. He's so not worth it." Millie reaches across the table and rubs my arm. "And I don't think you liked him all that much, if you're absolutely one hundred per cent honest about it."

"I did," I protest.

"Really?"

"Uh-huh." I fiddle with my silver bangle.

"Then tell me why."

"Do we have to do this? I don't really want to think about his good points right now."

"Just do it. Come on."

I sniff loudly. "Oh, all right. Um, okay. He's one of the best-looking people I've ever seen in real life. That smile, and those eyes, they're just delish. And his arms... Millie, you said yourself, he's yummy."

"We've already agreed that he's hot. But what about as a person?"

"Um, well..." I pause for a moment. Wow. This is harder than I thought. Zach's not funny. Or good to talk to. I was always second best to football, or his mates. He was rude. Arrogant. And terrible at kissing.

But there must be something. C'mon, Suzy, think.

But nothing's coming to mind. I'm totally stumped. Apart from his appearance I can't think of a single good thing about him.

"See?" Millie says. "Sure he's a hunky studmuffin of hotness, but he's got nothing else going on. And the way he's just treated you? Talk about a weasel. Why do you want to be with someone like that?"

Oh God. She's right. What was I *thinking*?

"Have I made a total tit of myself?"

"Only a little bit," Millie says. "But don't worry, I'll still be your bezzie." She pats my shoulder consolingly.

I collapse down onto the table again.

Why have I been such an *idiot*?

It takes another milkshake and a giant piece of carrot cake before I feel strong enough to venture back into the big wide world and head home.

"Hello?" I call, as I open the front door.

Now I'm here, I wonder how much that ticket to Outer Mongolia would cost. Anything to avoid everyone at school next week. I might get online and investigate. I can change my Facebook relationship status from *It's complicated* to *Single* at the same time.

"There you are, Suzy, you're ever so late," Mum says, rushing out of the kitchen. "Where've you been? You weren't answering your phone again." I don't even have a chance to put down my bag before she's grabbed me, spun me round and ushered me out of the house.

"Hey! What are you doing? I've got stuff to do."

"No time," Mum says, leaping into the car. "We're picking up your bridesmaid's dress tonight, remember?"

Oops. I'd completely forgotten about that.

"I've got so much to think about. We've got the dresses to collect now, thank goodness they open late tonight. Tomorrow I've got the favours to pack into bags, and the bakery is running late with the cake so I can't collect that until Saturday morning now. Heaven knows where I'm going to find the time for that with everything else I've got to do. I can't believe the wedding is this weekend. The time's gone so fast, don't you think? Now come on, buckle up, we're collecting Amber from work on the way."

Mum manoeuvres out of the drive and races off down the road, nearly taking the wing mirrors off several parked cars as she goes. Amber's driving skills are clearly inherited from the maternal side of the family.

I stare out of the window and sigh heavily.

"Are you okay?" she asks.

I shrug.

There are a couple of minutes of silence as Mum negotiates a right turn, then she asks, "Is this about Danny?"

I don't answer. Like I want to talk to *Mum*, of all people, about my love life. I mean, hers has been a complete disaster. The best man she ever managed to bag was Dad.

There's no way *she's* going to be able to help.

"Have you two not patched things up yet?" Mum says as we stop at traffic lights, and toots the horn in exasperation as the light turns green and the learner driver in front fails to set off in less than 0.1 seconds.

"Nothing to sort out. Danny's seeing someone else," I say flatly.

"Oh, come *on*," Mum says, as the learner lets out an old man who starts pootling along at about five miles an hour. "Sorry, Suzy, what were you saying?"

"Danny's got a new girlfriend," I remind her glumly.

"Well, you're seeing someone too, aren't you? What happened to Zach?"

"That kind of... ended." Even saying it makes me want to fling myself off the nearest cliff as I remember exactly how he ditched me.

Shuddersome.

Mum overtakes both the cars in front with an eye-wateringly scary manoeuvre. "Ah. Well, I didn't think he was right for you. Try not to worry, there's plenty more fish in the sea."

"You're a real help, Mum. Thanks," I say sarcastically.

"It's true. You're still young. And I know you're probably feeling pressured to find someone now you've broken up with Danny..."

"You *what?*" What's she babbling on about? My mother is officially asylum-certifiable loony tunes.

"It's only understandable," Mum says, reaching over and patting my knee comfortingly. "You'll get married one day, don't worry."

"Er, Mum, you do remember I'm *fourteen*, right? I'm not worried."

"If you say so," Mum says distractedly as we screech to a stop at the end of a long traffic queue. "Oh, what is going on with this road today?" She sticks her head out of the window. "Could you lot move out of the way?" she shouts. "I've got somewhere very important I need to be."

"Haven't we all, love?" I hear someone shout back, as I sink down into my seat, pull my hair over my face and hope nobody I know recognises me.

CHAPTER TWENTY-THREE

"OW!" I object as the seamstress, not for the first time, jabs me with a pin. Standing in a department store while someone pokes, prods and attacks me with sharp, pointy items is definitely not my idea of fun.

The pink dress is just as bad as I remember. It's kind of shiny, with large material flower rosettes all around the scoop neckline and circling the skirt. And it's just so, well, girly. Not me at all. But I suppose at least now it fits properly.

"How's your dress, Amber?" Mum says eagerly. "Does it look good?"

"Yeah, it's okay," Amber replies, her voice strangely flat.

That's weird. For a girl who gushed for a week about the hand-sewn pink sequins on her veil, she doesn't sound too happy.

"It's a good job it still fits. I must say, I do think it's strange you've managed to put on weight before the wedding," Mum says. "I lost half a stone before mine."

"I guess it's all the stress eating I've been doing," Amber says gloomily. I hear the curtain in her cubicle swish back. "I hope I don't look like a hippo."

"You don't, you're absolutely beautiful," Mum says, not seeming to notice Amber's lack of enthusiasm. "How are you getting on, Suzy?" Mum sticks her head past my curtain.

"Okay, thanks, Mum."

"You look beautiful too," Mum says, her voice catching in her throat. "Oh, my two little girls. I'm so proud of you both."

Uh oh. She's getting emotional. Any minute now she's going to demand a Puttock family hug, or something equally horrendous. I need to distract her. Fast.

"Mum, would you get me a pair of tights to try on with this dress, please?"

"What for? We've got plenty at home."

"Yes, but, um, I, er, want to get the full effect of the outfit. You know, how it's going to look on the big day, that kind of thing."

"Oh, well, in that case, not at all. Back in a mo."

Phew. She's gone.

"I need some more pins," the seamstress says snottily,

standing up. "This hem's coming loose. It'll need fixing now." She purses her lips, frowns like it's my fault and sweeps off.

And it's then I hear the noise.

Sniff. Sniff. SNIFF!

Sounds like someone's crying. And if it's not me, it must be…

"Amber?"

No answer.

Oh, I hope she's crying because she's happy. Please, please, please let that be it.

"Amber?" I repeat.

Sniff.

"Yes?" Amber replies shakily.

"Um, are you crying?"

SNIFF!

"Amber, are you okay?"

"Uh huh," Amber says, unconvincingly.

"Are you sure?"

Sniff. Sniff.

There's a pause and then a loud wail. "Noooooo! Suuuuuzy, I don't think I can do this!"

"Do what?" A heavy feeling of dread gives me an inkling of what she's about to say.

"I don't think I can get maaaaaarrrrrriiiiiieeeeed!"

Seriously? I *knew* something was going on with her.

This is the wedding of the century. Mum's been planning it for months. And Amber's supposed to be walking down the aisle in less than forty-eight hours. What does she mean, she doesn't think she can get married? And more importantly, what am I supposed to do about it? No way am I the right person to be speaking to about relationships, not with my love life so bruised and battered it's practically roadkill.

Suzy, think. *Think!*

First things first. There's no way Mum can find out about this. She'll spasm so hard they'll feel the repercussions worldwide.

I spot a shop assistant nearby, fluffing up dresses.

"Psssst!"

No response.

"Psssssst!" I hiss louder.

The shop assistant turns around. "Was there something you wanted?"

"Yes," I beckon to her wildly. "Can you do me a favour?"

The woman walks over warily. "How can I help?"

"You see that lady over there?" I show her Mum, who's currently frowning at the packets of tights. "I need you to take her to the very far side of the shop and not let her come back until I give you a signal."

The assistant's thinly plucked brows furrow together. "And why would this be necessary?"

"You hear that?" I whisper, as a loud sob comes from the next changing room along. "That's my sister and she's crying. Her wedding is on Saturday. I have a very, very bad feeling that things might have gone very, very wrong and my mum, who is borderline certifiable when it comes to this event, cannot find out about this under any circumstances. I need some help here."

The assistant suddenly becomes a lot more understanding. I bet she's one of those people that love a drama. "I understand," she says in a low voice. "I'm always happy to lend a hand in an emergency. Your sister hasn't had an affair has she? Or maybe she's pregnant with someone else's baby, or..."

"I don't know," I say through clenched teeth. "And the reason I don't know is because I haven't managed to talk to her yet. So please go and be distracting. Quick, Mum's coming."

Sure enough, Mum is heading towards the changing rooms, waving a box and beaming. "Suzy, I've got them..."

"I'm sure you haven't explored all the options," the shop assistant says, taking Mum's arm and steering her away. "It's so important to get the right denier in a tight, you know..."

Right. That's Mum taken care of. Now all I have to do is sort out Amber.

When I push the changing-room curtain aside, Amber is sitting on the floor, leaning up against the mirror. Her puffy gown is so huge it's practically up round her ears and her cheeks are streaked with dark mascara.

"Don't get make-up on your dress," I shriek.

"I don't care about the stupid dress," Amber says, picking up the hem of her skirt. She's about to blow her nose on it but I whisk the material out of her clutches just in time.

"What's wrong?" I ask her, sinking down onto the floor beside her, then yelp as a pin sticks into my tush. "Pin in a Puttock buttock," I explain, trying to raise a smile.

I fail.

Once I've removed the offending pin, and several more besides, I settle gingerly onto the floor.

"What's going on, Ambs?" I try again.

"I don't think I can do this," Amber says, ruffling the folds of her frock. "It's so, so, *big*, you know?"

"Your dress?" Well, phew. Thank all that is holy for that. Only Amber could have such a freak-out over clothes.

"No," Amber says crossly, frothing the material. "I mean the whole marriage thing. I've only known Mark a year, and now I'm going to be with him forever. Forever and ever and ever. Just Mark. Nobody else. Until I *die*."

Uh oh. This is more than the usual Amber wobbler. This actually sounds serious.

"Well... yeah," I say, gently. "That's kind of the point of getting hitched, isn't it?"

"I don't know. I always thought it was about the dress, and being a princess for a day." Amber's shamefaced. "I guess I hadn't really thought about the marriage part. I'm going to be someone's *wife*. I'm going to be Mrs Mycock!"

"You could always keep your maiden name," I say.

Amber glares.

"Sorry," I mutter. "Only trying to help."

"Ooooooh, what am I going to doooooo?" Amber moans, flapping her hands about and looking frantic.

"You love Mark, don't you?" I ask, cautiously.

"I guess so."

"You only guess so?"

"I'm just not sure how I know for certain he's The One," Amber says, sounding panicky.

Like I'm the person to ask. "I, um..."

"Suzy, you have to help meeeeee!"

"All right, all right. Give me a minute to think."

Then I remember Millie making me list everything I liked about Zach. Maybe that could work here, too. "Why don't you tell me everything you love about Mark?"

Amber sniffs and sits quietly for a moment. "Ummmm...
he's funny?"

"Yeah?"

"Yeah." Amber nods. "He makes me smile. He does
this impersonation of a dancing llama that always cracks
me up."

I smile encouragingly, while knowing I'll never be able to
look at Mark the same way again. Although, come to think
of it, it is really nice having someone who can make you
laugh that hard. Danny used to do these dumb impressions
of our parents that had me in stitches.

"What else?"

"He leaves me little love notes all over the place to let
me know he's thinking of me. Like in the car or my handbag
or in the bathroom."

"Yeah, I remember Dad wasn't happy that morning he
found one on the shaving mirror. But that's a good thing
too; it shows he cares."

"Um, he never makes me listen to heavy metal—"

"He doesn't *like* heavy metal," I interject.

"That's another good thing," Amber says, sounding
happier. "Mark likes songs from the shows as much as I do,
and he loves my chick flicks."

Danny and I liked the same music too. We used to love
listening to The Drifting together. We spent hours in the

garden last summer with a headphone each, staring up at the sky. Although I don't have such fond memories of his movie taste and non-stop *Star Wars* obsession. But I suppose it could have been worse, like those boring martial-arts films Jamie's always dragging Millie too.

"Plus Mark buys me loads of presents," Amber says, interrupting my thoughts. "He even promised he'd buy me an actual chihuahua after we got married."

"Those are all great reasons," I say. "Anything else?"

Amber's forehead wrinkles and she appears to be concentrating even harder than when she's choosing her lip-gloss colour in the morning. "What I think I love most about Mark... is that we can have proper conversations."

I have to try not to laugh at this point. A proper conversation? About what exactly?

Fortunately Amber doesn't notice and carries on oblivious. "We can really talk, you know? And even when we're not talking, and are thinking our own stuff, that's cool too. He knows me better than anybody in the world. He's like a best friend and nobody else could ever match up."

With the first sensible words I think I've ever heard my sister say in her life, the realisation hits me. Amber could be describing my feelings about Danny down to a T. Well, apart from the bits about the llama, the heavy metal and the chihuahuas, that is. But the sentiment's right. Danny was my best friend. And sure, we had some issues, but nothing we couldn't have talked about.

Oh. My. God.

I drop my head into my hands as the realisation of what I've lost hits me round the head like a sledgehammer.

Danny's the one I really want.

Danny's the one I'm still in love with.

My eyes well up. I've been a prize doofus, worrying about whether Danny and I had been together too long. And as for Zach... To be honest, I still feel sick when I think how stupid I was.

How could I have chucked away everything I had with Danny for him?

"I feel much better now, thanks, Suzy," says Amber. "Hey, what's wrong?"

"Nothing," I lie, and now it's my turn to sniff loudly.

"Suzy, I do love Mark, don't I?" says Amber, tentatively.

I can't let my sister make the same mistake I have. "Certainly sounds like it," I say firmly. "He's your best friend, you don't want to be with anyone else, and you shouldn't let that go."

Amber nods.

"Plus it would be a real shame for your stunning dress to go to waste," I add.

I'm impressed. I almost sound sincere.

"And *your* fabulous dress too, don't forget," Amber says, grinning and swiping at her wet cheeks. "How crazy was I to think I couldn't do this?"

"Look at these tights the lovely lady helped me find!" Mum says, charging in. "They've got a special sheen and a control panel to—"

She stops short when she sees Amber and me on the floor. The shop assistant shoots me an apologetic glance that says she couldn't hold back Mum any longer.

"What's going on?" Mum says shakily. "Amber, what's wrong? Why are you crying?"

"I—"

"She started blubbing when she saw my dress," I lie hurriedly. "It's still not the right length, and Amber's freaking out."

"Oh, don't be so silly," Mum says, rushing in and pulling Amber to her feet. "That can be easily sorted. A few more pins and a bit of hemming and it'll be perfect." She stands back to admire my sister. "Now, dry those tears. Let's get your veil and tiara out so you can try it all on one last time."

As I leave to have more pins stuck into various parts of my body, Amber mouths, *"Thank you"* over Mum's head.

277

I grin back, but my smile quickly fades.

I wish I'm as good at sorting out my own love life as I am at fixing my sister's.

CHAPTER
TWENTY-FOUR

"Suzy, where are you?" Mum bellows at the top of her increasingly hysterical voice.

It's Friday night, and most people my age are out with their mates, having a good time. Me? I'm hiding behind a tree in my garden, avoiding my mother. The wedding is tomorrow, and she's hit new levels of hyper since the wedding rehearsal. We left the church an hour ago, so at least now we know vaguely where we're supposed to stand and what we're meant to be doing. Everyone is happy and so excited.

Everyone except me.

I'm trying not to think about the smooch-fest ahead, but the word 'wedding' is mentioned whenever anyone opens their mouth. The whole flipping world is shoving love in my face. It's as if there's some kind of happy couple epidemic – they're on the street, at school, on TV – even Dad's got the bug and has been kissing and snuggling with Mum more than usual, which is too vomitous for words. *Nobody* wants to see that, not at their age.

So I'm coping with all that *and* having to skulk in the garden because Mum has finally shot right off the lunar scale of loopiness.

Obviously not thinking that planning and organising a wedding would give her enough to do, she decided to hold a barbecue at our house tonight, to 'welcome' Mark and his relatives into our family.

It's not the best idea Mum's ever had, it has to be said. I think she's come to the same conclusion too, because right now she's on the verge of a breakdown.

I mean, why did she think it would be a good plan to have a barbecue, when it's still practically winter and could chuck hailstones at any minute? Let alone leave *Dad* in charge of the cooking? Dad is a firm believer that if it's cremated on the outside, it's cooked. Never mind if it's still mooing on the inside.

The doorbell rings, and I can hear loud voices all speaking at once. Amber's cooing and gushing as she greets everyone. She's been totally different since our chat in the department store, returning to her mushtastic self and gushing over her future husband at every opportunity. I never thought the day would come when I'd be glad to hear them call each other 'Ambypamby' and 'Markymoo', but I'm genuinely relieved they're all right.

From my vantage point behind the tree, I watch as a long procession of people start to flood into the garden.

Wow, Mark's family is *huge*!

Mum was only expecting Mark, his parents and two brothers, but it seems like there are aunts, uncles, cousins and even a couple of next-door neighbours thrown in for good measure.

In the conservatory, Mum's trying to appear calm, but I can tell she's having a major panic, probably because she hasn't bought nearly enough food.

"You'll have to cut the sausages in half, Chris," she hisses frantically out of the door, which is when she spots me. "Suzy? Suzy, what are you doing behind that tree?"

Darn it. Busted.

"Where have you been?" Mum says tightly as I go over to her. "I need help. There's a jug of Pimm's in here that needs to go out."

I open my mouth to protest, but Mum's already gone.

I suppose it's my own fault. Harry's more savvy than to appear in Mum's eye line. I should have hidden round the corner of the house with her, where she's been busy replacing the cooked sausages with rubber imitations. You have to admire her. There aren't many people who'd have rubber sausages at the ready.

Over by the rockery, Mark's dad has made the mistake of attempting conversation with Aunty Loon.

"Who did you say you were?" she says, scowling fiercely.

"Mark's dad," Mr Mycock replies, a little nervously.

"Mark? Who's Mark?"

"Um, Amber's future husband?"

"Amber's *what*?" Aunt Loon looks aghast. "Don't be ridiculous, she's not getting married. Someone would have told me."

Good luck with that one, Mr M. You could be there some time.

As I head into the kitchen, I bump into Amber, who's balancing several large bowls of salad on top of each other. A fiver says they get dropped before they make it anywhere near the outside world.

"Isn't this great?" Amber gushes. "I'm so excited everyone's here." The top bowl wobbles precariously.

"Watch out!" I leap for the bowl and rescue it just in time. "Mum'll go even more schizoid if you drop these."

"Oh, she's fine," Amber says. "Just a teeny bit stressed cause I invited a few extra people, but that's all."

"A few?!"

Amber scrunches her nose guiltily. "Well, maybe more than a few. But Mark's relatives are so lovely, and then there are the neighbours, and all his friends, and I wanted everyone to meet each other because we're all going to be one big happy family tomorrow."

I lower my voice. "So you're definitely feeling better about everything?"

"Oooh yes, yes, yes!" Amber nods so frantically I fear for her brain cell. "I don't know what I was thinking the other day. How could I ever have doubted Mark? He's my little honeybunny, and I love him soooo much. I can't wait to be his wife!"

Amber dumps the bowls on a shelf behind her, and grabs me, squeezing tight.

"I love you too, you know, Suzy. You're the best sister in the world and I'm so lucky to have you."

"Amber..." I choke, running out of oxygen.

Amber squeezes even harder. "I'm so excited about tomorrow, aren't you? And it's all going ahead because of you. All because of *you*! I wish there was something I could do to thank you. I know you're getting to be my bridesmaid tomorrow, which is obviously amazing, but there's got to be something else..."

"You could buy me tickets for The Drifting," I offer hopefully, but Amber's not listening. She's released me to examine her long, perfectly manicured nails.

"It's such a shame you're single now," Amber says. "Everyone should be as happy and in love as I am. Did you never manage to sort things out with Danny?"

I gaze at my sister warily. "I guess we're kind of friends now. Sort of. But that's all. He's, um, seeing someone else."

Oof. It still hurts to say that out loud.

"Why do you want to know, anyway?" I ask, suspiciously.

"No reason," Amber says, reaching out to give me a hug. "I don't like to see you so sad, that's all."

Oh. Well, that's sweet. And surprisingly caring, coming from my sister.

"Now, you are going to make sure you cleanse properly tonight, aren't you?" As Amber pokes at my chin, I realise our special moment has passed. "It looks like you're still a bit spotty after that incident with the face pack. We don't want spots in the wedding pics, Suzypoos. Zap them quick!"

"Suzy, what are you doing?" Mum shouts, as Amber skips off with the salads. "People are dying of thirst out there. Take this out. And don't drop it, I know what you're like."

Grabbing the jug of Pimm's from Mum, and slopping half of it over the kitchen floor, I head back outside, and start to serve the drinks.

"So, Chris, you must be looking forward to getting rid

of these two," Mr Mycock says, holding out his glass to me as he tilts his head towards Amber and Mark.

"Understatement of the year," Dad says, shaking his head and trying to restrain the broad grin creeping across his face. "Just when you think one's about to leave, they start moving other people in."

Mr Mycock laughs. "So, Amber, have you seen any flats you like yet?"

"Um, well…" Amber exchanges a gooey smile with Mark. "We've actually got something to say about that. Mum, would you come here for a minute? We've got an announcement to make."

Dad's face lights up. "They've done it," I hear him mutter gleefully. "They've finally found somewhere to live and are moving out."

Mum bustles out into the garden, wiping her hands on her apron. I wonder if I should tell her she's got salad cream streaked down one cheek?

"We've got some exciting news," Amber says, beaming at Mark, who puts his arm around her waist and hugs her close. "And we wanted to tell all of you first, as you're our closest family. I did a test this morning and Markymoo and I are having a baby!"

Mum lets out a scream of delight and rushes forwards to hug Amber.

"A baby?" Mrs Mycock claps her hands in ecstasy.

"That's why I've been feeling so emotional, and eating strange things, and putting on so much weight." Amber giggles, rubbing her hand over her tummy. "It's all because of this ickle-pickle in here."

"You *are* still planning on moving out, though, aren't you?" Dad asks.

"Silly Daddy, babies are expensive, we won't be able to afford to," Amber laughs. "But we knew you and Mum wouldn't mind, because you won't want to miss out on a single precious moment with your new grandchild. Right, Mum?"

"Of course you and Mark must stay," Mum says. "Oooh, I'm so excited, I can't wait. Suzy and Harry, you're going to be aunties, isn't it wonderful?"

As Amber and Mum excitedly start the baby talk I suspect is going to take over from the wedding madness that's enveloped them for the last year, I notice Dad's gone horribly pale.

"Drink, Dad?" I offer, hastily.

Dad downs his beer in one, pours himself another, and retreats to the safety of the barbecue. As he goes, I hear him grumbling to himself. "Was only supposed to be temporary... weren't supposed to stay... nobody mentioned a baby. I'll never get any peace in this damn house… and it's *my* flaming house. Why won't they bloody leave?"

As Mark cuddles Amber into his side and she smiles up at him, I feel a big pang of sadness. Because I'm all on my own.

Danny always got on really well with my family, and I miss having him around for stuff like this.

But it's too late. I've got to try and move on.

Hopefully that'll be easier once the wedding's over.

CHAPTER TWENTY-FIVE

After countless hours of planning and preparation, Amber's wedding day is finally here. Between Mum and Amber, the levels of over-excitement in the Puttock household have reached intolerable heights. My eardrums are already ringing from all the shrieking.

I escaped as soon as I could after breakfast to go and start getting ready. I'm now standing in my bedroom, staring despondently at my reflection.

What's with these stupid material flowers anyway? *And* my eyes are all puffy, because I was up half the night crying. They're so swollen that Mum and Amber made me lie down on the kitchen floor with slices of cucumber covering them for forty minutes before they let me have my croissant and orange juice.

Urrrghh. Having to be bridesmaid today is the cherry

288

on top of my cacky cake.

Hello, people, I'm broken-hearted here! Don't you get that?

I don't *want* to fake happiness about other people's fabulous love lives. I want to skulk around gloomily, wearing black, listening to emo music and thinking how rubbish everything is.

"Will you give me a hand, Mil?" I ask.

"Sure," Millie says, putting down the magazine she's flicking through and hopping off the bed.

"I can't believe I've got to go out in public wearing this," I declare, swatting crossly at one of the dress's oversized flowers as Millie does up my zip.

Millie stands back to assess the whole outfit. "It's not that bad."

I make a face. "It's not that good, either."

"I'm sure you'll feel better when your hair and make-up is done," Millie offers.

She's doing her best to help, but I think I'm a lost cause. We're still waiting for the hair and make-up people to arrive, and all I can say is that I hope they can work miracles. It's going to take more than a dab of mascara and a touch of lippy to get me bridesmaidesque. Or even humanesque, for that matter.

My eyes are bloodshot, my face is pasty, and my

curls are more uncontrollable than usual after I tossed and turned all night. I'll need some industrial-strength product to get this mane behaving today.

"I look as rough as a badger's bum cheeks," I mutter.

"Oh, c'mon, this could have been a lot worse," Millie says. "You almost wore lime green, remember?"

"That's true," I say, shuddering. "I don't even want to think about how bad that would have been."

Over in the corner, Murphy lets out a whimper, then stands up and stretches.

"Don't let him near me," I screech, backing away. "If he trashes this dress, Mum and Amber will kill me. They'll think I did it on purpose. I knew you should have left him outside."

Murphy's tail wags furiously at the sound of my high-pitched voice and the homework on my desk goes flying.

"Murphy, gorgeous boy, sit, sit," Millie says, running over and trying to calm the dog. Eventually Murphy's persuaded to lie back down, using my beanbag as a headrest. Urgh. He's dribbling all over it.

"I still don't know why you had to bring him," I grumble.

"I couldn't leave the poor thing out on the street, could I?" Millie says. "And Mum refused to be in the house with him on her own. I took a huge risk bringing him by myself, anything could have happened to me."

"Yeah, well, thanks and all, but I'm not sure bringing him here, on Amber's wedding day when there are outfits and flowers and all kinds of things he could trash, was a great idea."

"He's been fine," Millie says, defensively. "And we'll go in a minute. Besides, you're the one that wanted me to come over."

"Because I needed moral support! Not some crazy great hound leaping all over me."

Millie rolls her eyes. "He's not leaped anywhere near you. Stop being so over-dramatic. Now what else have you got left to do to finish getting ready?"

"Um... Ooh, jewellery," I say, turning back to my dressing table and opening a couple of small boxes. I put in my earrings, and then fiddle with the clasp of my necklace, eventually getting it fastened round my neck.

"Can you do up my bracelet?" I ask, waggling my wrist at Millie.

"Sure." Millie peers closely at the silver bracelet. "Um, are these tiny *dog bones*?"

"Sadly, yes. In keeping with the doggy theme." I sigh. "The necklace and earrings match, see? Amber was originally planning on making my accessories out of actual dog biscuits. Thank God Mum found these on eBay before she got started."

291

Millie snorts with laughter. "What's with all the dog stuff?"

"Chihuahuas are part of the theme. Blame the influence of Conni G. She's totally obsessed with chihuahuas at the moment," I say, then point to the shoes I'm wearing. "These nearly had chihuahua stickers on each toe."

Millie bites her lip, trying to stop laughing. "Oh, Suze... no."

"And to make things worse, Mark told me last night that he's bought a chihuahua puppy and I have to take it down the aisle on a lead as a surprise for Amber. This whole day is going to be one long ritual of humiliation. If one more stupid suggestion is made by Mum, Ambypamby or Markymoo, I'm actually going to shoot myself."

"Poor Suze," Millie sympathises, casually wafting her mobile around.

"What are you doing?" I ask suspiciously.

"Nothing," Millie says, a picture of innocence. "Just trying to get some reception."

But when I hear a *click*, I realise exactly what's going on. "You cow, you're taking pictures, aren't you?"

"No!" Millie squeals, as I dive to wrestle the phone from her.

"You'd better delete those," I order.

"Okay, okay," Millie says, smiling as she taps away at

a few buttons. "They're gone, see? I'm sorry, but you have to admit this is the teensiest bit funny. Please, please let me come to the church to get a squiz at all of you together. I'm dying to see Amber."

"Don't you dare," I threaten. "If I see even a glimpse of you lurking I'll have you assassinated. Especially if you bring your camera along."

"You know I'm only messing. Don't stress it, Suze. You're going to have a fabby day," Millie says, hunting around in her bag and triumphantly extracting a packet of jelly babies.

Ugh. More jelly babies. Why didn't she bring something useful, like chocolate?

"I won't, Millie."

"You will. How can you not?" Millie asks. "People always have fun at weddings."

"I'm going to be surrounded by my family all day," I point out. "Where's the fun in that? And anyway, everyone's far too happy."

"Sweet?" Millie offers.

"Would you stop offering me those? Get it in your head. I. Don't. Like. Jelly babies."

Millie looks startled as she throws a jelly baby over to Murphy. "Seriously? You're winding me up. Everybody loves jelly babies."

"Not me. The idea of eating tiny babies made out of sugar freaks me out." I massage my forehead, feeling seriously stressed. "Oooh, everything's going to be a disaster."

"Oh, stop it," Millie says. "So your clothes are a bit dodge and your family's a bit crazy. You'll still have a laugh."

"I won't. Everyone will be going on all day about how wonderful it is to be in love and I don't... I haven't..." My voice falters.

All of a sudden it's got too much. I can't spend the whole day being reminded of how amazing relationships are when I chucked mine away.

"Suzy, what's wrong? You look like you're about to cry."

I blink rapidly, trying to stop my eyes watering. Come on, pull it together, Puttock.

"Hey, what's up? What were you going to say?" Millie sounds concerned.

"Nothing."

"You're *so* lying. Don't make me tickle your feet to get the truth."

A single tear spills down my cheek, dripping onto my chest before soaking into a fabric flower.

"I'm guessing this is about more than your dress?" Millie leads me gently over to the bed. "Is this about Zach? Are you still upset about what he did to you?"

"No," I sniff.

"Well, what then? It can't be about Danny…"

I wince and take a deep, shuddery breath.

"Suzy?"

There's no way I can meet Millie's eyes.

"Oh. My. God," Millie says. "It is about Danny. Do you still like him?"

"I screwed up, didn't I?" I say, tears starting to pour down my cheeks for the umpteenth time this week.

"I can't believe you still like Danny," Millie says in disbelief.

"Suzy?" Amber sticks her head around the open door, her hair in enormous rollers. Oh great, how much of the conversation has she heard? Hopefully none, although Millie isn't exactly known for her quiet voice. But even if Amber has heard anything, it's guaranteed she'll have forgotten it in seconds. Her head will be far too preoccupied with wedding stuff today.

"Hi, Ambs," I say, swiping my tears away quickly and forcing a smile.

"Just came to say the hair and make-up people are ready for you," Amber says, then squeals with terror when she sees Murphy. "Oh God, why's that mad dog here? Don't let him near me. I'm going back downstairs."

As she shuts the door behind her, Millie's face is still absolutely stunned.

"You're not allowed to say anything, not to anyone," I beg. "Promise me, Millie, promise you're not going to say anything. Especially not to Jamie. I don't want Danny to find out."

There's a long pause.

"Promise!"

"All right, all right, I promise," Millie says.

"Please, Mills, I really mean it."

"So do I," Millie says, biting the head off another jelly baby. "Cross my heart and hope to die. I won't breathe a word. I can be discreet when I want to. I've never told anyone that Jamie still slept with his teddy until last year. Oh. Oops."

"So, um, has Danny said anything about me lately?" I ask, deciding to ignore Millie's revelation.

"To be honest, I really haven't seen him that much," Millie says. She reaches over to the bedside cabinet and passes me a tissue. "We were supposed to meet up this afternoon but he blew Jamie and me off yet again because Jade wanted to go out with her mates."

"That's doesn't sound like Danny."

"Yeah, I know. But he told Jamie that Jade strops whenever he tries to get out of stuff, so it's easier just to do what she wants."

"He never used to be that willing to do things for me."

I pull the tissue into tiny pieces, rolling it into balls and dropping it onto the carpet round my feet. Murphy creeps forwards and starts chomping them enthusiastically.

"Are you crazy? Of course he did," Millie says. She stares at me, and then it's like a dam has burst. She just can't stop herself. "You guys were ten billion times better together than they are. He was always doing nice things for you, like buying your favourite ice cream whenever he came over to watch a movie. And he always remembered your birthday, unlike Jamie, who always forgets mine. Plus he got you presents you wanted, like that crazily expensive curl-defining lotion. Last Christmas Jamie gave me the soundtrack to *Kung Fu Madness*."

I guess I'd forgotten most of that.

"But he always wanted to stay in and watch *Star Wars*," I protest.

"So? He's a boy, Suze. That's what they *do*."

"Yeah, but..." I think hard. There's got to be something else. There was lots of stuff I found annoying about Danny. Wasn't there?

"He never showed me *any* affection," I say.

"That doesn't mean he didn't care," Millie says gently.

"Easy for you to say. Jamie's always all over you," I tell her.

Millie bites her lip. "But Danny's just a lot shyer than Jamie and not great at the emotional stuff. He's been a bit messed up since his parent's divorce. It doesn't mean he doesn't feel it, though."

"I suppose. But it's not like any of this matters anyway, does it? He's Jade's boyfriend now."

Millie appears to be thinking hard about what she wants to say. She fondles Murphy's ears distractedly. When she eventually speaks, her voice is guarded. "From the little I've seen of Danny lately, I'm not sure he's that happy."

My head snaps up. "What do you mean?"

Millie frowns slightly. "I don't know. Just something about the way he and Jade are together. Jade's dead bossy and she keeps trying to turn him into something he's not. She might be the prettiest girl in our year—"

I flinch.

"Sorry," Millie says, "but let me finish. I was going to say, she may be pretty, but she's not very nice. And I'm not sure how much longer Danny's going to put up with it."

"Do you think he's going to dump her?" I ask, trying not to sound too hopeful.

"I don't know, that's only the impression I've got," Millie hastily replies. "I wouldn't want you to get the wrong idea or anything."

As I wiggle uncomfortably, one of my pillows falls off

the bed and lands next to Murphy. The hackles on his neck rise as he growls at it, then starts barking furiously.

"Murphy!" Millie says in alarm. "Stop it, it's a pillow, you silly dog. Behave!"

But Murphy's not listening. He's barking away loudly, circling the pillow with a wild glint in his eye, and then he pounces, grabbing it in his jaws and shaking it furiously in the air.

"Millie, stop him!"

"Um, I think I'd better go now," Millie says hastily, grabbing Murphy by the collar. "I'll talk to you tomorrow, Suze, but text me later, yeah? Have a good day."

She blows me a kiss, yanks Murphy out of the room, and then she's gone.

CHAPTER TWENTY-SIX

A few short hours later and I'm standing outside the church, lost in a sea of pastel colours and giant hats as we wait for Amber and Dad. I came over in the car a bit ago with Mum and Harry, and have been trying to avoid Mark's nephew, Toby, ever since. The kid's eight, but seems to have taken a bit of a shine to me. Every time I turn around, he's standing behind me, smiling like a nutter. Like I don't have enough to worry about. After we arrived, Mum ran off like a crazy thing to greet everyone, so didn't spot Harry fiddling with her newly acquired fart machine.

"Suzy, over here." Mark waves from the church entrance. He's wearing a grey, not pink, suit (luckily for him Amber couldn't find a pink one that didn't make him look like a kid's entertainer), with a baby pink shirt and fuchsia tie, and has a giant pink gerbera as his buttonhole. Several disgusted-looking ushers are milling around nearby wearing similar outfits.

I can't believe Amber got these men to wear such girly clothes. My sister really is something else. But at least it's not just me looking ridiculous.

"Hi, Mark," I say, carefully negotiating my way over the damp grass. My heels keep sinking and I don't want to fall on my face in the mud. Which, given my track record, is a very real possibility.

"Here's the present for Amber," Mark says, tugging a tiny chihuahua in a pink dress out from behind his legs. It sits, shivering, by his feet. Ugh. I'm not a big fan of small dogs. Those bulgy eyes are just too freaky.

"Can you look after him until Amber arrives?" Mark asks. "She's going to be so excited when she sees him. You don't mind walking him down the aisle, do you? It's got a pink dress on, so it looks just like you."

"Um, sure." I force a smile and decide to ignore the unintended insult. I must be nice. This is Mark's wedding day too.

"Not long now," Mark says, checking his watch. "I'd best go inside. Don't want to see Ambypamby before she arrives."

Mark rounds up his groomsmen and I walk over to the road to wait for the limo.

301

And I wait. And wait. And wait some more.

After twenty minutes, everyone's getting restless. Inside the church, I can hear the vicar keeping the congregation occupied by leading a game of Simon Says.

"Simon says, wave your hands and praise God!"

Mum's almost gone into orbit with worry, and Mark's running in and out of the church, stressing about Amber not coming. I have to admit, the thought has crossed my mind. Dad's mobile is switched off, and there's no answer at the house.

Surely Amber wouldn't have changed her mind, would she? She was so hyped earlier and there wasn't a trace of wedding wobbles.

Another ten minutes pass, then, to everyone's great relief, a white limo finally pulls up at the church. Well, I say white, but you can hardly tell, because it's covered in mud. The front bumper's crumpled and half hanging off. What the flippin' heck's happened? It didn't look like that earlier.

As Amber scrambles out of the car, she's pouting and I think she's been crying. But even though her eyes are red, she's beautiful. I'm genuinely blown away.

Yes, admittedly, her dress is big enough to double as a marquee, but somehow she manages to carry it off. Her hair is loose and gently curled around her face, which is partly obscured by a full-length veil, and her tiara's twinkling prettily. She's achieved the perfect princess look that she's always dreamed of.

When I go over to greet them, Dad's practically squaring up to the limo driver.

"What were you thinking, going down there? My daughter's half an hour late for her wedding and she's devastated."

"I didn't know the car'd get stuck, did I?" the driver retorts.

"The limo got stuck?" I ask.

"Don't ask," Dad mutters darkly. There's a twig sticking out at a strange angle from his collar. "This idiot thought taking a car this size down tiny country lanes was a good idea. We had to find a farmer to tow us out of a ditch with his tractor. Bloody sat nav."

"I just want to get married," Amber says desperately. "Is Mark still here? And everyone else? Please tell me nobody's left."

"It's all fine, Amber," I say reassuringly. "Everyone's still here."

"But what about my timings?" Amber wails. "Now there won't be enough time for the photos and it was all supposed to be perfect and I feel like it's all ruined."

Amber's bottom lip wobbles furiously and then she

catches sight of the dog by my feet. Her eyes open wide in delight.

"Is that for me?" Amber screams at the top of her voice. The chihuahua practically leaps into the air with fright. "Oh my God, I love her. She's just too cute."

Amber's all smiles as the limo trauma's forgotten in an instant.

"It's from Mark," I explain. "He asked me to give it to you."

"I love the dog, Markymoo," Amber shouts. "Thank you soooo much."

Mark's voice echoes out of the church. "You're welcome, Ambypamby. Now hurry up and get in here so I can marry you."

"Baby, baby, come to Mummy," Amber says, grabbing the tiny dog and hugging it tightly to her chest. The chihuahua quivers and then starts to chew on her veil.

"I'm going to call her Crystal Fairybelle," Amber says.

"Um, I think it's a boy," I say.

"Oh." Amber looks downcast for a moment, then her face brightens. "Never mind, I'm going to call him Crystal Fairybelle anyway."

It must be awesome to live in Amber's world. Problems disappear so easily.

"Is everyone ready?" the vicar calls from the church

porch. "Poor Mark has been waiting long enough. Let's make you Mrs Mycock, Amber."

Amber reluctantly surrenders Crystal Fairybelle and I take hold of the lead as we head towards the church doors. The vicar scuttles inside, and gives the nod to the organist. The congregation rises to their feet and everyone turns around for a gawp at the bride.

As the opening bars of 'The Bridal March' echo from the organ, Dad pats Amber's hand and smiles proudly. Unless I'm very much mistaken, he's trying to hold back tears. They walk slowly down the aisle, although there's so much material surrounding Amber, Dad has to follow slightly behind.

I take a deep breath, and check on Crystal Fairybelle, who's chewing at my shoe strap. Giving him a gentle tug, we follow my sister. Amongst the congregation I spot Toby, who winks at me.

We're only about halfway to the altar when I hear muffled giggling. Everyone's pointing and laughing in my direction.

Oh no, what have I done now? Is my skirt stuck in my knickers or something?

But as I feel resistance on the end of the lead, I realise that for once, it's not me everyone's laughing at.

It's Crystal Fairybelle.

Because he's stopped to have a pee against the end of one of the pews.

What should I do now? There wasn't anything in the *Guide to Being a Perfect Bridesmaid* Amber gave me that covered this.

And there's no way in the world I'm picking him up to take him outside. As much as I hate this dress, I'm not getting covered in dog wee for *anyone*.

I gaze around helplessly, but Amber and Mark are too busy making gooey eyes at each other to notice, and Mum shrugs helplessly. So I just wait for him to finish. After the Niagara Falls of wees is over – for such a small dog, Crystal Fairybelle must have a disproportionately large bladder – we finally make it to the front of the church.

When the ceremony starts, the vicar starts talking about what it means to find your perfect match. How true love is the greatest gift of all, and that getting married means spending the rest of your life with your best friend. I manage to hold it together pretty well, but as soon as Amber and Mark start saying their vows, I'm blubbering away like a baby.

Because once again, all I can think about is how much I miss Danny.

CHAPTER TWENTY-SEVEN

Amber's evening reception has just kicked off in a hotel on the outskirts of Collinsbrooke. It already feels like this day's gone on forever. I can hardly believe that my big sister, instigator of the craziest nuptials this side of Hollywood, is officially a grown-up, married woman having a baby. Scary or what? Although that's nothing compared to the horror I'm witnessing right now.

Mark is swaying by the DJ booth, holding a microphone and serenading my sister with an out-of-tune rendition of 'The Power of Love'.

These two are so cringingly over-the-top sugary sweet they could rot your teeth.

As the final bars of Mark's song ring out and everyone applauds, the DJ announces the bride and groom are about to take to the floor for their first dance. Yep, the slush fest ain't over yet.

Mark and Amber wrap their arms around each other and start to sway to the music. The whole room breathes a collective, "Ahhhh," and I swallow back the urge to barf. But when Amber and Mark begin kissing very, very passionately and there's more than a glimpse of tongue, everyone starts shuffling and mumbling in an embarrassed fashion, not quite sure where to look.

Um, inappropriate, much? I'm out of here.

As I head towards the bar for a drink, I spot Aunty Lou gesturing at me from one of the tables.

Forcing a smile, I walk in her direction.

"Suzy, what's this music?" Aunty Lou shouts.

"It's the first dance song," I explain.

"Something's gone wrong?"

"Nothing's gone wrong. It's the first dance song," I try again.

"I heard you the first time. But what's gone wrong?" Aunty Lou asks, eagerly gazing around for the scene of the disaster.

I decide to change the subject.

"Are you having a nice time, Aunty Loon?" I say, then cringe as I realise my slip of the tongue.

"*What* did you just call me?" Aunty Lou snaps.

"Aunty Lou," I say, smiling so warmly she has no choice but to believe me.

"Hmmm," Aunty Lou growls suspiciously.

Phew. Got out of that one. I so *knew* she faked that whole deafness thing whenever it suited her. Just wait until I tell Mum.

"I'm just going to get a drink, I'll be right back," I fib.

At the bar, I ask for a lemonade, then find a quiet corner to go and sit down in. I'm trying not to be too depressed, but it's proving an impossible task.

Over the last few hours I've come to realise that when you are newly single, feeling cruddy about love, life, and, well, pretty much everything, the last place you want to be is at an all-singing, all-dancing, full-on romantic wedding reception, surrounded by every coupled-up member of your family and your own personal stalker. (Toby has been trailing me all afternoon.)

Everyone's in a twosome except me. Even Harry's befriended one of Mark's nephews and judging from the way they're whispering and laughing, they're plotting something we're going to wish they hadn't. She and her new partner-in-crime have already poured the cream left over from the coffees into the pockets of all the abandoned suit jackets, set off Harry's fart machine behind every person in the room and sucked several helium balloons so they're speaking like Minnie Mouse.

The whole flipping universe, including my seven-year-old sister, is paired off.

And I'm doomed to be alone forever.

Yawning, I sneak a peek at my watch. How can it only be eight o'clock? I'm zonked and the reception's not due to finish until after midnight. Being heartbroken is exhausting work.

Across the room, Toby's heading towards me with steely determination. Gah! I have to escape.

Where are the toilets? I'll definitely be safe from him there.

To my relief the loos are empty. I flip down the toilet lid, sinking onto it gratefully. The half-glass of champagne I drank earlier has left me a bit fuzzy. I'd like nothing more than to go home, but it's deffo not cool to sneak out early from your sister's wedding. Besides, Mum would kill me.

A loud bang makes me jump as the door to the ladies flies open, accompanied by the sound of rustling material.

"Now, little baby, Mummy just needs to go wee-wees," I hear Amber say as she shuts herself into the cubicle next to me. I can't believe she's talking to her baby already. It must only be the size of a peanut or something.

There's more rustling. "Oh no, my dress is too big." She knocks on the wall dividing us. "Suzypoos, that's you, isn't it? I saw you come in here a minute ago."

"Hi, Amber," I say wearily.

"Lovely sister, and my favourite bridesmaid," Amber says, as I wince. I *so* know what's coming. "I can't sit down properly in my pretty, pretty dress, and I'm bursting for a wee-wee. Please come and help?"

Yup. There it is. After everything else that's happened today, I've now got to be a toilet assistant to my sister.

I'm pretty confident *this* particular duty wasn't in the *Guide to Being a Perfect Bridesmaid* book either.

"Do I have to?"

"Please, Suzy. Pleeeeeeeeeeeeeeeeeeeeeeeeease. I'm desperate."

I roll my eyes heavenwards and stand up. "All right, all right, I'm coming."

Her dress is so huge it takes me a while to squeeze in next to Amber, but after a lot of twisting and turning, I finally manage to manoeuvre her skirt out of the way.

After Amber's finished the second-longest wee in world history, she heads over to the sinks to wash her hands.

"Come on, Amber, you'd better get back to your party," I say.

"In a minute," Amber says, staring in the mirror and fiddling with her hair. "I just want to have a little chat to you, first."

"Um, okay," I say warily. What's this all about? Probably some other crazy bridesmaid's thing she's just invented. Or she wants me to call the neighbours and check on Crystal Fairybelle again.

"When I came into your room this morning, you were talking to Millie, and I thought I heard you say that you still like Danny," Amber says.

I'm completely taken aback. This I was *not* expecting.

Amber looks at me expectantly. "Well?" she asks. "Do you?"

I lean back against the sinks. It's not going to make any difference if I tell her. "Yeah," I say gloomily. "But like I told you, he's got another girlfriend, so there's nothing I can do about it. Now, as there's nothing else to say about that, why don't we get you back to your reception."

"Okeydokes," Amber says cheerily as I gather up her train. "Have you had any wedding cake yet? It's delish. Make sure you get some. Ooh, look, there's Harry. I'm just going to go and have a quick word... See you later, Suzypoos."

Actually, I *am* pretty peckish. And the cake does look good. I'm making a beeline for it when Mum appears and grabs my arm.

"Suzy, come and dance. Your dad's refusing as usual and there's a horrible man out there who keeps making moves on me. Can you believe he keeps pinching my bottom?"

Without giving me time to object, Mum hauls me onto the dance floor. Her moves are excruciating. She's an even worse dancer than Danny, and that's saying something.

No! I must stop thinking about Danny. I must, I must.

"This is a terrible song, Mum," I protest.

Mum grabs my hands and starts swinging my arms backwards and forwards. Her bosom jiggles terrifyingly.

"What are you talking about?" Mum shouts over the music. "It's a classic! They don't make them this good these days. Now, just copy what I do."

To my horror, Mum starts doing some warped kind of body pumping, complete with improvised shimmies and jazz hands.

"Mum, stop," I beg. "Everyone's looking."

"Jealous, that's what they are, Suzy," Mum says. "It's not just anyone who can freestyle like this."

Mum keeps me on the dance floor for ages, but I eventually sneak away while she's fighting off the bum-pincher. Ignoring Aunty Loon, who seems to have made a miraculous recovery from her hip trouble and is urging me to join her in the actions to 'YMCA', I walk over to a nearby chair and sit down.

Ahhh… that feels so good. My feet were seriously starting to hurt. I lean back in relief, then immediately jolt back upright. Because someone who's the spitting image of Danny has just walked across the room with Harry.

But when I look again, he's disappeared, swallowed up by the crowd. Danny's out with Jade at that party, I remind myself. Of course it wasn't him.

Darnation, I'm thinking about Danny *again*. I'm obsessed. But I just miss him so much. It's like there's a massive cloud of gloom following me everywhere, constantly reminding me Danny's not my boyfriend any more.

I *have* to work out some way to stop this and get my head under control.

"Ladies and gentleman, can I have your attention for a moment?" Amber's voice echoes around the room accompanied by a sharp squeal of feedback.

A loud cheer breaks out as everyone stops dancing and turns to face Amber expectantly. She's standing by the DJ booth, clutching a microphone.

Oh no. She can't be doing a song for Mark now. One serenade this evening was more than enough. My ears can't take another.

The DJ quickly adjusts the mike before Amber speaks again. "I hope you're all enjoying yourselves?"

Everyone whoops their agreement and Amber beams. "That's great. Okay, most of you here know Suzy, my sister, who's been an amazing bridesmaid today. Where are you, Suzypoos?"

As the crowd starts to clap, I reluctantly get to my feet and half-heartedly wave. Now what's she up to? Haven't I been embarrassed enough?

"I've got someone here who's got a special message for Suzy," Amber says. "Can you put the record on now?" she asks, turning to the DJ.

I'm confused. What's going on? What record?

The opening bars of a familiar song echo through the room and my heart leaps in response.

It's The Drifting, 'All I Can Think of is You'.

And then Danny's walking towards me, making his way through the crowd of aging rellies.

It can't be... how can it be... I mean, he wouldn't be here, would he?

But unless I'm hallucinating, it definitely is Danny who stops in front of me, smiling nervously.

"Hi, Suzy," he says.

I think I'm about to pass out.

CHAPTER TWENTY-EIGHT

Danny's here.

Danny's actually here, at Amber's wedding reception. Like, right in front of me. I'm tempted to do that cartoon thing of rubbing my eyes with my fists before doing a double take. He's wearing a white top with a long-sleeved shirt over it and some new jeans, and his hair's all tousled.

I've never seen him looking so good.

My cheeks are on fire because everyone's eyes are on me. Yes, I'm blown away that Danny's here, but at the same time, I'm very aware my whole family is watching this.

Wow. From the guy who never made any public gestures, this is a pretty big deal.

"Dance with me?" Danny says, over the music.

I nod my head, unable to speak. I'm still not entirely convinced I'm not hallucinating the whole thing.

But when Danny wraps his arms around me and I nestle into his chest, I know this is real. I breathe in the scent of him, so different to Zach's, but so overwhelmingly familiar. Danny's heart's pounding so fast I can feel it as our bodies press together, which makes me smile to myself.

We move to the music, but it's hard. The beat's all wrong for a slow dance and so we're bobbing around awkwardly.

But it feels great. Embarrassing, but great.

"Everyone's staring," he whispers.

"Do you blame them?" I ask. "You just crashed my sister's wedding reception."

"I didn't crash it," Danny says. He stops dancing and moves me away slightly to see my face. "I got a call from Harry on your phone asking me to come. She said you wanted to see me but were busy having your photo taken and couldn't talk to me yourself."

"Wait a minute," I say. "Harry called you on my phone? I gave that to Mum to look after."

A quick glance around the room and I spot Harry with Amber, watching us intently. What's going on?

Then it all clicks into place.

The conversation I had with Amber in the toilets. The chat Amber had with Harry straight after. And Harry was always nicking my phone to text Danny.

"My sisters appear to have set us up," I say. "I didn't know anything about this."

"Oh. Right," Danny says, tightly. "Well, in that case, I'd better go."

"No, don't," I say, grabbing hold of his arm. "Please stay. Although… I need to know. Did they choose the song, as well?"

"No. That was me," Danny says, his cheeks turning pink.

In that case, I'll temporarily hold off murdering my siblings. Just until I find out what's going on here.

"Look, Suzy, we seriously need to talk," Danny says. "I… I found out some stuff this evening, and when I got Harry's text I realised I had to see you. When I got here, Amber said I should dedicate a song to you, and I thought of The Drifting, and, well, the name of this song kind of said everything perfectly. All I can think of is you, Suzy. God, I can't believe I just said that out loud. Talk about lame. It sounded much better in my head."

Did I hear that right? Is this Danny's way of saying he wants me back?

I'm *so* confused.

As The Drifting dies away and the intro to 'The Locomotion' blasts around the room, Danny cringes. "Do you want to head outside, go for a walk or something?"

"Sounds good," I say gratefully.

In the gardens, we find a bench and sit down. An awkward silence falls between us and at first I have no idea what to say. I'm majorly weirded out. Why is Danny here? What does he want to talk about? What was the deal with the Drifting song back there? And, for that matter, why is he here with me and not with his girlfriend? There are just too many questions I need answers to. I'll start with the most important.

"So, um, why aren't you with Jade?" I ask, trying to sound casual as I curl my legs up underneath me.

"I broke it off." Danny gazes off into the distance.

Say WHAT now??? Did my ears hear that correctly? Stay cool, Suze. For once in your life, be calm and composed.

"You did?" I say, eagerly. "When?"

Okay. My calm and composed still needs work.

Danny's quiet for ages. "Earlier this evening."

"And is that what you wanted to talk to me about?" I ask.

"Not exactly," Danny says. "Wow, this whole thing is such a mess. Suze, there's no easy way to tell you this... You and I, we broke up because of Jade and Kara."

"What? No, we didn't. What are you talking about?" This is getting more befuddling by the second.

"The whole thing was a bet. Kara told me this evening."

It takes me a moment to absorb what he's just said. "You... you *what?*" I splutter, when his words sink in. "What do you mean it was a bet?"

"Jade apparently claimed she could get any boy she wanted to go out with her. Kara bet that she couldn't get me and..." Danny's voice trails off.

My mouth falls open. I knew those two were low, but this takes the flipping biscuit.

"Kara only told me because Jade's really close to winning," Danny says sadly. "She had to go out with me for a full month and the time's nearly up. Kara knew if she told me, I'd break up with Jade. I don't think she'd expected Jade to stick it out for so long, to be honest."

I'm shaking my head in disbelief. "No. This doesn't make sense. It can't have been a bet because you liked Jade, didn't you?"

Danny doesn't answer.

"I'm right, aren't I?" I press. Hard as it's going to be to hear, I need to know the truth.

"At first I kind of did," Danny confesses. "I was flattered. Jade's hot and girls like that don't usually look twice at people like me."

Ouch. That hurt. But... I suppose he does kind of have a point – I felt the same about Zach. I fiddle with my bracelet as Danny continues.

"But I realised soon enough that Jade's not exactly easy to be around. She's moody about everything, and her friends are *so* annoying – all they want to do is party. She never wanted to just hang out either, although Kara told me one of the terms of the bet was that we had to be seen in public together regularly. Jade put her all into winning; you know how competitive she is. She's a girl who doesn't like losing. At anything." He shrugs like he doesn't care, but I can tell how hurt he is by the whole thing. "I left Bryony's party after Kara told me, and dumped Jade by text as I was walking home. I've been ignoring her calls since, so I can only imagine how well that went down."

"Bet or not, you still kissed Jade on the night of the party," I say frostily. "Nobody forced you to do that."

"I keep trying to tell you, *she* kissed me."

"You kissed her back," I protest.

"I know what it must have looked like, but listen. The night at the party, I went to the toilet, remember? And on the way back, I bumped into Jade, who said that you were in the courtyard and wanted to talk to me. I don't know why I believed her, but I couldn't see any reason why she'd lie. When we got out there, I saw you in the courtyard holding hands with Zach, just like she'd wanted me to see. She kissed me while I was too shocked to react. I did pull away, but by then you'd already run off. Honestly, Suze, she made all the moves, and, um, that wasn't the first thing she'd done, either."

"Huh?" I don't like the sound of this.

Danny flushes. "She'd been texting me, and while we were doing that art project together she kept telling me she thought I was cute, stroking my hair and all that. I was stupid enough to think it was genuine. I hate myself for falling for their crap."

I don't know what to do. I want to trust him, but...

"How can I be sure you're telling the truth?"

"I *am*," Danny says in frustration. "And you have to stop making out like it's all my fault. You're not exactly an innocent party here, are you? You were holding hands with Zach."

I've got zilch left to lose. "I was, and I'm sorry, but I swear, *nothing* went on that night," I say. "It nearly did, but only because I was messed up about a lot of stuff. Zach was about to kiss me, but I stopped him. I couldn't do it to you."

Danny doesn't respond.

"I know how stupid I was to even go outside with him in the first place," I say. "I'm really, really sorry."

"Is Zach the reason why you started acting all distant and weird when we were together?" Danny says.

"Partly, yeah," I confess.

Danny nods slowly. "I knew you fancied him."

"I thought I did," I say. "But like you realised with Jade, I know now that Zach's a complete moron. You saw the way he dumped me."

"I. . . " Danny tries to interrupt.

"Let me finish,' I say gently. "I only liked him because you never made me feel special when we were going out. It was like we were brother and sister, or mates or something. You get that, right?"

Danny nods then fiddles with a button on his cuff for the longest time. "Suze, there's something else I've got to tell you," he says, eventually. "Um, it's about Zach. I don't exactly know how to say this. Please don't be too upset. But he was kind of in on the bet too."

My eyes open wide in shock.

"Jade promised she'd buy him an iPod if he took you out, to keep you out of the way," Danny says quietly. "I'm really sorry, Suze, but like I said, Jade did everything she could to win."

Oh. My. God.

This is a whole new level of humiliation.

Zach was *bribed* to go out with me? He pretended to fancy me, when actually he couldn't have cared less? It was all because of a flipping bet?

"I can't believe this," I say furiously. "That's outrageous."

"You're not wrong," Danny agrees.

"We can't let them get away with treating us like this," I seethe.

"I know," Danny says, "but before we talk about that, there's one more thing I need to tell you."

There's *more*? I don't know if I can cope with anything else.

"I, um..." Danny clears his throat. "I, er, still like you. And, um, just wanted to check, that, uh, you do know that, right?"

A slow smile spreads across my face. Is Danny saying he'd like to be my boyfriend again?

"You only *like* me?" I need to be clear about this.

"C'mon, Suzy, you know it's more than that," Danny objects, a hurt expression on his face.

"Do I?"

"Don't you?" Danny sounds surprised.

"Nuh-uh. I mean, you never told me when we were going out together. And you weren't exactly the most affectionate boyfriend in the world."

"Just because I wasn't all over you like Jamie is with Millie, it doesn't mean I didn't care," Danny says.

"But something to show we were together would have been good," I point out. "Like wanting to hold my hand or kissing me in public without dying of embarrassment.

I know you're not great at the romantic stuff, but it felt like you never made an effort. You always wanted to hang out with Harry."

Danny nods. "I'm sorry. If you give me another chance, I promise I'll try. Because I… I love you." He mumbles the last part at top speed then reaches out to gently twang one of the curls framing my face. And this time, it doesn't annoy me.

I've gone all tingly. Danny's just told me he loves me, for the very first time.

I'm lost in happy thoughts when Danny clears his throat pointedly.

Oh. Right. He's waiting for me to say it back.

"I love you, too," I whisper shyly.

We smile at each other like a pair of crazies, before Danny slowly leans in. Staring deep into my eyes, he raises his hand to my cheek and strokes it gently with his thumb. Then he lowers his mouth towards mine.

Danny's lips are soft and tender, and I melt into his body, relishing the feel of his arms pulling me closer. The kiss is perfect, like we've never been apart. I don't want it to stop. Ever.

But that plan's scuppered pretty darn quickly when we hear a whooping noise coming from the nearby hedge and we pull apart in alarm.

I'm all dazed, like I've just woken up from a deep sleep. "What the... ?"

Amber and Harry emerge and are dancing around happily, high-fiving and yelling.

"Woohoo, it worked!" Amber crows triumphantly.

Oh, *right*. My sisters. I'd forgotten that it was their meddling that got Danny here in the first place.

"We got you back together, we got you back together," Amber singsongs. "Are you pleased, Suzypoos? I hope so." She bounds over to give me a huge hug. Then she hugs Danny, who turns purple with embarrassment and coughs awkwardly.

It's only because I'm so happy that I'm not going to kill the pair of them.

"It all worked out perfectly," Amber says, beaming at me with pride. "You helped me realise Mark was my handsome prince, and all my dreams have come true, so I wanted to give you a happy ending too."

"But how... ?" I ask, still trying to understand.

"All I had to do was find out for sure you still liked Danny, so when you said you did, Harry texted him and got him to come," Amber explains. "We hoped you'd do the rest, and we were right."

I listen in astonishment. I'm amazed that she master-minded this. Most of the time Amber acts like she's had a lobotomy. I'm actually really touched.

"Our plan was good, wasn't it?" Harry says.

"Hmmm," I growl, but I'm smiling.

"Are you coming over to our house soon?" Harry asks Danny. "We haven't watched *Star Wars* for weeks!"

"Yeah, I'm sure it won't be long," Danny replies.

Harry wriggles onto the bench on the other side of Danny. "I've got loads to tell you. There's this new joke I've heard about and it's really funny. You put a person's hand in a bowl of warm water while they're sleeping and they wet themselves. Will you help me do it? I'm thinking about trying it on..." She points non-subtly in my direction.

"Harry, not now," Amber says. "Come on, let's go back inside. These two need some time on their own."

"Awww," Harry whines. "I haven't seen Danny for ages."

"You'll see him soon enough," Amber says. "Now c'mon, we're leaving."

Amber drags Harry off and then it's just me and Danny sitting in the dark again. I lean my head onto his shoulder.

"So, what are we going to do about everything?" Danny asks, jerking me out of the dream-like haze I've been in since our kiss. The fury I feel about the bet bubbles up again.

"I don't know, but we need to do *something*," I say. "Have you got any ideas?"

Danny shakes his head. "No. Maybe we should talk to Jamie and Millie, see if they can help?"

"Good thinking," I say. "Let's get them to meet us in Bojangles tomorrow."

Danny takes his phone, taps out a couple of texts, and hits send. "Done. So, um, what shall we do now?"

"Well, you could always kiss me again," I suggest.

So he does.

CHAPTER TWENTY-NINE

"**Hey, you're** actually on time," Danny says as he greets me outside Bojangles. He's wearing his *Star Wars* T-shirt and looks gorgeous. He smiles as he leans forwards to give me a kiss hello.

A proper kiss. In public and everything.

"You look great," he says.

I'm glad he noticed, because I made an extra effort today. Yesterday the wedding hairdresser used this incredible hair softener and my curls are still in pretty tendrils, plus the make-up artist showed me some great tips so my eyes seem enormous. I'm wearing a funky, slouchy black jumper under my jacket, teamed with leggings and Amber's favourite knee-high boots. Well, it's not like she'll be needing them – she's off on honeymoon today.

"When I told Jamie and Millie I wanted to meet here I didn't say you were coming, or that we'd sorted things out," Danny says, a small smile playing around his lips. His delicious, kissable lips. Ooooh, I'm so glad he's my boyfriend again!

"C'mon. Let's go and surprise them," Danny says, clasping my hand in his and pulling me through the door to Bojangles. Mille and Jamie are already sitting inside. Millie's chattering away but turns when the bell rings. Her jaw drops open and then she screams at the top of her voice.

"Oh. My. Goooooood!" she yells, dashing around the tables and chairs towards us, nearly sending the poor waitress flying. "You're holding hands! So does this mean you're back together? Why didn't you tell me?" Millie swats my arm with pretend annoyance.

"Are you going to give us a chance to sit down, Mil?" Danny says.

"But I want to know everything now!" Millie says, bouncing up and down. "When did all this happen? You are definitely back together, right?"

"Yep," I say, grinning happily.

"Aaargh!" Millie screams again. "I'm sooooo happy for you! This is the best news ever." She grabs hold of me and dances around, almost knocking a stack of dirty plates and glasses over.

"I knew you'd sort things out," Millie says, finally releasing her hold.

"I'm glad someone did," I say. "Cause I sure as heck didn't."

"Oh pffft," Millie says, flapping her hand. "You two are meant for each other."

As we sit down, Jamie's shaking his head and laughing. "Millie, what are you like? You're crazy."

"What?" Millie says. "I'm just happy for my friends. What's wrong with that?"

"Well, I'm happy too, but you don't see me leaping and screeching all over the place, do you?"

Millie sticks out her tongue, and Jamie plants an affectionate kiss on her cheek.

"What can I get you guys?" the waitress asks.

"I'll have a cola," Danny says. "Actually, no. I won't. I'm going to have something different. I'd like a berry smoothie, please. And, Suzy, I'm guessing you'll have the usual?"

"Yep. Hot chocolate with cream and marshmallows, please."

I lean back in my chair and sigh contently. This is perfect, and exactly as it should be. Everything's back to normal.

The waitress heads off to the kitchen and Millie

wiggles on her seat with excitement. "So, c'mon you two, spill."

"It's kind of a long story," Danny says, his voice becoming serious. "Wait until you hear what's happened..."

At lunchtime on Monday, I'm standing with my friends outside the canteen. I feel a bit sick. I can't honestly believe we're going to confront Jade and Zach. But at the same time, I know we have to. They need to know they can't treat people like that, and my feelings of anger and mortification about the whole thing haven't gone away. Every time I picture their smug faces I want to pummel something. Hard.

How could they pretend they liked us, just to break us up?

Not only is what they did the lowest of the low, it's majorly humiliating. And I'm a girl who's no stranger to humiliation. Not to mention I even ate fish to try and impress Zach. *Plus* they made me miss out on The Drifting.

All in all, it's completely unforgivable.

"So, you ready?" Danny says.

"Ready," I reply, taking a deep, steadying breath.

We push open the double doors and scan the cafeteria.

"Over there." Millie indicates a table in the middle of the room. "C'mon. They're all together."

Jade and Kara are sitting opposite each other, while Zach's next to Jade, chatting to several of his football mates and a pretty redhead from the year below.

We stop at the end of the table and I cross my arms, trying to make myself appear tougher. In reality, I'm shaking with fear and I've never felt so squirmy.

"What do *you* want?" Jade says.

"I just wanted to let you know your plan to break us up failed," I say, forcing my voice to stay steady.

"Nobody cares, and you're putting me off my lunch," Jade says coldly, taking a bite of her salad. "Go away."

"We're not going anywhere," Danny says.

"Not until you apologise," I add.

"As *if*." Jade laughs nastily. "On what planet do you think that would actually happen? You're pathetic, Suzy Puttock, you know that? Which is probably the reason Zach couldn't handle going out with you for more than two minutes."

"Too right," Zach interjects, through a mouthful of shepherd's pie.

"Like you're such a catch, Zach," I say loudly. "Snogging you was like being slobbered on by an Alsatian. I'd take a towel along if you're planning on getting some action later," I tell the redhead. "You'll need it. It was seriously revolting."

As everyone bursts out laughing, the girl grimaces and moves away from Zach.

"Like I care what you think," Zach says scornfully, pulling an iPod Nano out of his pocket. "I only went out with you to get this."

"Zach, shut up," Jade hisses.

"What's the problem, Jade?" Danny asks. "Worried we'll find out about the bet you made with Kara? Too late. She already told me."

"You *told* him?" Jade slams down her fork.

"You weren't supposed to say anything," Kara snaps at Danny furiously.

"You *bitch*," Jade shouts. "This means I win the bet, you know that?"

"As *if!*" Kara yells back. "*You're* the loser. He dumped you before the month was up."

"And all of a sudden it makes sense why," Jade says. She grabs a handful of salad, and throws it at Kara, so it splatters all over her. "Who's the loser now?" Jade snaps.

"What are you doing, you crazy freak?" Kara shrieks. She swipes salad dressing out of her eye and stands blinking for a moment, as pieces of grated carrot slide down her cheek. There's lettuce on her shoulder, tomato in her eyebrow and sweetcorn all over her tie. Then, scowling fiercely, she grabs her smoothie and chucks it into Jade's face.

"What the——?" Jade splutters.

My friends and I stare in delight as all around us, people start clapping and whooping, abandoning their meals to hustle in for a better look. Jade's soaking, her usually perfect hair clinging to her face in soggy pink tendrils, and her shirt's drenched. Jade and Kara are never seen in public looking anything less than immaculate, so to see the pair of them like this is pretty darn satisfying for everyone they've tormented over the years.

I try to hold it in, but a gurgle of laughter escapes as Jade pushes back her chair and runs at Kara with a primal yowl. Are they for *real*? This is too hilarious. Kara attempts to shove Jade away, then the two girls are tussling and tugging at each other's hair as hard as they can.

They lurch into the table, causing all of the glasses to wobble and shake. Zach's cola tips over, spilling into his lap.

"Hey…" Zach leaps up, trying to get out of the way, but it's too late. "My iPod," he yells, holding the now dripping device between his thumb and finger. "It's trashed!"

"Did you do a stress wee?" Jamie asks loudly, pointing to Zach's soaked crotch, and causing everyone to laugh even louder.

"Shut up!" Zach lunges angrily for Jamie, but Kara and Jade stagger into him, causing him to stumble. In the process, Zach gets jabbed in the eye by Jade's elbow.

It looks like it hurts. A lot. Oh, happy, happy days.

"Right, that's enough," Mrs Lewis says, forcing her way through the crowd. "What's going on? Jade, Kara, Zach, break it up *now*."

"But it was them who started it," Zach says, gesturing at us.

We all gaze innocently at Miss Lewis.

"I doubt that very much. They're not the ones filthy and brawling in the middle of the dining hall," Miss Lewis says. "I expect to be able to eat my lunch in peace, not have to deal with this pathetic behaviour."

"But they—"

"Not another word," Miss Lewis snaps, finally hauling Kara and Jade apart. They stand either side of her, glowering fiercely at each other. "Head's office. Now. Zach, you too."

As my friends and I stand aside to let Miss Lewis past, Jade, Kara and Zach glare at us as they leave to a chorus of laughter, hissing and applause. Zach's walking strangely, trying to disguise the fact it looks as if he's wet his pants.

"There's just one more thing…" Danny says and, in front of everyone, he leans over to give me a full-on snog. People are hollering at us to get a room, but I don't care.

When he pulls back, Danny's cheeks are scarlet. "Public enough for you?"

"For now," I say, grinning. He puts his arm around me and we follow Jamie and Millie out of the dining hall and into the corridor.

In the distance we can see Kara, Jade and Zach waiting outside the Head's office.

Jamie lets out a small snigger, which is all it takes to set us all off. We laugh so hard we're bent practically double.

"Did you see Jade's face when that smoothie went over her?" Danny says.

"And the stuff about snogging like an Alsatian. That was genius," Millie says.

"It was true," I giggle. "He was disgusting."

"Can we not talk about you kissing Zach?" Danny says, sounding slightly pained.

"Sorry. I'll never mention it again," I promise, nestling into Danny's side.

"That was amazing," Jamie says, as he and Millie put their arms around each other. "I never imagined they'd turn on each other like that."

And he's right. It *was* amazing.

Right now, I couldn't be happier. I'm with my fabulous boyfriend. I have the best friends on the planet, and justice has been served. All is good in the world.

"*Star Wars* tomorrow night at Jamie's, then?" Danny asks, grabbing hold of my hand tightly. "You up for that, guys?"

"Sounds good," Millie says.

"Deffo," Jamie adds.

I roll my eyes. I guess some things will never change.

But deep down, I wouldn't really want them to.

ACKNOWLEDGEMENTS

Hurrah, hurrah, this is as close to an Oscar acceptance speech moment that I'm ever likely to get, so I fully intend to make the most of it. There are heaps of people I need to thank who have helped in various ways over the years, so I hope I don't forget anyone. I'm sorry if it's you.

First of all, a million thank yous to Adrian Hughes, because I honestly couldn't have done this without you. You're the world's greatest husband, supporter and ego booster, and always have an enormous amount of faith in everything I do.

Mum and Dad, for being fantastic parents and always ensuring there were stacks of books around while I was growing up. One of the greatest gifts you gave me was the love of reading. Mum, I wish you could see this, you would be so excited. I miss you, and your unfailing support, every single day.

Oliver, who has the best laugh in the world and always makes me smile.

The rest of my family, (Saunders, Wood and Griffiths alike), especially Rob, Laurie and Grace.

My lovely editor, Sara Starbuck, and the fantastic team at Templar, with shout outs to Helen Boyle, Emma Goldhawk and Will Steele.

Marie-Louise Jensen, Kelley Townley, Karen Priest, Gemma Green and Eleanor Hawken, who always had genius suggestions on how to improve things.

Gill and John McLay, for their friendship, encouragement and support.

Julia Green, for helping in so many ways during my time on the MA in Writing for Young People.

Ali Hill, Catherine & Ian Sparrowhawk, Jo Nadin, Moira Bowler, Kay Woodward and Vicki Shepherdson, for providing laughter, encouragement and kicks up the backside when needed.

Sarah Henley for the science advice, although the science scenes eventually got cut out. Sorry, Sarah.

Evan Green, who wasn't at all fazed when I randomly asked him to translate 'I've lost my sausage' into German.

And last, but by no means least, Lindsey Fraser, who has always been there with her pom-poms, cheering for Suzy the loudest of them all.

FIVE FACTS ABOUT ME, Karen Saunders xxx

1) I'm a walking disaster area. I once ended up with a broken nose during a tickling fight.

2) My favourite words are eclectic and catkin.

3) I've done a heap of random jobs. Like stuffing Christmas crackers. And covering hundreds of library books in sticky back plastic.

4) When I was at university, everyone said I looked like the twins from B*witched. (Google them - I couldn't wear dark denim for *years*.)

5) I can fluently mirror write. It's my best party trick.

For more about me, come and have a nosy around my website: www.karensaunders.co.uk

Other Templar books you might enjoy...

ISBN 978-1-84877-134-5
Also available as an ebook

ISBN 978-1-84877-146-8
Also available as an ebook

forgive my fins

by Tera Lynn Childs

Half-human, half-mermaid Lily has a crush on Brody, a human boy. Trouble is, when mermaids kiss someone, they bond for life. So when her attempt to win Brody's love leads to a case of mistaken identity, she finds herself facing a tidal wave of relationship drama.

'I simply adored this book!'
Alyson Noël, author of
The Immortals series

fins are forever

by Tera Lynn Childs

Don't miss the tail-flicking sequel to *Forgive my Fins*! Can Lily stay true to her duty as princess, her true love and her dreams, or will she decide that living on land means living a lie?

ISBN 978-1-84877-683-8
Also available as an ebook

Don't Call Me Ishmael

by Michael Gerard Bauer

As far as I know, I'm the only recorded case of Ishmael Leseur's Syndrome in the world. It is capable of turning an otherwise almost normal person into a walking disaster registering 9.9 on the open-ended imbecile scale. And that is why I've decided to write all this down.

'Comic genius and a great read.'

The Bookseller

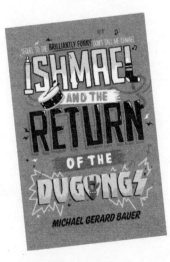

ISBN 978-1-84877-712-5
Also available as an ebook

Ishmael and the Return of the Dugongs

Don't miss the brilliantly funny sequel to *Don't Call Me Ishmael*!